Also by Gordon Gravley

Gospel for the Damned

Subscribe to the author's newsletter *from...Another Writer*
via his website www.gordongravley.com

The

Quieting

West

Gordon Gravley

The Quieting West

Copyright © 2017 by Gordon Gravley

The Quieting West is a work of fiction.
All incidents and dialogue, and all characters, with the exception of some
well-known historical and public figures, are products of the author's
imagination and are not to be construed as real. Where real-life historical or
public figures appear, the situations, incidents, and dialogues concerning
those persons are entirely fictional and are not intended to depict actual
events or to change the entirely fictional nature of the work. In all other
respects, any resemblance to persons living or dead is entirely coincidental.

First IngramSpark Edition.

ISBN-13: 978-1-948718-02-8

LCCN: 201-7907-704

Cover by Bespoke Book Covers

Subscribe to the author's newsletter *from….Another Writer*
via his website www.gordongravley.com

To Dad.

I think you'll like this one.

CONTENTS

❧   ❧   ❧

The

Quieting

West

Prologue

In the Central Arizona mountain town of Prescott, on a rocky and secluded ranch west of the landmark known as Thumb Butte, upon a desk in the library of a house more than a hundred years old, I found this manuscript. It was written by my great-grandfather, William "Billy" Colter, whom I was named after. I spent a little time with him as a child; I mostly remember playing on the large rocks that made up much of his ranch's landscape. He used to complain about those rocks like a man might complain about an old, half-blind dog with chronic flatulence, with a tone more of everlasting endearment than of contempt or annoyance.

"It's hard to get a good ride. And stupid cattle love to get stuck up in there," he'd grumble with his rough voice, scarred by a wound to his throat decades before. But he adored those rocks and the land they rested upon.

I don't recall ever seeing cattle on his ranch. He shut down that business before I was born. He did love to ride though, and took me out with him on occasion. My memory is still fresh with the beauty of the dry Arizona forest, permeated by the smell of dust and pine.

The last time I saw Billy was for his one hundred third birthday. Although his hearing was all but gone, he was remarkably lucid and coherent. "I don't feel a day over a hundred and two," he joked.

He asked me how my writing career was going, and he told me about some producers of a documentary who had approached him regarding his life and his association with Thomas Andrew Benton. But Billy refused to be interviewed. Instead, he told them he would write down some notes that they could use in their research.

Those "notes" are this manuscript that I found in his library in 1997, almost two years after his passing at the age of one hundred six. Nothing of what he wrote was used in the documentary. After nearly two decades of legal battles with relatives and relatives-of-relatives over rights to the manuscript, I finally present it here, in its entirety, in my great-grandfather's words. There's been minimal editing, mostly in the process of dividing his continuous narrative into chapters and sections, adding italics for emphasis, and I've headed the chapters with excerpts from Benton's own poetry.

I hope you enjoy.

W. C.

One

A fine young man has come to the ranch.
Not tall, but sturdy in stance,
Looking for all kinds of work, by chance

S ome gentlemen have asked me to write a few things about Thomas Andrew Benton. Partly because he was my friend, but mostly, I think, because I'm the only person still alive who knew him. Keeping the memory of others is a responsibility that comes with living as long as I have, I guess.

It was the autumn of 1909, and I had been looking for steady work for some time. It was especially hard with winter coming. A man isn't likely to give up hot meals and a warm bed too easily, so jobs were scarce even for someone with my experience. Since I was about ten years old I'd been doing just about everything a cowboy knew how to do and then some. But when my wanders took me into Scofield, Utah, I was desperate and about to do something rash, like work one of the mines (it's a different kind of man than me that works deep under the ground rather than on top of it) or commit some petty crime to spend a few nights in a dry cell.

I got word of a ranch just outside of town called the Triple-T where not one but three top hands had just up and left. I didn't question why, but rode out to the ranch as quickly as I could. The Triple-T was the property of Maxwell Jackson. He'd had the T longer than I'd been alive, surviving the Indian wars, and the mine disaster of 1900, but all that mattered to me when we met was that he had three jobs needing to be filled.

It turned out that he was as desperate to hire as I was to work. Not to say he was hasty. You don't keep a ranch as long as he had being hasty. We talked for a bit. He told me he was going to work me hard and that I would probably end up hating him. I told him if he was fair I would hold no grudges. When I shook his calloused hand I knew I was going to like working for him.

He showed me the bunkhouse, told me to pick a bunk, put my stuff away and that I was needed out on the north range. He would have someone take me out there. The bunkhouse was bigger than many I'd seen. One room, but eight beds, each with a side table and a small shelf and window above it. A black kettle stove in the middle of the room gave it all the comfort of home.

There were three vacant beds next to each other for me to choose from. I picked the one in the middle to give me room on either side. I've always liked my space. Since I travel light, in a minute I was ready to head out. I took a moment to look over the other bunks and see what kind of men I would be working with.

Only one other bed was occupied on my side of the room, in a corner furthest from the door. Leaning against the wall there was a guitar partially wrapped in a thick blanket. Both the blanket and the guitar strap, which lay across the half-made bed, were decorated with Mexican patterns.

Across the room, on the bed closest to the door, sat a deck of cards and on the side table was an abundance of grooming supplies–various sized combs and brushes, scissors and razors, tonics, colognes and a tin of mustache wax. There was enough stuff to fill a damned barbershop.

Next to that was an impatiently-made bed. A copy of *Tom Sawyer* and a picture of a very pretty girl were on the shelf above it. Something told me I would like the fellow who slept there. And next to him, I gathered, was probably the dirtiest person I would ever meet. There was an odd odor coming from the pile of clothes under his bunk, which was not made. I could only imagine he either told a good joke or worked as hard as two men for the others to put up with him.

The last bed was meticulously neat. His shelf was

stacked with a respectable collection of books, including some Dickens and one by Elizabeth Custer about her husband George. On the side table was a leather-bound journal and a pencil. A suitcase was tucked under the bed, and in the corner stood a Winchester hunting rifle. Clearly, everything was in its place.

The door opened just enough for a Mexican fellow to put his head in without letting in too much cold. My Spanish was never very good but I could tell he wanted me to hurry. As I followed him out to the horses I saw the flakes of snow falling and understood his urgency. He told me his name was Miguel, and he explained we were heading out to collect strays and bring the herd in closer.

The T wasn't the biggest spread I'd worked but it was a good size. We rode steady for a good ten minutes before meeting up with the other cowboys and a herd. Miguel took me directly to a man who rode tall in his saddle.

"¿Quién diablos es?" the man asked Miguel. I couldn't help noticing his long, curly hair flowing out from under his hat, and his remarkably trimmed mustache and beard.

"Se trata de Billy Colter," Miguel answered. *"El Señor Jackson solo lo contrató."*

"Well, I'll be damned! That old bastard got us some help! Billy Colter, I'm Frank Johnston," the groomed man said and tipped his hat. At that moment two other hands rode up. Frank nodded towards one of them. "That's my brother, Jamie." The brother was slender and looked even younger than me. We reached across our horses and shook hands. "That there is Clarence Stoud. Be careful to stay upwind of him." Clarence nodded without smiling through his ragged beard.

"We've got a lot of strays to round up," Frank then said. "The three of us will do that. Miguel, you and Billy take this herd in."

"*¿Dónde está el Señor Benton?*" asked Miguel.

"He's in the south range doing the same thing we are. This bad weather coming in has the cattle all spooked. We've got cows scattered all over the place." Frank turned his horse and rode off with his brother and Clarence following.

I wanted to ride with them. I was hankering to get my hands dirty and know the land, but I was given an instruction and I was going to do it. The two of us tightened what there was of the herd and started moving them in the direction from where we'd come. It turned out to be more like us following them because where the cattle wanted to go and where we were taking them were the same.

Like many a cowboy, Miguel loved to talk. In a mix of English and Spanish he told me about the Triple-T. It seemed that a neighboring spread, run by a Joseph Thorne, was growing all around Mr. Jackson's ranch, surrounding it on nearly three sides. For a year, Thorne pressured Jackson to sell his land to him. Mr. Jackson was not interested in the deal, so much so that their relationship became heated, anything but neighborly. To retaliate, Thorne set some of Jackson's own men to sabotaging the T. They would "lose" cattle, and misplace supplies and equipment.

"Señor Benton, he figured it out," explained Miguel, "and who it was doing it."

"What happened?" I asked.

"*Habia tres hombres.* They cornered Señor Benton in the bunkhouse. *Pero no importaba. No lo sé. No lo sabía…* They did not know… Señor Benton has killed many men. They had knives and guns. *Pero no importaba…* It did not matter. They fought and he took away their guns. I found a knife on the floor. He had shot it from one of their hands. I gave it to Señor Benton, because he earned it, but he told me to keep it. I searched the bunkhouse for more things. *Pero no encontré nada.*"

"Do you have that knife?" I asked.

Miguel sadly dropped his head. "I lost it yesterday when my horse and I took a fall," he said. He stroked the neck of his mount. *"Pero él está bien."*

The cattle lumbered along obligingly in front of us. It wasn't long before the corral was in sight. Miguel rode ahead to make sure it was open and ready. As night and snow began to fall and we got the last cow corralled, the Johnston brothers and Clarence came in with the few stragglers they had found. In all it seemed a modest herd for the size of Mr. Jackson's spread. I blamed that on the actions of Joseph Thorne and his saboteurs.

"I'd say we did good," Jamie stated proudly.

"I hope so," said Frank, very matter-of-fact.

We tended our horses then got ourselves to supper. I'll never forget that first meal on the T. It was as fine a supper as I've ever had in any restaurant anywhere. Beef stew spiced with red pepper, cinnamon and cloves, honey cornbread and the sweetest baked apples. Mr. Jackson knew the best thing for morale was a good meal. He prepared everything, as he'd never been married. I'm sure those three that had lost their jobs sorely regretted it whenever it came time to eat.

As we sat I noticed we were a man short. "Maybe I should see if Mr. Benton needs help," I said.

"Thomas would rather all of you have something to eat," replied Mr. Jackson. "If he's not in by then, a couple of you could head back out."

"Besides, he don't know you," Clarence said to me. "If you found him he'd probably shoot you on sight."

They all laughed. The rest of the meal was in silence as we were all famished. After, the two brothers headed back out to help Thomas. Miguel, Clarence and I settled in the bunkhouse. I started a fire in the stove and made coffee for when the others returned. Miguel sat on his bed in the corner and strummed his guitar while Clarence enjoyed the stove's heat from his unkempt bunk.

"How long you been working ranches, Billy?" Clarence asked.

"Since I was pretty young," I said, "eight or nine, maybe ten."

"You ain't sure?"

"Well, I've never quite known how old I was. My parents died when I was too young to remember, and my uncle who took me in didn't know, either. Anyway, I worked my first round-up to move on from my uncle. I told the boss I was fourteen, but I'm sure I was much younger."

"How old do you guess to be now?"

"Twenty, maybe."

"I figured you been riding a while. Didn't I say, Miguel, that I thought he'd been riding a while?"

Miguel nodded without looking up.

"How long have you been with the T?" I asked Clarence.

"Almost three years. You won't find a fairer boss than Maxwell Jackson. He may work you into the grave, but he don't ask you to do nothing he don't do himself."

"Miguel was telling me there's been some excitement here recently."

Clarence leaned close to me, and I leaned away from the stench of his breath. "Don't believe everything that Mexican tells you."

Miguel stopped his strumming and glared at Clarence who smiled big and laughed even bigger.

"We did have an incident," Clarence continued, "when Benton found out those three men you replaced were undermining our work here. He went after them, chased them into the woods. Three gunshots later, Benton came out of the woods...alone."

"This happened in the woods?" I asked.

"Yep. Left the bodies to the coyotes."

I looked at Miguel who had gone back to his playing. He did not respond to Clarence's rather different version of what happened.

"Benton has killed men before," Clarence said. "He was a lawman once. You ain't heard of him?"

I shrugged.

"And you never heard of young Tom Benton's great manhunt?"

I shrugged.

"Where you been in your life that no one never talked about Thomas Andrew Benton?"

Once again, I shrugged.

"Well, Benton's father was a lawman. He was the sheriff of some town in Texas that ain't there no more. Hell, Texas wasn't even a state then, it was still part of Mexico. A day didn't go by that there wasn't some sort of trouble. Well, when Benton was twelve years old he watched his father get killed breaking up a meaningless bar fight." Clarence paused to make sure I was listening to him. I looked him in the eye and he continued. "For ten years Benton tracked that man that killed his father. Through seven states and two territories. Finally, at the age of fifteen, Benton found that man and put an axe in his head. Thomas Andrew Benton is not a man you want to have a problem with."

I nodded to let him think I was more impressed than I was. Not to say his story was anything to scoff. But I had seen many hard men in my life. I once knew a man who searched for three days without sleep for a stray calf. When he found its carcass being gnawed on by a cougar he spent another three days hunting that cat down. Another time I saw one man take on a whole saloon of drunken soldiers. They took him to be a dandy, but he was a skilled fighter and as mean as a badger. Sometimes you just had to be. Yes, I've known plenty of hard men. The West was made by them.

Clarence fell back on his bunk and went right to snoring like a hibernating bear. Miguel set his guitar down, also to lay to sleep. I put some more wood in the stove so it would be plenty warm for the others when they returned. This happened about an hour later. I'm a light sleeper, and I sat right up when the Johnston brothers came in.

"What are you doing up?" Frank said.

"I heard you ride up. Everything go okay?"

Jamie fell dead asleep on his bed, right below the picture of the pretty girl, without even taking his boots off. Frank took them off for him and covered him with a blanket. "A lot of trouble for one runt calf. But that's how Thomas is."

"So I've been hearing."

"Yes? I'll bet you've been hearing a lot from these two," Frank said with a quiet laugh.

"They were telling me about how Mr. Benton ran those three men off the ranch."

"I'll bet they have." Frank warmed himself by the stove and got ready for bed as he spoke. "What's happened here lately is probably the most excitement either of them have seen all their lives."

"I've heard different things. Do you know what happened?"

"Well, you know that we had three hands here that were making trouble for us. When Thomas caught them letting our horses loose from the corral they ambushed him and drug him back to the bunkhouse. It was a hell of a fight. But it takes more than three men to put down Thomas, and once he got a hold of his gun, well they would've needed an army."

"Did he kill them?"

"Can't say for sure, nobody actually saw what happened," said Frank. He laid back and curled up beneath his blanket. "All we know is there was a fight, shots were fired and those three are gone. And we all know Thomas. Now get some sleep."

I dropped my head back onto my pillow and closed my eyes. It wasn't long before Thomas finally entered the bunkhouse, letting in a gust of cold that nearly caused me to sit up again. But I lay still with my eyes closed. I guess, after all the talk, I was intimidated about meeting him. I listened as he removed his holster and hung it by his bed. *Within reach*, I thought to myself. Then he took off his coat and sat on the bed to pull off his boots. He did all this very quietly so as not to wake the others, and he then went to warm himself by the stove. After a minute, I had the feeling I was being watched and I opened my eyes.

Thomas was looking down at me from the foot of my bed. He was tall. From my angle, he looked near to hitting his head on the rafter above. At first, I thought he was still covered in snow, but it was his grey hair. He was as old as a grandfather. And he had huge hands that seemed designed more for wrestling a steer than skillfully handling a pistol. The rest of his features were shadowed in silhouette as he stood with the room's only lamp behind him. My first impression of Thomas Andrew Benton will always be as a towering, old cowpuncher.

"I thought you might be awake," he whispered and held out one of those big hands to me. "I'm Thomas. I look forward to working with you."

I shook his hand. "I'm Billy Colter."

"Well, get some rest, Billy. We have plenty to do tomorrow."

I caught a glimpse of a grin, as though he took pleasure in working his crew hard. Then he put out the lamp, and I fell right to sleep.

Two

Beneath the skyline of the mountains
Is where I live
Their peaks draw the horizon,
Their trees scrape the sky

E very morning, Thomas would have a list of work for us to do scrawled upon a black-board by the door. He said it was to help his aging memory. The hands, however, said it was to make sure they got all their work done. Moving the herd from one pasture to another, collecting strays, repairing fences, chopping wood. Any number of things. Always on the list was for Clarence to wash either himself or his clothes or both. Where it was on the list determined how important it was to get done. On my first morning there, it was the number one item. Clarence knew he could put it off no longer and begrudgingly gathered up his clothes and himself to get it done before breakfast.

Because Mr. Jackson didn't employ house staff, we had to take care of our own domestic duties like mending and laundry. Having once expected to have a wife, Mr. Jackson added the most modern indoor bathroom and laundering facility I'd ever seen to the back of his modest ranch house. With the prospects of acquiring a wife long dwindled, Mr. Jackson gave us cowhands full use of it. The finely carved wooden cabinets, marble counters, and claw-foot tub were certainly nice to look at, but as out-of-place to us as an elephant at a rodeo.

The previous night's storm, after all our fretting, left only a dusting of snow. Clear skies made for an icy cold morning. The ground crunched beneath our boots and Frank's breath instantly turned to frost upon his mustache. Thomas was nowhere to be seen, which is how it would be most mornings. He was up and out before the rest of us. But we would always have our list and set to doing it.

Thomas had a list of his own, and he nearly always worked by himself. He would check on us throughout the day, of course, to know we were completing our tasks in a timely manner and help when necessary. To be honest, we found it embarrassing to need the help of that old man. We did our damnedest to work "quick but thorough." The highlight of our day was to have Thomas offer nothing more than a "good work," and ride off.

I never met a cowboy that didn't have some sort of quirk. Thomas's was solitude. Getting up before the rest of us, being scarce as a coyote all day, and getting in after we've all retired was just his way. Of course, we all had our speculations about what he was doing.

"He's getting away from the stench," Frank stated with a glance to Clarence.

"*Él tiene una señiorita,*" Miguel said with an envious grin.

"He has a lady friend?" I said.

"A whore, more like it," Clarence snorted.

"Thomas does have a fondness for prostitutes," Frank explained to me, "but none of them around here." Then to all of us, "What Thomas does is his own business."

"He's probably out mending fences," Jamie said. The others laughed, which Jamie took offense to. With a frown, he added, "There's a lot of down fences, especially up north."

"Why would that old man be sweat'n work he could get us to do?" challenged Clarence.

"Maybe he likes it," Jamie sheepishly replied.

"I like that he's not always hovering," I said. The others quietly agreed. We'd all had our share of bosses that had their hands in our work as much as our own. In some respects, Thomas made us feel like we were our own bosses.

One morning, when winter was finally making way for spring, as I lay listening to him go through his routine,

Thomas did something different. He knew I was awake and handed me a cup of hot coffee. "Since you're up," he said, "you've volunteered to help me out today."

I quickly sat up, took the cup, and burned my tongue drinking so fast.

"Slow down. I'll get the horses and see you out front in fifteen minutes."

He went outside and the morning rushed in and slapped my feet. I don't remember it having been a particularly hard winter, but usually come March I was tired of the cold and would prefer to stay under the covers until the sun was warm. I wasn't going to disappoint Thomas, though. All of us respected him too much. We'd do whatever small things we could to impress him.

He had our horses ready by the time I made it outside, and he waited while I double-checked my saddle, then we rode off. The mountains were a silhouette with the sun getting near to begin its rise. It promised to be another day without a cloud in the sky.

"We need to repair some fence damaged by a snowdrift," he told me after a bit of riding. "I've just been waiting for the snow to melt enough. Even if you hadn't been awake, I would've waked you up. I like how you build. I don't want it coming down again anytime soon."

I wasn't modest enough to argue with him. *The others*

were good riders and ropers, but sloppy at building, I thought. I liked that Thomas thought so too, but we said nothing more about it. We had work to do. And it turned out we worked well together, in silence, like an old married couple. I must admit it was kind of eerie. For Thomas, although he enjoyed his solitude, I think it was more about having someone around him he could tolerate let alone work with.

The others asked me about what we were doing.

"Mending fences, mostly," I told them, "like Jamie said."

"I knew it! I was right, wasn't I?" crowed Jamie. He smirked proudly in big-brother-Frank's direction.

Again, there were speculations. This time about what it was like to work with Thomas.

"He's telling you exactly what to do and how to do it, ain't he?" said Clarence.

"I'll bet he lets you go about your work and then has you re-do it," Jamie guessed.

"I don't think I would like to work so close to Señor Benton," commented Miguel.

"It hasn't been bad, actually," I told them. "He does let me go about my work. And he does give some direction, but mostly suggestions. No, it hasn't been bad."

As the days slowly warmed, Thomas requested my help more and more. It became routine. As I said, we would work in silence. When Thomas took to a task he did it. There was no interrupting him. We would also take our breaks in silence as he would wander off to the shade of some tree. It had to be the right tree, too. Many a time he would move from one to another in search of the perfect trunk, the perfect set of roots, and the perfect amount of shade. Once found, he'd take out his leather notebook and begin to write and think and write.

It was after the work was done, as we rode at a turtle's pace back to the corral and the house, that we would talk. Our conversations were never about anything important like politics or philosophy. They were about places we've been and people we've met. Of course, being forty-some years older than me, he had a lot more to talk about than I did. He'd been nearly everywhere: Texas, Colorado, Arizona and Utah. As far south as Mexico and as north as the Dakotas.

"What's your favorite city?" I asked, thinking he must've seen them all.

"I am partial to Denver," he said. "But this here is my favorite kind of skyline." He gestured to the trees and the surrounding mountains and the range that stretched before us.

"I haven't been to too many places much bigger than Scofield."

"Everyone should see a big city at least once. You

should go to Denver someday."

"Maybe I will," I said.

On another of our slow rides I asked him about the notebook he writes in.

"I like to put down my thoughts," he replied.

"Like in a diary?"

"No. More like in...verse."

"You mean poetry?" I said. I sounded a bit more shocked than I meant to, but Thomas just laughed.

"A cowboy can't be a poet? Many I've known that sing. Miguel strums a fine guitar. And I've yet to meet a hand that didn't enjoy a dance now and again. So why not a little poetry?"

I looked away, duly chastised, and then asked, "What do you write about?"

"My life. Things I see."

On occasion, he would elucidate about common things. Like fences. "They're a godsend to the cowboy...and our damnation. Fences give us work to do, and make our job easier by keeping cattle from straying too far. Yet, they keep us hemmed-in, and may someday make us obsolete. Mr. Jackson didn't need to replace those three men, as I see it. Mind you, I'm glad you've joined us, Billy, but there are days when there's not enough to keep us all busy, partly because of fences."

By then I was comfortable enough with him to bring up something that had been nagging me. "What happened with those three men you chased off?" I asked him.

"What have you heard?"

"Different things."

"Everyone loves a good story, don't they?"

"I suppose they do. So, what happened?"

"Well," Thomas began, then gave pause to make sure he told it to me right. It had been several months since it happened. "I'd suspected them three of ill-doings for a while, and I was riding to the house for a confrontation."

"Readied for a fight?"

"Luckily, it never got to that. I was planning to deal with them the best way I knew how—with the truth. The truth makes men like them all squirrelly and nervous. I caught up to them at the corral, about to let our horses loose, and I flat out told them I knew what all they'd been up to. Of course, they hemmed-and-hawed about one thing and another, but realized there was no fighting the truth. And the fact that I had my hand on my gun.

"I escorted them to the bunkhouse and gave them two minutes to gather up their belongings and get off Mr. Jackson's ranch. They tore through that bunkhouse like they had badgers in their pants, leaving it a shamble and a lot of their things behind. Then they jumped on their horses—"

Thomas took a moment to laugh, and then continued, still laughing. "One of them barely got his left foot in a stirrup before his horse took off, his free leg flailing.

"I followed close behind in case any of them suddenly got brave. The moment I saw the slightest hesitation from them to keep moving on, I drew my gun and fired three shots right over their heads." Again, Thomas laughed. "They were far beyond the horizon before their dust settled to the ground."

I was laughing, too, at Thomas's story, but also at the stories of Frank and the others, all talking like they alone had seen what happened. I shouldn't have been surprised. They were like so many cowboys I've known. They do love a good story. That night at supper I was still laughing, on the inside, knowing what really happened.

Mr. Jackson would change my jovial mood, however. All our moods. He announced after supper, so as not to ruin our appetites, that he was selling the T. Not to Joseph Thorne, but to some men from Texas to who Thorne owed a lot of money. More money than his huge spread was worth. None of us could imagine that kind of money.

"I've been talking with those Texans all week," Mr. Jackson explained. "I don't normally like Texans, no offense Thomas, but like me they are no friends of Thorne, and they made me a right fair offer. It's about time I settled myself down anyway, away from ranching."

"What are you going to do, Max?" Thomas asked.

"I've been thinking a long time about having a store, maybe in a city, like San Francisco. Anything would be better than wrestling with these ornery cattle."

I knew what Mr. Jackson was telling us wasn't true. Like all of us, he loved the life, even the dumb, stubborn cattle. I knew he was just trying to make it easier on us.

"These men say they have room for only two of you on their crew," he then told us.

"I don't understand that," Clarence blurted. "There never seems to be a shortage of work around here."

"I imagine these men run their ranches a little more efficiently than I do."

"More fences," I heard Thomas say to himself.

"It won't happen for a couple more weeks," Mr. Jackson continued. "You can decide among yourselves who's going to stay on. Those of you who move on, you'll be paid what's owed you for the season." He turned from us. Then he stopped before leaving the room. "By the way, Joseph Thorne shot himself in the head earlier today. I didn't like him much, but I do feel for his family."

We all felt for them, too, and sat in silence for a time. Then Thomas said, "No one needs to decide anything right now. Let's give it a few days."

We sat a little longer with our coffees, and then a question came to me. "What would you do if you couldn't be a cowboy?"

The others laughed a bit nervously. Clarence was the first to answer. "I don't much care what I do as long as I've got a place to sleep and a roof over my head."

Miguel reached over and slapped Clarence's belly. "And plenty to eat!"

"You'd work in the mines?" I asked Clarence. He shrugged.

"A man shouldn't be in the ground 'til he's dead," Thomas said.

"I would be a farmer," Miguel stated, "like my father."

"Growing beans ain't much work," Clarence grumbled.

"I could see me and Jamie running some kind of business," Frank said. Jamie's expression said otherwise and his brother told him, "Don't take that manner. You won't get far with that pretty gal of yours working someone else's cattle. I don't know any rich cowboys."

"Not of money, anyway," Thomas added.

Jamie looked over at Thomas. "What would you do, Mr. Benton?"

As common to Thomas, he thought a moment before answering. "I've done a lot of different things in my life. But,

I honestly can't imagine doing anything else anymore." Then he smelled his coffee and took a long sip.

I didn't give an answer to my own question, but I thought about it the rest of the night. I couldn't think of anything else I'd do because being a cowboy isn't as much about what you do as it is about how you do it. If you're a cowboy, it doesn't matter what you do. You're still a cowboy. It made sense to me, yet I didn't share my thoughts because I didn't know how sensible it would sound.

A few days passed and we went about our work with that decision hanging over us. Then one night Thomas walked into the bunkhouse with the look of a man who had made a choice. "Before everyone goes to sleep," he said, "I just wanted to say that I'll be leaving the T at the end of next week."

"Where you head'n?" Frank asked him.

"To Denver first. Then, who knows?"

Right then in a blink, I made a decision, too, and said to Thomas, "Mind if I ride along? You said I should see Denver."

"I'd welcome your company, Billy," he told me, and then said to the others, "Well, I hope that helps the rest of you make up your minds. If I forget to say it later, I've enjoyed working with all of you. You're all fine hands. I'd be glad to work with any of you again one day."

And that was that.

Three

Listen to the whispering west

Its stories what defined us

Its trails what shaped us

Its cowboy's hands what made us

Not two weeks later, Thomas and I were on a train that would take us to a train that would take us to another rail line that would take us to Denver. Fortunately, he paid my way and the way for our horses, as travel like that was a luxury to me. I agreed, on the condition that I pay him back one day, and because I could see he was long ready to get there. Traveling horseback wasn't the best option when you wanted to be somewhere sooner than later. For the most part, Thomas was one of the most even-tempered men I'd met, but he had times when his restlessness all but possessed him. Wanting to get to Denver in that late summer of 1910 was one of those times.

On the train, he often wrote in his notebook. Other times he stared out the window as though he was looking for something. But mostly, he told me stories.

He told me about the Mexican town where he was born, the one that's not there anymore. He was born in 1833. Texas wasn't yet a state. It wasn't even a Republic. His father was a Mexican lawman, and his mother a soiled dove who did little in the way of mothering. But his father loved her. When she died, his father took it hard and drank himself into a sulky mess. Then he got himself shot and killed breaking up a saloon brawl. Thomas was thirteen about that time.

"That's when you began to hunt your father's killer?" I asked him. I felt I knew him well enough by then I could ask him anything. His response was a gut-busting laugh.

"No. That's when I went to work," Thomas said as he caught his breath. "I had nothing because my father had nothing. I stole a horse, I'm not proud to say, and rode away from that dirty old town as fast as I could. I didn't know what I was going to do. But, I did know that I wanted to see a big city."

So, Thomas rode to New Orleans. Tall for his age, folk always thought he was older than he was which made it easy for him to find odd jobs with ranches and farms along the way. Once there, he found work as a bootblack, polishing shoes and boots, and then took on the unforgiving labor of the wharves, loading ships bound for faraway places, right beside many a Black.

But, Thomas told me, "There was something stifling

to the spirit there, as well as a lot of rats and mosquitos. I first saw slavery there, and I was not fond of it. The treatment of the Blacks after the war was particularly distasteful. I worked right along many a black man and found them to be more trustworthy and hardworking than the Whites in that city. If only we were to judge men on those qualities alone. No, New Orleans wasn't to my liking."

Thomas hopped a steamboat up the Mississippi to St. Louis. "I wasn't going to let one bad city dissuade me from further experiences."

He found much of what he left in New Orleans again in St. Louis. "Shipping and trade, slavery, and the French." But he also found something new—friendship, in the form of the du Bois family. Thomas took a job as a hostler with an inn run by Joseph du Bois, his wife Cherise, and their three daughters: Laurette, Tilly and Marie. Thomas was given a room at the back of the house.

"I was fourteen," Thomas recalled. "A far lesser man would have succumbed to the temptation of those daughters. Well, two of them. Marie was only three. But I held my own against the beguiling presence of Laurette and Tilly. It was only my respect for Joseph and his kindness that kept me corralled, and my fear of Cherise. That woman would have skinned me to the bone if I'd done anything untoward with her girls."

Thomas was with them for two idyllic, though often frustrating, years. Until cholera struck. Of the du Bois household, all but Thomas and young Marie perished to the condition. In a dying wish, Joseph asked Thomas to take Marie away from St. Louis and the disease.

"Joseph had a brother in Chicago. But I'd heard rumors of the disease spreading there, as well. Instead, I took Marie with me to Texas—it was a state by then—to Franklin Bodell's ranch, where I had worked for a time. Franklin gave me a job, and his family took little Marie in as one of their own. I was with the Bodells for only a few years before I was once again overcome by wanderlust."

This time his restlessness would take him as far west as one could go. With hungry prospectors in California, cattle were being driven there from the areas of San Antonio and Fredericksburg. Thomas was quickly hired on for the experience of a lifetime—a cattle drive through the New Mexico Territory and up the California coast to San Francisco. He ended up working a number of those drives until the need for beef along the Pacific Coast waned. In 1857, Thomas found himself back at the Bodell ranch.

But not for long.

There was talk of gold in the Territory of Kansas, near the Rocky Mountains. After having been to California and having seen the opportunities that yellow rock could offer,

Thomas got hit with gold fever. In 1858, at the age of twenty-five, he travelled northward.

Thomas gained no fortune as a miner, though. Instead, he found success in running a more legitimate livelihood: a livery stable. He also had a hand in the making of a small mining town into a vital community known as Denver. "It's a wondrous thing to grow a city," he said. "Where once there were tents and shacks there are buildings of brick and mortar. Muddy trails become streets. Hoodlums replaced by upstanding citizens and families…for the most part, at least."

Thomas corresponded with the Bodells on a regular basis. In one letter, Franklin Bodell expressed concern about the war over slavery coming to Texas and, specifically, to his ranch. This time, it was Thomas's idea to take Marie out of harm's way by bringing her to Colorado.

"I wasn't a fool. I knew that ugly war would leave every part of this country fouled by its touch. It would come to Denver just as sure as it would go to Texas. But I'd made a promise to Joseph that I would take care of Marie, and I felt I could best do that if she were with me."

Marie was not alone, however. In the early spring of 1860 she had given birth to a daughter of her own, the father being a transient cowhand who quickly rode away from his responsibilities. Come that fall, Thomas took fifteen-year-old Marie and her baby, Ellen Marie, away to Denver.

Thomas was there for twelve years, giving only financial support to Marie. He didn't feel it was his place to tell a mother how to raise a daughter that wasn't his. In 1868 his livery stable burned down. He borrowed money from a saloon owner to rebuild the stable and worked as a barkeep to repay the debt.

Eventually, city life and the caring for other men's horses began to take its toll upon Thomas. He longed to be on the range once again, and at the age of forty, Thomas left Denver and the run of his business to Marie and returned to the hard life of a cowboy.

Marie died a few years later. Ellen Marie, then nineteen, took over run of the stable while Thomas continued to send money from wherever he found himself employed: the territories of Wyoming, Montana and Arizona, and the state of Utah. Thomas worked outfits throughout the west. "And every few years I satisfy my hankering for the city and return to Denver," he said.

One time he returned to find Ellen Marie had sold the livery stable and invested in a much more lucrative business—a brothel. Thomas couldn't argue her choice of venture as it brought in more money than his stable ever did and she no longer needed his support. Not financially, anyway.

Their unique relationship had spanned thirty years in this manner. Thomas would come to spend a week or a few with her in the big city, and then go off in search of a ranch that needed a hand for months, sometimes years, at a time. If no ranchers were hiring, he found odd jobs in small towns. For a brief period he was even a lawman. "But I couldn't help but think about how thankless my father's life was," he explained. "I didn't wear that badge for but a few weeks."

Mostly, though, he had been a cowboy.

"Any run-ins with Indians?" I asked him at one point, not ever having met one myself.

"Not the way you might think. I've been fortunate in that way. An Osage did save my life once."

"An Indian saved a cowboy?" I naïvely questioned.

"I was chasing a stray down a wash when a rainstorm hit. The flash flood swept me and my horse away like we were leaves in a gust of wind. If it hadn't been for Eagle Heart, I would have been dead. My lungs were filled with water, and I had a pretty good knot on my head. He healed me back to health."

Thomas left it at that and went strangely quiet.

"What's your favorite part about being a cowboy, Thomas?"

"There's little I've enjoyed more than a cattle drive. I've ridden about every trail. The Chisholm and the Dodge

City, from Texas to the Dakota Territory. But riding that long is too hard these days. An afternoon mending fences suits me better now."

"Maybe we'll find work like that in Colorado," I said.

"Maybe."

I gave a little thought to how different it was for me as a cowboy as it had been for Thomas. Oh, much of the work I did was the same, moving cattle from one place to another, branding, busting broncos. Oftentimes, I'd had to take on the duties of a mere farm hand as some ranchers took to growing crops for their cattle. But I'd never ridden a cattle drive. Railroads connected nearly every part of the country by my time and moved cattle much faster along than those bygone trails. Long gone were the open range and endless rides. The land was by and far already tamed by cowboys like Thomas when cowboys like me came along. And I'd never run into an Indian. The government had long confined them to reservations.

The train ride through the Rockies was as beautiful as it was long. I'd not yet experienced their majesty up close. Along pine covered mountainsides and through deep canyons, we chugged. When Thomas was done with stories about himself, he shared many of those he had read. He'd read a great deal, too: Dickens, Twain, Cooper, Hawthorne. One author he didn't care for was Jules Verne. "The world is interesting enough as it is. I don't have any need for fantastical things that could never happen." But he was right when he said that everyone loves a good story. I know I do. And I don't think anyone loved telling them more than Thomas. By the time we finally reached Denver, I felt like I'd heard them all.

Four

When I take her, she takes me away,

my weariness forgets why I found her

and I welcome the new day.

Her gift to me is tomorrow.

Without her, I'd go no further.

I was plenty ready to get off the hard seats of that lumbering train as we pulled into Denver's Union Station. Sure, it was days faster than horseback, but the confines of the car had gotten to me. I quickly forgot all my discomforts, though, as the city of Denver was a sight to see. The immense buildings of brick and stone were like castles. The station itself was a fortress with a clock tower that reached a great height. Street cars ran up the center of the wide avenue in front of us and horse-carriages moved along on either side of them. A grandly decorative arch "welcomed" our arrival to the city. It was hard to imagine the rough and tumble beginnings, the tents and shacks Thomas had described. Denver was a real metropolis.

It was a daunting and unfamiliar scene. One that made me wish for my Colt at my side, but Thomas had us pack our pistols away before leaving Scofield saying that we would be better received without them. He did, however, keep a Colt Thunderer—its 2½" barrel made it a perfect pocket pistol—concealed in his coat. Truthfully, though I owned a gun, I never had a reason to use it outside of killing a rattler, and I rarely even carried it. I'd more likely use my pistol to hammer a loose nail than shoot it.

I walked through that grand arch and into the busyness of the city and thought it odd how the circumstances of my life had never led me to a place like Denver. Maybe I avoided them on purpose, as I don't like to be crowded. But I was nearly twenty-one and felt myself greatly lacking in many of life's experiences. I'd never been on a train nor seen a real city. Hell, I'd never been in a fight nor broken a bone. I was feeling as raw and simple as an Eastern tenderfoot. It consoled me a little to know I had at least kissed a girl or two by that time in my life.

Thomas spared no expense in our travel. He paid for the transport and stabling of our horses, and he covered our accommodations at the Oxford Hotel, which was just a couple of blocks from the station. It stood five or six stories, if I recall. What mattered was that it was the tallest building I'd ever seen, and the streets of Denver were lined with buildings just like it. There was a drug store on the first floor where I would end up having my first taste of ice cream, just one of several firsts for me during my stay there.

Thomas got us each a room. I objected, telling him we could share one and I'd sleep on the floor, but he ignored me. What I remember the most about the room was the bed. It was like a cloud, and I slept right on into the next day. It had been a long train ride that offered little rest for me. When I woke, I thought it was dawn when it was dusk. Thomas took me downstairs to the Oxford's restaurant for a fine steak dinner in a room of rich wood paneling, sconce lamps, and tables set with crystal and white linen. He told me how he had spent the day visiting an old friend, and that he was going back after we ate. I was welcome to go along if I wanted.

We walked a few blocks to Market Street, and then Thomas took us to a modest brick house where two ladies eyed our approach from the porch. "Have you ever been to a parlor?" Thomas asked me.

"I can't say that I have."

"This one isn't no 'House of Mirrors,' but it's nice enough."

I didn't tell him I hadn't any idea what he was talking about.

The ladies came down the steps to meet us. "You're back so soon!" said one of them to Thomas. "And you brought a friend," said the other.

"I'm here to see Ellen Marie," Thomas told them.

"Of course you are," said the first, a bit snidely.

Both women had handsome figures and held themselves in a manner that was anything but shy. The second put her arm through mine and started to lead me up the steps. I looked up and down the street at the many other houses with women in front of them, and suddenly I felt quite foolish as it came to me that these 'parlors' were brothels, and the ladies were prostitutes. Denver's Red Light District was as nearly famous as New Orleans's and San Francisco's which I had heard about, and I was standing right in the middle of it.

I stopped at the top step and released my companion's determined grip. "I think, perhaps, I'll be heading back to the hotel," I said to Thomas.

"That's fine, Billy," he replied. "Most likely I'll see you in the morning."

As I made my way in the direction we had come I heard my lady's sweet and forlorn voice. "Don't be a stranger, Billy."

Now, you may think my behavior a bit prudish, or perhaps it was an experience I was not yet ready for. Truth is, that kind of attention from a woman was never my preference. What I mean is, I could never buy into its insincerity. A prostitute's only interest in a man is how much money he has, and how she can get it from him. When his money runs out, so does her interest. I would discover, years later, that those soiled doves were only one kind of whore our modern society has to offer.

Back at the hotel I stopped into the drug store and had that first ice cream I'd mentioned earlier and bought myself a newspaper. Then I went up to my room and fell asleep while reading about a drunkard injured in a fall from a moving streetcar, the high cost of a finely carved parasol handle, how crosswalks have added comfort and beauty to the streets, and the darn wretchedness of constipation. Stories you would only expect from a big city like Denver.

The next morning, Thomas had not returned to the hotel. I ate breakfast alone and finished my paper from the night before. Then I went for a walk. No destination in mind. I just walked.

Every tall building looked the same to me, and there were a lot of them. So that I wouldn't get lost, I went along named streets, like Wynkoop or Wazee, as much as possible and kept my bearings by counting the numbered streets I passed as I remembered that the Oxford was somewhere on 17th. I've easily made my way across vast open plains and through thickly wooded forests, but navigating those cavernous city streets was something else.

I walked for hours, peering into store fronts as I went.

So many services and so much merchandise I had no use for. Bicycle repair and photographic developing. Sewing machines and telephones. I even saw those fancy-handled parasols I had read about the night before. When I got hungry, I stopped in a store and picked up some jerky and licorice. And there was no shortage of saloons for other refreshments.

My favorite part of the city was Larimer Square. The development of Denver, with Thomas's help, began there a little over fifty years before, and although the original wood buildings had burnt down and been replaced by splendid structures of brick and concrete, you could still feel its history, as brief as it was.

I also enjoyed the stares I got because of my cowboy attire. I'm sure I looked as strange to them as the men did to me in their heavy suits and vests, and the ladies in their high-necked, bustled dresses. And the hats! No practical use for them that I could see beyond mere decoration. A group of young ladies giggled and whispered as I walked past and giggled some more as I flashed them a smile. Now that I think about it all these years later, the attention I received may not have been all that flattering. They may have been laughing at me rather than with me. Well, no matter now as I'm sure they're all dead and gone.

When I found myself on Market Street, I decided to

check in on Thomas, but I couldn't remember exactly which parlor we had stopped at the night before. I ignored the invitations of the prostitutes as I walked and hoped something would look familiar to me. Eventually something did. It was Thomas himself strolling in my direction with a woman on his arm. She was a waif of a thing with a sweet smile and large, tired eyes. Unlike the other women around the city the dress she wore exposed her smooth, thin neck. Next to Thomas she almost looked like a child, though I guessed her to be well into her forties.

Thomas was very happy to see me, like a drunk spying a bottle of whiskey. "Billy!" he shouted with an outstretched hand. We shook and he about broke my fingers in his exuberance. "Billy, I'd like you to meet Ellen Marie. Ellen, this is Billy."

"Pleased to meet you, ma'am," I said. I gently took her tiny hand, afraid I might crush it like Thomas did mine.

"Likewise, Billy," she said with the slightest curtsey. Her deep, mature voice did not match her delicate appearance. Then to Thomas she said, *"Il est un jeune homme poli, non?"*

"Oui, il est un beau jeune homme," Thomas replied.

Thomas and Ellen Marie continued their stroll, speaking a little more French, and I went along beside them. "Did you come here looking for me?" Thomas asked me.

"Well, I suppose I did. But I have been out taking in the city."

"There's a lot to see, isn't there?"

"Yes, there is."

Ellen interjected, "Have you been to the vaudeville theater down on Welton Street?"

"No, ma'am, I haven't."

"It's just a few more streets that way," she said with a flick of her wrist that I admit I found somewhat becoming. In fact, her whole manner was quite womanly, natural and supple. The opposite of the stiff postured ladies I had seen throughout my walk earlier. Whatever it was about Ellen Marie, it was impossible not to watch her. "It's a lovely theater, really. And they have the most entertaining acts you've ever seen. You must go, Billy."

"How could I not?" I replied, my eyes fixed upon her.

Then Thomas said, "I have some good news, Billy." He pulled a crumpled envelope from his breast pocket and showed me the letter inside it. "An old friend of mine, Jack McElroy, wrote me saying he's got some work if I'm interested. He has a ranch in Arizona, outside of Prescott. It sounds like he may even have enough to do for the both of us."

The news of work was exciting, but I had to ask, "How did he know you were here?"

"He knows me too well," Thomas replied. "He knew I'd be around to visit Ellen Marie sooner or later. The letter's only dated a month ago."

"It was fortuitous you're being here," Ellen said with a smile to Thomas and wink at me. I didn't know what that word meant, but I could have listened to her say it all day and night.

"How about we head south in a few days, Billy?"

"That would be fine," I said. I excused myself to continue my walk and left them to continue their stroll.

"Au revoir, Billy," said Ellen Marie, and I vowed to myself to one day learn French.

ॐ   ॐ   ॐ

Welton Street was a little more than a few blocks away. Having walked as much as I had already, I was well in need of a sit and cool refreshment by the time I found the theater. It clearly stood out from the other buildings around it. It was only three stories, but long, and a partial domed roof gave it the appearance of a small palace. Signs out front proclaimed "Modern Vaudeville," and I was drawn inside.

There was a refreshment counter with a marble soda fountain where I enjoyed a treat before going into the auditorium. The seats were comfortable, and I slipped my boots off to give my feet a treat of their own. The feeling of being in a palace was all around me. Ornamental trim framed the balconies, upper levels, and the immense stage. Everything sparkled underneath the many lights.

The theater was less than half full. The audience was mostly men. Maybe the acts weren't refined enough for ladies, I thought. The women that were in attendance did seem a little rough around the edges. Their laughs and demeanor were as bawdy as the men's.

The show started with a pair of slapstick comedians. It was utter nonsense but funny. The more the big guy smacked the little guy around the more the audience roared. But when the little guy got the best of his partner in the end, we all cheered. Then a magician came on and most of his tricks didn't work too well, so the crowd jeered and booed him off the stage.

A pair of singers seemed to be the crowd favorite, but my personal favorite was the animal act. There was a dancing dog, a monkey playing a fiddle, and a bear riding a bicycle. They were all so impressive, and smarter than many a cowboy I've worked with.

After that, a strong man performed amazing feats of strength and acrobatics. He was followed by a burlesque dancer whose manner reminded me of the women on Market Street. Knowing there were women in the audience, her gyrations made me a little uncomfortable.

Then, the evening's entertainment concluded with something I had once heard about but never seen. It was a moving picture. It was more than eighty years ago, but I remember it like it was last week. It was called *His Majesty the Queen,* and it was about a king who, for reasons not clearly explained, had to dress as a queen to foil some plot to overthrow his rule. For the most part, the comedy was much like the rowdy slapstick from earlier. What made it different, though, was that it told a story. An absurd story, but a story nonetheless. It wasn't just the pranks I was laughing at, but the situation and the characters as well. With the live acts, I recall still being aware of the auditorium and the crowd. But the motion picture screen was like a window to another place and everything around me disappeared.

I left the theater wanting to see more and wanting to share it with Thomas. It was growing dark as I made my way back to Market Street. I had to ask everyone I met if they knew of the house where Ellen Marie worked. If the men I asked responded to me at all, it was either with a laugh or a "one whore's as good as another." The prostitutes I spoke to either didn't know her or they tried to turn my attention upon them instead. Finally, I found a young woman as ragged as the day was long who pointed me in the right direction.

The front room of the parlor house was elegant yet musty. A few men sat there, each in the company of a lady. Two of them were particularly boisterous. When I asked for Ellen Marie, I was directed to a kind of ballroom that glowed in the light of a crystal chandelier where a piano player performed in the nearest corner. Some of the women danced with their customers before leading them up the stairs that were covered with an Oriental carpet and framed by a finely carved banister. Other "couples" sat together along the perimeter of the room. They drank champagne and laughed. It was there that I spotted Thomas with Ellen Marie sitting in his lap. They were so comfortable together that for a moment I forgot the true nature of their relationship. They could have easily been a pair of newlyweds enjoying an evening out.

The two of them were happy to see me. "How was your tour of our city?" Ellen asked me with genuine interest. "Did you get to see a show?"

"I did, and I thoroughly enjoyed it!" I answered and told them both all about it. I suggested to Thomas that we go the next day as I thought it would be something he would enjoy as well.

He listened with pleasant attention, but then his eyes narrowed and he motioned to the front room. "Did you see a pair of men when you came in? Loud, like they felt they had something to say that everyone should hear?"

"Yes, as a matter of fact I did. Why?"

Thomas didn't answer right away. He watched the front room for a time before saying, "Be careful who you share stories about your life with, Billy."

Ellen Marie noticed the confusion on my face and explained, "Some unfriendly acquaintances of Thomas's are here. We're hoping they keep their distance."

"They came here looking for you?" I asked Thomas.

"No. I only told them about some of the places I've been. It seems they wanted to come here for themselves. It's an unfortunate coincidence."

Laughter and boasting from the two men could be heard over the piano playing and conversations around us. Ellen Marie tried to distract Thomas. "Let's go to my room. We certainly won't run into them there, will we?" she told him with a sly smile.

"Too late," Thomas said.

The two men entered the room. They were both long and lean and could've been brothers with the similarity of their expressions and mannerisms, or maybe they had simply been riding together for some time. They were drunk, and there was a stagger to their swagger. These were not men you would have to seek out to pick a fight with. They would come to you. And as soon as they saw Thomas, they did.

Thomas stood immediately, setting Ellen Marie aside like a precious doll and taking his hat from the side table there. I remember Ellen Marie looking at him with concern, yet a certain longing that said she truly enjoyed seeing this side of her man. Thomas stood his ground like a bull, and I made sure to take a step back. Both men stopped when Thomas stood. One of them laughed in such a high-pitched, nervous tone that it made me laugh, which then made him surly.

The other loudly cursed Thomas. "I can't find no real work 'cuz a you, you son-of-a-bitch!"

"You only brought it on yourself," Thomas replied.

"I'm stuck workin' a damn factory!"

"Work is work. You should be glad you found any."

"It's demeanin', I'm tellin' you!"

"Then maybe it suits you," I heard myself say. Their business certainly wasn't my business but I didn't like anyone talking to my friend that way.

The loud cowboy looked at me with such disgust and surprise that he didn't know how to respond so he turned to Ellen Marie instead, which proved to be a grave mistake for him. "That's the skinny, old whore you always talked about? Talk about demeanin'!" His right arm rose up to shoo her away, but his drunkenness was such that he misjudged the distance and ended up slapping her forehead with the back of his hand.

Thomas burst forward. The cowboy reached beneath his coat. Who knows if he was reaching for a gun or a knife, but he never got the chance to pull it out. Thomas threw his hat into the cowboy's face and then brought one of his huge fists down upon the poor drunk's cheek, sending him hard to the floor.

His partner made a move at Thomas. I thrust a hand inside my empty jacket and gave him a warning. He fell for my bluff and stopped. Then Thomas did something I still can't believe I saw. He lifted the loud drunkard to his feet and hit him again. Then again. And again. The cowboy was only half conscious but Thomas kept picking him up and beating him down. It was brutal. After the fifth time his partner turned and got out of the house as fast as he could. After the eighth time Ellen Marie had to grab Thomas's shoulder.

"Stop! You'll kill him!" she shouted.

Thomas let the bloodied cowboy drop one last time and left him there. He wasn't dead, but he didn't move.

"You better get of here, Thomas," Ellen said, scolding him like a child. "The both of you!"

Thomas grabbed his hat that lay next to the crumpled drunk and took long, hurried strides out to the street. I followed him in practically a run all the way back to the hotel.

"Maybe we can go back there tomorrow after things settle down," I said to Thomas.

"No," he said, "she meant we better get out of Denver."

We gathered our things. Thomas paid the bill. We got our horses from the livery stable and rode out of the city. There wasn't time to wait for the next train south. I've never returned to Denver, but I'll always remember my first taste of ice cream, my first (and last) Red Light District, and my first silent movie.

Five

I know 'em all
those dreamers and fortune seekers...
men and women who left their marks,
or scars, some say,
but indelible, remembered.

Thomas was quiet for much of the first two days of our ride south. We just rode. It was on our second night that I couldn't bear the crackling sound of our campfire and nothing else any longer.

"Who were those two cowboys, anyway, Thomas?" I asked him. "Were they from the Triple-T?"

He only gave a sullen nod.

"Is there more going on between you three than I think? I mean, the way we hurried out of town and all."

"Perhaps I'd had a little too much to drink, but I don't tolerate any mistreatment to a woman. And I wasn't in the mood to deal with some fool sheriff. I took it all as our sign to move on."

I tried to console him by saying, "I'm sure he's

recovering just fine." But my friend sat there miserable and quiet.

"Beating down that stupid cowboy isn't what bothers me," Thomas finally confessed. "I didn't say goodbye to Ellen Marie. And who knows when I'll be seeing her again." After a moment, he added, "Make sure you always tell folk goodbye, Billy. Don't leave that kind of thing undone."

Even if Thomas had never told me of his history with Ellen Marie it wouldn't have mattered, all anyone would ever need to know was there in his wretched posture. If he did happen to look up, it was just like he had on our train ride, like he was looking for something not out on any horizon, but somewhere in his head.

The next morning and for the rest of our ride into Arizona, things were back to normal. Except now, I was telling him a bit about me, about how I didn't remember my parents or where I'd been born. I told him how I'd come out of Kansas to get away from an uncle who didn't much want me around, and how I'd worked and rode through the states of Nebraska, Wyoming, and Utah. I told him how the men I'd worked for were like fathers to me, some of them teaching me to read and write. Then I apologized to him for not having had a very interesting life or good stories to tell.

"You will, Billy," he told me. "Besides, it's been getting more interesting lately, hasn't it?"

"Yes, I suppose it has," I said with a laugh.

What did interest Thomas was the fact that I didn't know who my parents were. "Your uncle never told you about them? You never wondered?" he asked me.

"He never said much of anything to me. I guess I never considered knowing."

"A man should know where he comes from. His history is who he is. You should learn as much as you can about your mother and father. Then you'll learn a lot about yourself."

"I wouldn't know where to begin."

"Start with your uncle. Find him and make him tell you everything he knows."

I stopped talking about it. I knew he was right, but my uncle could've been dead for all I knew, and I just didn't want to go looking for him. I put my attention, instead, on what was ahead for us—a new job in a new place.

I asked Thomas about his friend, Jack McElroy, the man who was offering us work.

"I've known Jack longer than I've known anybody that's still alive," Thomas said. "Hell, I've known him so long I can't remember how long I've known him. When we first met we didn't much like each other, though. He thought I was a know-it-all. And I didn't like him for a couple of reasons. One, because he was a bully."

"What was the other reason?"

"He's the son of the man who killed my father."

"Wait. I thought you said you never went hunting for that man."

"I didn't. Our paths crossed by mere dumb luck down in San Antonio."

"I guess this Jack McElroy didn't much appreciate you killing his father, then."

"I didn't kill Old McElroy. It was Jack done that."

I stopped my horse. "Wait. Now, I'm confused."

With a light laugh, Thomas explained. "There was one thing Jack and I agreed upon—that his father was a royal son-of-a-bitch. He'd made a real unpleasant life for Jack and his brothers and sisters. I won't tell you the things he'd done, but if there was ever a man who needed to be killed it was John McElroy. But I didn't think it was right for a son to kill his own father, so one day I went looking to do it for him. I got to their ranch and found the old man dead with an axe in his skull. One of Jack's sisters saw me and I ran."

"All these years you've taken the blame for a murder you didn't do?"

"Jack was going to go to the sheriff, but I told him that he and his family had had a hard enough life already. He didn't need any trouble with the law. His father and I had a history, and I imagine I would have killed him sooner or later."

"So, you've been a wanted man ever since," I said.

"Yep."

"And that's why we left Denver in such a hurry."

"Yep. I can't risk the chance of running into some old lawman with a good memory."

We rode on in silence for a time. Then Thomas said, "I'd appreciate it if that's one story you don't share with anyone, at least 'til after I'm dead and buried."

"I don't see any reason to be sharing that with anyone," I told him.

Late the next day we made it to Central Arizona.

Prescott was one of those mining towns that survived when the gold ran out, thanks to ranching. Spreads were established all around, mostly in the valleys north of town. Not the Willow Ranch, however. It was tucked away in the woods, established by Mr. McElroy's friends, Henry and Pauline Mitchell. Jack McElroy came there to help Pauline when her husband passed on. When she died shortly after that, she left the Willow to Mr. McElroy.

From a distance, Prescott looked like any other small mountain town. Buildings congregated upon a mesa, surrounded by trees and a horizon of peaks faraway. Closer in, just outside of town, was a butte that stuck out of the landscape like a thumb. Thomas pointed out that that was where we were heading.

Up close, the town had charm and character that I immediately took a liking to. At its center was a courthouse, as stately as any building I saw in Denver, and all around it were clean, welcoming storefronts. I remember feeling that I didn't need to be going anywhere else. I was ready to stay put for good as we rode past the elegant Hotel St. Michael in the direction of that butte.

The Willow Ranch's acreage was wooded and rocky. A narrow, deeply rutted road wound itself over a rough contour of hills and washes. It was not land I would want to be chasing cattle across. But, according to what Thomas had told me about in Mr. McElroy's letter, the job offered had little to do with ranching. That was all I knew.

We came to a curve in the road where on the far side sat an old wagon, eroded from lack of care and use, and on the other was an area flat and clear that presented a ranch house, a bunkhouse, a barn and a corral. Parked beside the bunkhouse was a car. A Willys-Overland touring car, if I recall correctly. As popular as automobiles were becoming then, it was still a sight to see one outside of town. The car was covered in dirt, but otherwise looked fairly new.

Standing on the front porch was Jack McElroy. He was just as Thomas had described him, not tall but built as solid as a rock with wide shoulders and an equally wide stomach. Atop those shoulders was a beaming, red face. We were still approaching the house when Thomas shouted, "Mac, damn you! Who the hell did you steal this piece of land from?"

"Steal?" Mr. McElroy yelled back. "This was given me by a woman madly smitten with my beautiful face!" He stepped down from the porch and came our way.

Thomas got off his horse. "She was mad, alright! Mad with syphilis!"

The two old men jeered at each other like schoolboys, then bear-hugged like long, lost brothers. When Mr. McElroy shook my hand, he impressed me as a man who underestimated his own strength. He might snap your back with a jovial slap or break a rib under his embrace, and then give a robust laugh at your pain.

"This is a terrible piece of land for cattle, Mac," Thomas said.

"Henry never did have a head for business, or beef," Mr. McElroy admitted. "I sold every last one of them and had to let all my hands go. I was about to sell off the land as well when some folk from Chicago offered to lease it from me, which is why I have a job for you."

"What is it these Chicagoans are doing?" Thomas asked.

"Come on, I'll show you," Mr. McElroy said with a

broad grin. "I think they're shooting over this way today."

"Shooting?" I asked. "What are they shooting at?"

Mr. McElroy laughed so loudly that it made me laugh even though I had no idea what I was laughing at. He said, "I guess you could say they're shooting each other!"

We walked for a bit along a narrow path. Except for a breeze through the pines, it was quiet. There weren't any sounds of gunfire or anything. We crested a ridge that overlooked a dry creek bed lined with boulders as big as horses. Among those large rocks some people were jumping and running around. Some were dressed like Indians. Not that I'd seen a lot of Indians before, but they looked kind of odd, mostly because they weren't Indians: they were White. They were as much Indian as I was. The others were townsfolk or settlers, I guessed. They shouted and screamed and ran from the not-so-menacing Whites-dressed-like-Indians.

Thomas summed it up pretty well when he asked his friend, "What's all this nonsense?"

Mr. McElroy pointed to two men we hadn't yet noticed. They stood on higher ground than the others, and they were dressed like regular folk. One of the men looked into a box that was pointed at those running around the rocks, and he turned a crank attached to the side of the box. "They're shooting a motion picture," Mr. McElroy said. The other fellow began yelling down to the others, instructing them on how to act being chased by Whites-dressed-like-Indians and all.

"I saw one in Denver," I said. "Remember, Thomas? I told you about it."

Thomas didn't answer. He couldn't take his eyes off the nonsense. He seemed pleasantly mesmerized, however. There was a hint of a smile on his face.

"That gentleman there," Mr. McElroy explained as he pointed to the man cranking the box, "is taking moving pictures of those others play acting a story."

I couldn't make any sense of a story from the way they were running around. It wasn't anything like the movie I had seen in Denver. But I had to admit it was fun to watch. There were six of them, four men and two women. Two of the men were the Indians, wearing what looked like leather pajamas with fringes and large, feathered head-dresses. The others were the townsfolk. All of them wore a significant amount of stage make-up. Satisfied they had run around sufficiently, the man who had been yelling got them to stop by shouting, "Cut!"

The players wandered off to rest in the shade while the camera operator moved his equipment to more level ground. The last fellow, the yeller, came over to where we were. He was thin, with sloping shoulders and a slumped back. Mr. McElroy introduced him as Alan Grady, the director.

"Director?" Thomas replied. He respected men in positions of authority to some degree, but I could see he had his doubts about Grady.

"Yes, well, somebody has to be in charge," Grady answered with a snort. His voice was pinched, so much so that it was a bit hard to listen to him. "What do you gentlemen think of our little story here?"

Again, Thomas was surprised. "Story? I can't say that we saw much of a story."

"Well, no, I guess not. It still has to be put together," Grady replied.

"What is the story?" I asked.

"It's about a young woman who is captured by Indians, and the man who rescues her at all costs," said Grady proudly.

"Not original, but tried and true," said Thomas. Grady was about to respond when Thomas continued. "Of what tribe are those two supposed to be?"

"Well, they're, well, Indians."

"With those head-dresses, they could be Plains Indians, but this doesn't look much like the plains. And they're wearing boots. Couldn't find any moccasins?"

"No. No, we couldn't, as a matter of fact. But I

decided boots were acceptable," Grady answered, feebly standing his ground. "Mr. McElroy, who are these two cowboys, anyway?"

"These are the men I hired to protect you from them Patents Detectives you're so worried about," Mr. McElroy answered. "By your request, you might recall."

"Well, perhaps they should get around to doing their job and leave me to mine."

With his arms crossed Grady stomped off in the direction of the actors. The cameraman had been nearby enough to hear our conversation and when Grady left he stepped closer.

"I warned him about those damn boots," he whispered to us. Then he said, "My name's Toby Greene. Pleased to meet you." We shook his hand and introduced ourselves. He had soft skin and gentle features, but a genuineness in his eyes that made you trust him. Before he left us to join the others he added with a shrug, "I've been trying to keep the boots out of the camera's frame."

On our walk back to the house, Mr. McElroy explained to Thomas and me just what our job would be. "As I understand it, there's this bunch called the Picture Patents Company or something like that, and they don't want nobody making motion pictures but themselves, so they send out detectives, gunmen really, to find and stop people like Grady."

"Is that legal?" Thomas asked.

"The Patents seem to think so."

"That means Grady's a criminal?"

The two old men had a belly of a laugh at the idea of the thin, chinless movie director an outlaw. "I don't know if what the Patents Company is doing is in the right," Mr. McElroy said eventually, "but they're doing it, which is why I asked you here."

"I don't understand," I confessed.

"Well, Billy, let's say you owned some land and you wanted to farm it."

"I'm not much of a farmer."

"In this example, you are. Just pretend. Okay?"

"Okay."

"Now, let's say you buy a plow and the fellow you bought it from says you have to give him a share of your crop, and if you don't, or if you try to use someone else's plow he'll send out some men to break your plow or shoot your horse."

"That's why I'm not a farmer," I said, "ranching seems a lot simpler."

"So, you want us to keep a watch for these patents men," Thomas said to his friend.

"That's right," Mr. McElroy replied. "Grady and his

people have come all the way out here to make pictures and avoid these Patents. The men Grady works for have been leasing my land for a few months now, and there hasn't been any trouble so far."

Mr. McElroy showed us where we were staying, which was in the main house with him. The movie people stayed in the bunkhouse. You can't imagine how important I felt having a whole room and bed to myself. There was even an indoor bathroom just like a hotel. As I took in the accommodations, I heard Mr. McElroy tell Thomas, "I wrote everyone I knew that might be interested in this job. I'm glad you were the only one to respond."

I remember feeling the same way.

Six

He can ride, as every cowboy should,
Rope, brand, round the herd
and chop the wood.
He'd do it all, sun-up to down, if he could.

The work Thomas and I were hired to do wasn't work at all. The way Thomas figured it, the Willow's land was so difficult to traverse that any visitors would have to come straight up the road. "We have the advantage of being hard to find and even harder to get to," he explained. And it was so quiet that we could hear anyone arriving from miles off, especially if they came by automobile. So, we just watched the road. There were days when I felt a bit of the outlaw because of the money I was stealing from the Chicago-men who paid Grady and the others.

We stood watch in shifts, me strapped with my Colt and he wearing his Schofield with his Winchester in reach. When it wasn't his watch, Thomas helped Mr. McElroy with any odd chores, or they would ride the property together. Whether they spent that time reminiscing old times or scheming new plans, I can't say. Sometimes Thomas would sit on the porch and write in his notebook or read something from Mr. McElroy's library. Whatever he was doing, it was apparent that Thomas was very content during our stay there.

When I wasn't on watch, I spent time with the movie actors. If they were working, I had free entertainment. If they weren't, they were good company. As I said, there were six of them. Two of the men had the same first name. John, I think, but I can't remember their last names. What I do recall is that they were both very handsome. Nearly perfect, I would say. Does it make any sense that because they lacked any sort of distinguishing marks or imperfections they became so unmemorable?

The other two gentlemen actors were quite different. I've never forgotten them. Artemis Franks and Charles Benz. Artemis, who everyone called Arty, was a portly but active character. The things he could do with that large body of his! Run, twist, tumble, and fall, in the movies he was always falling. He was like a clumsy acrobat in an over-sized clown suit.

Charles Benz was an old stage actor whose face was as craggy as the surrounding landscape, and maybe just as ancient. The reason I knew he was a stage actor was because he said so. A lot. It was the one thing that the others complained most about his company. He was a ham of a performer, and he spoke with a highly-affected tone. His words always came out very round and full. The two actresses often made fun of him, especially when they referred to Artemis and Charles together as "franks-and-beans," imitating Charles's snooty tone to make "beans" sound more like his name, "Benz."

"I say, what is this delicious delicacy?" one of the ladies would ask in the exaggerated accent of a well-bred Easterner.

The other would reply similarly, "Why, it's franks-and-benz, my dear. Franks-and-*Benz*."

Neither actor took to the ladies' humor kindly—Charles simply because he was crotchety, but Artemis, who was generally good-natured, wasn't amused because he had favor for one of the actresses. I tried to tell him it was Charles they were poking fun at, yet it didn't settle his embarrassment much. I felt especially bad for Artemis because the gal he favored, well, she favored me. Both actresses did, to be honest. I don't think it had anything to do with me being some great catch or anything. I think they were bored with the handsome Johns, bored with their surroundings, just plain bored. Then I come along, something a little different. Whatever their reasons, though, I didn't care.

The object of Artemis' affection was Faith Monroe. She was young like me, with a face that the camera adored, as Toby Greene put it. To me, she had all the fine features I look for in a woman—a petite nose, soft chin, a slight but fetching figure, and bold, expressive eyes. She caught my attention that first day across the rugged land of the Willow Ranch like a fawn in the forest.

The other woman was Anna Beth Cranston. She was old enough and attractive enough to pass for Faith's mother and not at all shy about her full, hour-glass figure. There were two sides to Anna Beth. When she was in front of the camera she was warm and motherly. Away from the camera, she was surly and rough with a voice to match. Thinking back, in her case, it was a good thing the movies were silent.

Whenever I was on watch, and the ladies weren't busy shooting, one or the other of them would keep me company. To my relief, they never visited at the same time. Being in the middle of a pair of jealous women was the last thing I wanted.

Wait a minute now. I never thought about this before, but why didn't they cross paths? Maybe it had nothing to do with coincidence or dumb luck. Maybe they were sharing me, and arranged their visits accordingly? I'll be damned. I'm feeling a little bit taken right now, all these years later.

Anna Beth's maturity and experience was hard to

resist, but my preference was for Faith. Up to that point in my life I had not seen a prettier woman. And she seemed to like me, which made her even prettier. "She's like a young Ellen Marie," Thomas noted one day. "You best be careful." He also warned me, "You better not let those Patents Detectives catch you with your pants down." It wouldn't be right for me to go into details about my rendezvouses with those two ladies, but Thomas was not entirely wrong.

The attention I received did not put me in the best light with the other men, especially Artemis. As much as I tried to be friendly with him, I was just one more obstacle between him and Faith. I felt for Artemis, yet with or without me she had no interest in him so it didn't much matter.

Grady, too, was enamored of Faith. There was no question he put the camera on her more than anyone else, and he spent a good deal more time "directing" her than the others. But she was not impressed. He was as invisible to her as a drop of rain in the ocean. To compensate for his lack of presence, Alan Grady would yell. He would yell at Toby Greene to set up his camera. He would yell at the actors to perform the way he wanted. He would yell at the clouds overhead for taking away his light. He was a man forever under pressure.

The movie-making only happened a few hours a day.

The sun's best angle was in the morning and the late afternoon. If the sun was too high their features would lengthen and droop, or be lost altogether if they were wearing hats. It was details like that which interested Thomas. On occasion, I spied him talking to Toby Greene and asking questions. I, on the other hand, enjoyed watching the actors rehearse and perform. That was the part of the process that Thomas found boring and repetitious. "They do it over and over again until there's no more surprises," he criticized.

"But when someone watches it in a theater, it will be for the first time," I explained, as though I were some kind of expert.

But I suppose I was learning *something*. For instance, one afternoon I learned how to fake a hanging. They were shooting a scene where some ranchers (Charles and the two Johns) pretend to hang a man (Artemis) suspected of being a little too friendly with the daughter (Faith) of one of them. Mr. McElroy stepped in to help. It seemed mock-hangings were something he was strangely experienced in.

"Nothing scares away a miscreant faster than nearly dyin'," he stated, and had the others bind Artemis's hands behind him, lift him to the back of a horse, and drop a noose around his neck. The rope was flung over the sturdiest branch of a big cottonwood that stood near the rock from where I would normally watch the road.

"Pull the rope just taut enough so that he thinks you mean business," Mr. McElroy instructed the "ranchers." Then he demonstrated how to loop it off so that it would slip loose when the horse rode away.

"Are you sure this will work?" asked Artemis, a nervous crack to his voice.

"I guess we'll see. It's been awhile since I've done this," replied Mr. McElroy, with a wink to the rest of us.

It worked, of course. Grady gave himself credit for a good piece of directing that day, though it seemed to me Mr. McElroy did most of it.

I watched them make movies every chance I could. I was fascinated by how I could be sitting with Faith and the others one moment, and the next see the women as pioneers or the men as prospectors or soldiers. It was like watching stories I'd heard come to life.

"I've lived the stories," Thomas said, "and what they're doing ain't nothing like them."

"Well, for those of us who haven't lived them, these versions are the next best thing," I replied.

I told Faith what I'd said to Thomas. "That's very insightful, Billy," she sweetly commented and shared my insight with the others.

"Well said, young man," said Charles. "This isn't

some frivolous pastime we're engaged in here. Acting and storytelling is a great art."

"Hear that, everyone?" responded Anna Beth in her upturned-Easterner tone. "We're great *artists*!"

The two Johns laughed. Even Charles had a chuckle and replied to her, "Well, some of us are, anyway."

The movie crew was like a family. Amidst all the bickering and teasing you could see they genuinely enjoyed each other. Not ever having a family of my own, I guess that's what I wanted the most from being around them. But they never quite took me in as part of the group.

Not until one day, that is.

I remember it was a particularly hot afternoon and Grady approached me with the question, "You're a pretty good rider, aren't you?"

"Not as good as some, better than many," I answered.

"I need someone to ride a horse, *fast*," Grady explained. "None of the actors are up to it. How about it? Want to be in a movie?"

"I don't know the first thing about acting."

"You won't be acting. You'll be riding. You'll be doubling for John."

"Doubling?"

"You'll be doing the dangerous stuff. You know, the stunt. I can't afford to have John injured. I'll pay you two dollars."

"You're going to pay me to ride?"

"And do a fall."

I'd ridden horses most of my life. And I'd fallen plenty of times. But I never knew someone to *pay* me to do those things. I also liked the idea of doing something "dangerous," so I agreed.

They were making a movie about a pony express rider delivering an important letter. A villain shoots the rider off his horse and steals the letter as its contents would be detrimental to his nefarious plans. One of the Johns played the express rider, Faith was the woman who nurses him back to health, and Charles was the villain. It was a role he often played as he had a face that leant itself well to villainy.

Artemis expressed a strong desire to play the rider. I suspected that he knew there would be an opportunity to kiss Faith. But, as Grady had to explain, "That won't work, Arty, because Billy can't double for you. The two of you, well, you don't look anything alike."

"I can ride well enough," Artemis argued, "and anyone can fall from a horse. What's there to it? You just fall! I take falls all the time!"

"It's not the same."

"Why not?"

"You're an actor, Arty. Actors don't fall off horses.

Anyway, I need you to play the sheriff. It's an important role."

Truthfully, I felt to be the one in an important role, more so than the actors. You might say I had a specialized skill by keeping another from harm. It had been Toby Greene's suggestion to use me (although Grady acted like it was his own idea), and he was the one who gave me real direction.

"You don't have to ride too fast," he told me. "I can crank the camera a tad slower than normal so that when it plays on the screen you'll appear to be riding faster than you actually are."

"How can that be?" I asked.

Seeing the bewilderment on my face he said, "It's movie magic. I'll explain it to you sometime."

I rode back and forth across the Willow's land so many times that afternoon that I thought I'd covered enough miles to take me back to Denver. Also, like Toby told me, I kept my head down and my hat low to help conceal that I-the-rider was not John-the-actor. "The audience has to think you're the same person," Toby explained.

"More movie magic?" I said.

"Exactly."

When it came time to do the fall, hiding my face would prove to be a little trickier. Toby suggested I roll from the saddle, away from the camera, and let the horse obscure my features. But Grady was not happy with the result.

"What was that?" he yelled. "You look like you went to sleep and fell off! You've been shot! Let's see the shock and the agony!"

I did it again, and Grady yelled at me again. And again. And again. My shoulder began to ache from landing on the ground so many times. But Grady still was not happy. It was Anna Beth who came to my rescue.

"Pretend to do it the way Charles would do it," she whispered to me as she brushed me off for another go.

So, on the next ride, when I got "shot," I jerked and reared back so violently my hat flew off and my poor horse lost its balance and tumbled to the hard earth right along with me. Dust and gravel filled the air around us. He scrambled to stand and run off, leaving me upon the ground in the most agonizing stiffness I could muster. When the dirt cloud cleared, I heard Grady shout, "Cut! That was great! Perfect!"

I don't know exactly what Toby said to Grady, but I'm sure it had something to do with the visibility of my face. Sure, the John and I may have had the same build, but otherwise we looked nothing alike.

"It won't matter. It happens so fast that most people won't even notice, and the rest of them won't care," was

Grady's response.

"It's the one person that does notice and care that I worry about," said Toby.

"Don't worry. It's good enough."

As Grady walked away, I heard Toby mumble, "Another Grady creation, where good enough is good enough."

That night, all I could do with Faith was talk. My body and my ego were too sore to partake in our normal "recreational" activities.

"You did fine today, Billy," she told me.

"I don't feel like I did."

"You mean Grady? Oh, he yells at everyone. You've seen him. That's what directors do."

"He doesn't yell at you."

"That's because he's sweet on me."

"True. But you are a good actress. You don't give him call to yell at you."

She laughed at me, not for the compliment I gave her but for my apparent foolishness. "Oh, Billy, you don't know anything about acting. If you did, you would know that I'm a mediocre actress at best. I don't expect to have much of a future in this business. My pretty face will only get me so far."

"Then what are you doing here?"

"I intend to be the wife of an important movie man someday, and being in the movies is the only way to get noticed by a man like that."

"Just how 'important' a man?" I asked, now *feeling* a bit foolish.

"A studio head. Or a producer on his way to being a studio head. Or a director on his way to being a producer on his way to being a studio head. But nothing less than that."

"Then why aren't you with Grady?"

She laughed at me again. "Because Alan is, at best, a mediocre director. He'll never be anything more than that."

I *was* the fool. Like Artemis Franks. Like Alan Grady. Faith must have seen it in my face. "But we're having fun, aren't we, Billy?" she quickly added with a squeeze of my hand.

She was right. I was having fun. I wrote earlier that Thomas was content in Prescott. I was too. Those months in Arizona were some of my fondest. Faith may have had her plans to move onwards, but I never wanted to leave.

Seven

...there's nothing like the smell of gunpowder
and the metal-blue of its smoke.
Freedom, justice, triumph and power.
Words to be lived than merely spoke.

The next day I wanted to talk to Thomas about what our plans were going to be. The movie folk wouldn't be there forever. Then what would become of us? I found him on watch, keeping vigilance by the road, sitting on a rock with his notebook by his side. He didn't notice me as I walked up. He was in one of his stares, this one being longer and deeper than any of the others so far. He looked outward so hard I thought he might fall from the rock to the ground.

"Thomas?" I said after a minute of not being acknowledged.

"Did you hear that?" he said in a kind of daze.

"What? What is it?" I asked.

He still did not seem to recognize me. "It's from over there! Can you hear it?"

I followed his line of sight but saw nothing but woods

and rocks and the crumbling wagon. Faintly, I could hear the clinking of a chain on the wagon as it swung in the breeze.

"Ringer's bell!" Thomas shouted with a strange, childlike glee. "He's there! In those trees!"

Then, like a confused child waking from a nightmare, he finally saw me and gasped for air in surprise. "Billy?"

"Yes, Thomas, it's me. Are you okay?"

"Billy," he said with an embarrassed sigh and a confused laugh. Catching his breath, Thomas peered off to something over my shoulder, something that quickly brought him back to reality and turned his harried expression into a frown, then a scowl, and then he said, "What the hell is that?"

I turned to see Toby Greene with his camera in front of the corral. On the barn beside it hung a make-shift sign of rotted wood. It read: O.K. Corral. At one end of the corral stood Charles and Artemis, wearing the best gunfighter costumes they could put together–black hats, dark long-coats and leather holsters that drooped under the weight of heavy pistols. The two Johns emerged from the barn in similar attire. Faith and Anna Beth were there, off camera, but in full make-up and dressed as modest frontier wives.

"Okay, Wyatt," Grady shouted to Charles, "let those McLaury's know you mean business!"

Charles pointed a finger at the Johns and said, "I'm

warning you. We mean to run the two of you out of Tombstone."

"Okay, Doc," Grady yelled at Artemis, "pull your coat back to reveal your gun. Show them you're more than ready to use it!"

Artemis did as he was directed. The Johns did their best to look like hardened and tough men. But, frankly, they were just too handsome.

"Cut!" shouted Grady. "McLaurys, move out of the way so we can shoot Wyatt and Doc drawing and firing their guns. Everybody stay clear. Wyatt and Doc? Load your pistols with only one bullet, and remember to fire into that hillside."

Once Toby had repositioned his camera and began cranking, Grady yelled, "Action!" Charles and Artemis drew their guns. Poor old Charles didn't have the strength to pull back the hammer of his Colt Navy with one hand so he took the gun in both, cocked it, shakily aimed, and fired. The pistol's kick jolted itself from Charles's two-handed grip and fell to the dirt. Artemis tried drawing his unwieldy Dragoon so fast that he fired before the tip of the barrel cleared the rim of his holster. It left a hole in the leather and sent the bullet into the ground just a few feet in front of him.

"Cut!" yelled Grady, shaking his head in disappointment.

Thomas's eyes narrowed. He stood and walked toward them with the determination of someone ready for a fight, like he looked that night in the Denver brothel.

"What's going on here, Toby?" he asked.

But it was Grady who answered. "We're recreating a gunfight in Tombstone, once a mining town in the southern part of this state. I read an article about it."

"Like hell you're recreating anything. This is as close to the truth as a piss-pot is to the Grand Canyon."

"And what makes you an expert, Mr. Benton? We're you there?"

"Yes, I was," Thomas replied, and he suddenly had everyone's attention. It was easy to forget Thomas's advanced years and how much of what the rest of us only thought as history he had actually lived. He would have been almost fifty at the time of the infamous gunfight. "It was October of '81. I was there tending to some cattle business. Arizona was still a territory at the time."

"You were there?" said Toby. "You knew The Earps and Doc Holliday?"

"I'd seen them around."

"You saw the gunfight?" Artemis asked, stepping closer.

"What there was. It only lasted half a minute, but a long time when someone's shooting at you."

● ● ●

We all moved in to listen to Thomas. Everyone except Grady, who announced, "We need to keep working while we still have the light."

"I won't allow you to demean the truth with this nonsense," Thomas snapped.

"Alan, let's hear what Thomas has to say," Toby said. "You have to admit there's something missing here."

"Actors who can fire a gun, perhaps?" Grady uttered tersely.

The others ignored his remark and readied themselves for Thomas's comments.

"First, the shoot-out didn't happen at the corral. It actually happened in a vacant lot between two boarding houses behind it. Next, there were as many as nine men involved with the incident, and you've got only four. Where's Billy Clanton, one of the men who was killed? And his brother, Ike, and Billy Claiborne, and Virgil and Morgan Earp? And who are these women supposed to be? And where the hell are the mustaches? They all had mustaches!"

None of us said anything as Thomas went quiet. We felt there was more and we didn't dare tread upon his oration. But Thomas stayed quiet. His eyes were wide, so riled he seemed to be frozen in time. He turned his back on us and stepped away.

Toby went to Grady. I couldn't hear what he said but

it made Grady straighten and state, "I'm the director here!"

"Yes, and you will continue to be," Toby consoled, "but perhaps we should invite Thomas as a–um–historical advisor. He could be a valuable resource."

Artemis leaned in between the two of them and added, "Please, Mr. Grady. I, for one, am feeling quite silly here."

As was his manner to make someone else's idea seem like his own, Grady walked over to Thomas, and said, "Mr. Benton, it appears we could use your, well, your assistance and expertise. Would you be so kind as to advise us in this matter?"

Thomas considered the notion. With a nod, he replied, "I would." And like Thomas, he got right to work. "We need more men. Billy, you'd make a good Morgan Earp. You two, John is it? You're both fine as McLaurys, you just need to be mussed-up a bit. But you, Charles, you should be Ike Clanton. He doesn't do any shooting. And Arty? You'd be better as Virgil Earp. You can't be Doc Holliday, you're too stout. Doc was dying of consumption. He may have been an ornery cuss but he was thin and wasted. Grady, you'd be a perfect Doc Holliday. Also, Doc began the gunfight with a shot gun and pulled his pistol later."

"I've got one in the house," declared Mr. McElroy, who had been quietly watching from the porch up until then.

"I don't get in front of the camera," Grady stated. "I'm a director, not an actor."

"Oh, come on Alan, you'd be great," Anna Beth told him.

"We need men, Alan," Toby told him. When Grady crossed his arms in protest, he added, "No one says you can't direct *and* act."

"You can do it, Alan," Faith told him and gave his arm a gentle squeeze.

I'm sure it was Faith's touch that convinced him, yet Grady chewed on the idea for a moment before agreeing. I can't say for sure, but I think Alan Grady was one of the first to do such, to direct himself in a moving picture. Before Chaplin, Keaton, or von Stroheim.

Then Grady asked Thomas, "What was that you said about mustaches?"

"They all had mustaches, especially The Earps. Theirs were quite full," Thomas explained. "Ike Clanton had a goatee, as well, I recall. But I don't remember Billy Clairborne. He was a minor player in the incident, so I guess it doesn't matter too much."

Grady turned to Faith and Anna Beth, "Ladies would you see what you can do about mustaches?"

Whether they were happy about doing something different or being directed without being yelled at I can't say, but the women were giddy with excitement in their new roles as make-up artists. They hurried off to the bunkhouse to prepare.

"We still need four more men," Thomas said.

"Wait," said Toby, counting in his head. "Only three more, right?"

"I think we should have someone to represent County Sheriff Johnny Behan. He was not a friend of The Earps, and he made an attempt to stop the fight."

"It's going to be hard enough just to get three men."

"No, I like that idea," Grady interjected. "It would add an extra dramatic element. More story. We need four more men."

Mr. McElroy came out of the house with a shotgun and heard the exchange. "There's plenty of men in town that'll do anything to earn a few dollars. How 'bout I ride in and rustle up four of them?"

With a nod from Thomas, Mr. McElroy was off to fetch his horse. First, though, he handed his shotgun to Grady, and assured him it was not loaded.

"Now, let's talk about these guns," Thomas said to everyone, mostly Grady. "Who's the damned fool who thought using real bullets was a good idea? Isn't there such a thing as a prop that shoots duds or something, like in a stage play?"

"Well, yes," Grady admitted, "but we don't have any more, and the studio has been demanding more gunfights. It seems they are very popular."

"I suppose that is fair enough," Thomas said, "and you've taken precautions to avoid serious injury. But you men need to learn a bit about handling a pistol."

Thomas took Arty's Dragoon from him and gave him his own Schofield to use, unloading it first, of course. Then began our lesson in the art of the quick draw, which was really very simple. Start slow, very slow, and do it over and over and over. When Thomas felt we were ready, he would have us go a little faster (but still very slow). First, we were like snails. Then, like dripping molasses. Then honey. Artemis, Grady, the Johns, and me repeatedly took our empty guns from their holsters at least a thousand times until we could pull them as smooth as cream. And that would be fast enough, Thomas told us. "I don't imagine most folks today have ever seen a gunfight. We'll have them believing you're true shootists."

More movie magic, I thought to myself.

I also thought about how Thomas, just like he had back on the Triple-T, was getting a ragged bunch to work together like seasoned craftsmen. It was the first time the actors performed without bickering. They were all feeling pretty good about what they were doing. Thomas had that way. It was his own kind of magic, and it made the perfect bedfellow for the business of making motion pictures.

A little over an hour later, Mr. McElroy returned with four men. They were common cowboys, like many I had ridden with. They were lean and calloused and ready to work, with just a bit of the only-rooster-in-the-hen-house way about them. Most importantly—they all had mustaches! I could see the disappointment in Faith and Anna Beth knowing they weren't going to be able to get their make-up kits close to those rugged men, none of whose names I can recall.

Thomas sorted out who of them was going to be who in the movie. None of them had to prove their skill with a gun. It was evident to Thomas. Then came the task of picking a place to shoot, or rather, to *film* the action. It was Grady who suggested the space between the main house and the bunkhouse as both could pass well enough for the boarding houses Thomas had mentioned earlier. One of the Johns, who was very proud of the 'O.K. Corral' sign he had made, wondered if it could be used in a scene somehow.

"The McLaurys and the Clantons did walk through the corral on their way to the vacant lot," Thomas said. "No reason we shouldn't have them do the same."

"I'd like to see the Earps and Doc Holliday do that as well," said Grady. "I mean, walk to the gunfight, you know, to build tension."

"We would need a street and a saloon," said Thomas.

"There's plenty of each of those in town," Mr. McElroy replied.

So Grady had us shoot all the scenes we could on the ranch–the McLaury and Clantons' approach through the corral, Sheriff Behan's attempt to stop the fight, and the gunfight itself–with Thomas explaining in great detail where everyone stood and who did what when. He would also offer advice like, "Ike was a bit of a coward. He drank a lot and talked a lot to make up for it," and "We need a cane for Doc. But Virgil was carrying it. And Doc held the shotgun under his coat. Also, about Doc, he was a sick and dying man. That made him not afraid of anything, especially death."

Then actors and equipment were loaded into the Willys and driven into town with me, Thomas, and the hired cowboys following on horseback. The car was only meant for five people, but with all eight of them and Toby's equipment, Artemis and the Johns rode standing on the running boards, hanging off either side for dear life. Grady had the ladies don their costumes again so they could participate as town folk.

A crowd quickly drew around us as Toby set up his camera in front of the Palace Saloon at the town's center. Thomas suggested he avoid getting the saloon's name in the picture as it was a well-known establishment and any illusion of Tombstone would be gone. This appealed to Toby's not-settling-for-good-enough sensibility. With Grady (Doc), Artemis (Virgil), me (Morgan), and one of the cowboys (Wyatt) standing there in the street, a glimpse of the saloon behind us, Thomas took a moment to share a story.

"The four of you are crossing paths with history right now," he said. "Virgil Earp was the constable here in Prescott at one time. He and Wyatt and Doc Holliday have been in that very bar behind you. They may have even walked right where you're standing. And Wyatt and Doc? You two had a powerful close friendship. Such that, once, when Doc had gotten himself into some trouble with the law in Denver, another of Wyatt's friends, Bat Masterson, testified on his behalf when Wyatt couldn't. Now Bat didn't care too much for Doc, but he stepped in to help anyway, because he knew how important Doc was to Wyatt. Everybody knew."

The four of us looked back toward the saloon and at the ground under our feet. Even though Morgan was not a part of Thomas's story I imagined myself as the younger Earp, visiting his brother Virgil there in Prescott. I didn't know it at the time, but that was my first lesson in acting. I began to feel who I was supposed to be, and I could tell the others were experiencing the same. I could swear Grady-as-

Doc was coming down with consumption right before my eyes, and our hired hand, who until then had never been anything but a cowboy like me, stood as tall as Wyatt Earp. And it was all because of Thomas's directing.

Later, Grady received a telegram from the movie studio, congratulating him and his crew on "some fine motion picture footage." It was edited and billed as "so authentic, even real bullets were used!" There have been many reenactments of that gunfight in the movies over the years, some as false and absurd as a pig with lipstick. I still consider ours to be one of the best ever done.

ॐ   ॐ   ॐ

Though Thomas had become a little more interested in the movie-making process, he still proclaimed it as nonsense. A few weeks had passed since our reenactment of the Tombstone shoot-out, and I felt it was time to convince him otherwise. In town was the Elks' Theater that presented live acts and showed motion pictures, so I proposed that all of us go there for an evening out. It was a riot as all eleven of us piled into that Willys. Once again, Artemis and the Johns hung off the sides. They were joined by Mr. McElroy who clung to the back and whooped and hollered like he was busting a bronco as we bounced along that rutted road.

Thomas and I had a fun ride as well. We were crowded into the backseat with Faith and Anna Beth on our laps, giggling the entire time. Ever since Thomas demonstrated his potential as a movie director the ladies had turned their attention upon him. I knew what Faith's intentions were. Thomas had all the necessary qualities to run his own business, be it a livery stable or the empire of a movie studio. As for Anna Beth, the novelty of me had simply run out.

We arrived to the theater, falling out of the car, laughing and breathless, and onto the street and sidewalk. Thomas escorted both of the ladies into Prescott's grand Elks Theatre. I must confess to a bit of jealousy toward that old man. I was learning how Artemis had felt about me. In fact, it was Arty who helped me up from the sidewalk, brushed me off and accompanied me up the steps to the lobby.

Though smaller than the theater I had seen in Denver, the Elks was just as elegant. From its red-velvet carpet to the epaulet-like ornamentations framing the stage and mezzanine above us, we all anticipated a first-rate evening of entertainment. And we were not disappointed.

It began with a woman who sang and told jokes. She reminded me of Anna Beth by her boisterous manner, but she also had a beautiful singing voice. We applauded for more as she left the stage.

The next act made up for our want of more. It was a pair of brothers who could dance in ways I never knew possible. They were acrobatic in the way they went back-and-forth in precise, syncopated moves. The music they danced to was so lively I couldn't help but tap my feet, wishing I was up there performing with them.

Then came the moving pictures, and that window to another place. There were three of them: one was a comedy that had the entire theatre in an uproar of gaiety—inept policemen chasing a criminal as acrobatic as the previous dancers; the next, a Victorian romance, had the ladies (and a few of the men) in tears; and lastly, a western. I can't remember any more details than that because I was interested in watching Thomas. I was determined he see the movies as something other than nonsense.

As the first one started, he stretched his neck and tilted his head to peer behind the screen, in search of actors and scenery. Then he looked behind him at the light coming from the projection booth. Just like Thomas, he was trying to figure things out. Finally, he sat still, watched, and smiled. He laughed at the silly police, cheered for the heroes and booed the villains. During the western, he looked about to pull his Thunderer from his coat and fire at the gunslingers. I felt vindicated as I saw my friend experiencing the magic of his first motion pictures.

Afterward, Thomas stood and announced to all of us, "Drinks are on me!"

We drank at the Palace Saloon until the old man decided he wanted to experience another first for himself—driving an automobile! We stumbled from the bar and into the Willys once again. This time, the Johns and Artemis *sat* on the sideboards because they were too drunk to stand. Their legs dangled over the road. As it was, they each nearly rolled onto the street with every turn. The rest of us were piled upon one another like a litter of newborn piglets–in a stupor of squeals and snorts. Mr. McElroy navigated as Thomas drove.

We went all through Prescott and eventually down a road that took us out of town and into the black of night. The contours of the gravel road barely appeared in our headlights before Thomas would react. He would turn too sharply, apply the brakes too suddenly, and accelerate with a jolt. A couple of times he sent the car into a slide. On horseback, Thomas may have been as nimble as a mountain goat, but as a driver he was like a gangly colt.

Mr. McElroy had him stop beside a clearing. We got out of the car, still squealing and laughing from the exhilaration of our ride, and then gathered firewood in the dark. Soon we were all sitting and lying around a roaring blaze. Summer was about over, the chill of fall was looming, and there seemed to be a million more stars above us in that clearing than over at the Willow. I was very happy, and once again I had the attention of the ladies. But it wasn't about me. No, they wanted to hear me tell them all about Thomas.

So I became the storyteller, relating everything I knew about my friend. Not to say I exactly told the truth. Rather, I told the stories just as I had heard them from Clarence Stoud and Frank Johnston, and the other cowboys of the Triple-T. I carried on the tradition and the lore, no matter how fabricated it was.

"Where have you been in your life that you never heard of the lawman Thomas Andrew Benton?" I said.

The ladies were dumbfounded, embarrassed, but mostly drunk.

"And you never heard of young Tom Benton's great manhunt for the man who killed his father?"

I had their full attention as I wove the tale, all the while knowing the truth. At one point, I glanced over at Thomas and Mr. McElroy, and they gave me approving nods. Then I told of my own adventure in the big city of Denver, leaving out certain details about Ellen Marie as I didn't think it appropriate. Thomas gave me another look of approval and stretched himself out in the warmth of the fire. Before long, we succumbed to its sleepy glow and curled into a single, snoring heap beneath the stars.

The dawn was cold. All of us, but Thomas and Mr. McElroy, were groggy from too much drink and not enough sleep. We grumbled like children to get back to the Willow as soon as possible instead of starting another fire. Mr. McElroy drove, thankfully, yet still we groaned our pains from every bump and sharp turn.

Upon our arrival to the ranch, there were three men, strangers, waiting for us—one very large fellow flanked by two that were not so large. The broad-shouldered, barrel-chested giant wore a bowler and a jacket, each a size too small. His ill-fitting coat revealed a holstered pistol upon which his hand rested. The other two held rifles. We knew exactly what their business was.

"We shouldn't have filmed in town," Grady said quietly. "I knew word would get out."

I heard Artemis and the other actors whispering among themselves but I couldn't make out what they were scheming. Suddenly, they jumped from the car, screaming in terror—the ladies *and* the men—and ran in a panic to the bunkhouse for safety.

One of the smaller men took a step to follow but the

big man stopped him. "Let them go," he told him. "They're of no concern." He never took his eyes from the rest of us still sitting in the car. "Which of you is in charge here?"

Mr. McElroy answered, "This is my ranch. What do you want?"

"You don't look like motion picture people."

"That's 'cuz I'm not."

"I know there's been pictures made here. Give us the cameras and we'll be on our way."

Thomas climbed from the car and walked towards the three with firm determination. The big man put out a hand and said, "You can stop right there old-timer." He mistook Thomas for a yokel. Before he could start another sentence, Thomas whipped out his Thunderer and aimed it directly at the man's giant chest. If the big man was surprised, he didn't show it. He was a cool customer and wise to keep his gun holstered. Thomas kept on walking until they stood just a foot apart. The giant stood his ground and cracked a confident smile. "What about them?" he said.

His two smaller partners had their rifles raised at Thomas.

"What about them?" Thomas replied. He leaned forward and pressed the barrel of his pistol to the man's heart. "You're the only one I'm aiming to kill." The big man's smile went flat. Then, with a glance behind all three of the strangers, Thomas added, "Besides…"

They turned to see Artemis and the Johns staring the agents down and wearing the holsters and guns from our O.K. Corral movie. They had been so quiet in sneaking out of the bunkhouse that none of us had noticed. The moment they had everyone's attention, the three actors drew their pistols as quick and smooth as hired gunmen—just like they had learned weeks before!

The two small men were so startled they immediately let their rifles to the ground and put their hands in the air. The big man went pale as Thomas took his gun from its holster and dropped it to the dirt. With a growl, the man said, "You all are making a big mistake."

"It's you who's made the mistake," Mr. McElroy responded as he climbed out of the Willys. The rest of us followed. "The mistake of the wrong profession and the mistake of coming onto my land in a threatening manner. I got every right to shoot the lot of you right here and now."

"But you're not going to, are you?" whimpered one of the smaller men.

Mr. McElroy mulled the thought for a long minute. "No. We're not going to shoot you." He looked around to make sure he had the attention of the rest of us. "We're going to hang you."

"You can't do that," the big man snarled as the other

two went sickly white.

"We can, and we will."

Mr. McElroy gave a nod to the Johns and they ran off to fetch three lengths of rope while the ladies gathered the men's horses. The small men sobbed at the realization of their fate as me and Toby bound their hands behind them. I felt a little bad for them. With the big man tied as well, Thomas lowered his pistol, and Artemis gave a relieved sigh and said, "I'm sure glad this worked. We couldn't find any bullets for our guns."

We all burst into laughter–well, all of us but the three detectives–and the big man went as sickly white as his partners. But instead of crying he bravely argued for their defense. "You've got no right to be doing this. We were only doing a job," he said.

"You were trespassing," stated Mr. McElroy, "and you aimed your rifles upon us. If that's your job, I don't take kindly to it."

We got them on their horses and led them to our "hanging" tree, the big cottonwood by the road.

"You three got any kin we should notify?" Mr. McElroy asked as we quickly laid the nooses around their necks and pulled them taut so they knew we meant business.

"I ain't got nobody," cried one of the small men.

"Me neither," sobbed the other.

"They're not gonna do this, boys," said the big man. "They're just putting a scare into us."

At that, Mr. McElroy reached up, grabbed the big man's lapel and pulled down on him, which caused the noose to give the detective a choke. "Next time," Mr. McElroy told him with grave seriousness, "we'll do this for real!"

Mr. McElroy signaled for us to smack the horses. Those back-end slaps echoed through the silent pines, and away the mounts galloped down the road with their riders—nooses snug around their throats—still in their saddles, ropes streaming loosely behind like long tails, tied to nothing.

As the horses carried the three men out of our sight, the clopping of their hooves fading in the breeze, we all went quiet and solemn-like. Not out of sympathy for those poor, miserable detectives, but because it felt like the end of something, like a fade-to-black at the close of a good movie.

It was when we turned from the road and toward the house that we saw something that made us smile. It was Grady cranking away at Toby's camera. He had sneaked away and set up the equipment to document our little scene forever to film. In all of his short motion picture career, I think Alan Grady will be most remembered for that brief clip, seen only by a few within the industry, never by the public.

სი   სი   სი

After our little fun with the Patents Detectives, Grady decided it was time to pack up his crew and move on to Los Angeles. Thomas agreed. "I don't doubt they'll be back," he said, "either with more men or the authorities. And I, for one, am not inclined to stay and find out which it will be."

"Let 'em come," challenged Mr. McElroy. "I still say I was in the right, the way they came onto my property and all. Hell, all we really did was make them to soil themselves a bit. They'll get over it."

Besides avoiding The Patents, Grady had his own reasons for wanting to leave Prescott. "I think I've proven myself here. We all have. It's time we had the chance to make some real movies."

I don't know what we'd been making if we weren't making *real* movies, but all the others agreed. I, for one, didn't want to go anywhere.

"What are we going to do?" I asked Thomas.

"I don't know, Billy," he answered, "but I don't think it's wise we stay around here much longer."

When I shared my concern with the others, it was Faith who suggested Thomas and I go to California with them. "You'd love it, Billy. The weather's beautiful all the time. No more winters. And you've got some experience with motion pictures now. I'll bet you could snatch up some work like that," she explained with the snap of a finger.

And it was Toby who reiterated Faith's idea to Thomas. "You're a smart man, Thomas, and God knows there's a shortage of those in the picture business. You've got the makings of a fine director. You should think about it."

"I will," Thomas told him, and they shook hands.

A day later, Thomas, Mr. McElroy, and I watched as the lot of them, all crowded into the Willys, equipment strapped to the roof, drive off down the rutted road that would eventually take them to Los Angeles. They left our sight, and soon we could no longer hear the sputtering of the Willys's motor. Motion pictures wouldn't return to Prescott until the following year, with the arrival of cowboy star Tom Mix.

It wasn't but a couple of days later when Thomas asked, "Billy?"

"Yes, Thomas?"

"You ever been to California?"

Eight

The West ends at the ocean

and a new frontier begins

One of turmoil and storms, waves

to wash away our sins,

Making way for new ones

It took Thomas a week after that, with winter looming, to ready himself to leave for California. "I have to get my affairs in order," he explained, "and I want to write a letter to Ellen Marie."

I understood wanting to write a letter, but what affairs did he have to get in order? From what I could see, we just had to figure out what to do with our horses, and Mr. McElroy had already offered to keep them for us until we needed them again. Thomas even gave him money to pay for their stabling. So what else was left?

Although I knew he'd travelled plenty beyond the Colorado River, I saw Thomas was somehow apprehensive to move on. I found him a couple of times in Mr. McElroy's library, the letter to Ellen Marie on the desk in front of him.

Instead of writing he was fidgeting, staring out the window and talking to himself. His nervousness made me nervous. I did what I could to console him, saying things like, "I hear the Pacific Ocean is a sight to see. Magnificent beyond words I've been told. Won't it be nice to see it again?" Or, "Faith says the weather is beautiful all the time there. No more winters. That will be something, won't it Thomas?" It helped a little, I think.

It wasn't until we boarded a train to Ash Fork, from where we would then go to Los Angeles, that Thomas would finally sit at ease. And only when we ate at the Escalante Harvey House, enjoying a good meal served by ladies in unflattering black-and-white uniforms (prompting him to comment with distaste, "The Spanish missionary Father Silvestre Velez de Escalante explored this area in the late 1700's, and this is how his name is honored") did I recognize my friend once more.

Like the train ride through Colorado, I was aching to reach our destination. Although the sandy red, blue, and purple hills along the horizon were nice to look at, for the most part, the desert up close wasn't much too my liking– flat and colorless. It also seemed Thomas had told me all the stories he had to tell. We spent a lot of our time in silence. If we did converse, it was more to reminisce about our brief time in Prescott, and at one point, Thomas got tired of me wishing we had never left that little mountain town.

"You could have stayed, you know," he said. "Mac would have welcomed you. You're free to make up your own mind about what you want to do next in your life."

"I suppose you're right," I replied, and resigned to say nothing more about it. (At least for a while, anyway.)

Los Angeles was only the second big city I had seen in my life. It had a different look to it than Denver. It was spread out, stretching across the rolling landscape, and its buildings were clean and white, with many touches of Spanish design. The two cities had different personalities, as well. I was in Denver for just a few days but that city came across like an old, reliable work-horse–sturdy and steadfast. Los Angeles, I quickly came to learn, was more an unbroken stallion–beautiful, yet unruly. The year before, in 1910, there had been a bombing of the *Los Angeles Times* newspaper building. It killed some twenty people. I didn't know what to think of a place where such a thing could happen.

"It's not so much a stallion," Thomas corrected me later, "but a gangly colt fighting with itself to run before it can barely stand up."

People had been going to California for decades wanting to get rich and make the city of Los Angeles their own, no matter what the cost. But Thomas and I were looking for just a small piece of its opportunities. We got off the train at La Grande Station. (Anyone who's seen the movie *Meet Me in St. Louis* with Judy Garland has seen that depot. It was a popular shooting location.) We then walked central Los Angeles like a pair of tenderfoots on the open range, yet as eager to work as racehorses at the starting gate.

Our excitement was short-lived. The city was an endless sprawl. We could make neither heads nor tails about where to begin. Whenever we asked someone if they knew Alan Grady or Toby Greene or Faith Monroe or any of the others all we got were bemused looks. It seemed we were quite the pair of strange strangers, and it quickly wore down our spirits.

Then Thomas asked someone if they knew where the movies were made. You might be surprised to learn it wasn't Hollywood. No, in early 1911 Hollywood was still but a sleepy town about eight miles away from Los Angeles, famous for its fruit. It was a respectable community that did not welcome the already sordid reputation of the movie industry. In fact, for a time, movie theaters were banned there. It wasn't until later that year, I think, that a roadside tavern on Sunset Boulevard was taken over by some movie makers from New Jersey, the Nestor Motion Picture Company, which would become the first movie studio in Hollywood.

Thomas and I were directed, instead, to Edendale.

That's where many of the West Coast's movie studios were located at the time. It was easy to see why, once we got there. It was a movie-making Eden. You could see the Pacific Ocean. There were views of snowcapped mountains on three sides of the horizon, and groves of fruit trees and ranches closer in. And so much sunshine you were wishing it would cloud up and rain just for a change of pace.

Our first day there was coming quickly to an end, and the two of us had to give up our job search for a place to sleep. And that became our next challenge. All too often at the local hotels and boarding houses was a sign in the window that read, "No Movies"—"movies" being a derogatory term for people who work in the motion picture industry. After a few of those signs, I said to Thomas, "We're not actually in the movie business, yet. And even if we were, it really isn't anyone's concern if we don't want it to be."

"That's very true, Billy," Thomas replied, and we went into the next hotel we found. We got ourselves a room, and the next day we were fresh to continue our hunt for employment. It was Thomas's idea that we divide our efforts. "One man is more likely to be hired than two," he said. So he went in one direction, and I in the other.

‌‌
ớ   ớ   ớ

Half the morning was gone by the time I found a group of men standing in front of a non-descript building, much like a warehouse. At that time, Selig Polyscope and Bison were a couple of the better known studios in the area. Sheldon Pictures, run by the notorious Anthony Sheldon, was one of the lesser known ones. It was in front of his studio where the group of men gathered. Some leaned against the wall. Three men sat on empty fruit crates and played cards on the bottom of an overturned trash can. Others paced and agitated at the warehouse's front door.

"If you're looking for work," one of them said to me, "get in line." He motioned with his red, sleepless eyes toward the end of the group, which stretched the length of the building.

I responded with a friendly nod–he did not reciprocate–and I walked to the end of the line. There, another tired-looking fellow offered me a cigarette. I declined as smoking was a pastime I had never grown fond of.

A good quarter-of-an-hour passed before someone came out of the door. He was a skinny character with a nose like a bird's beak and an Adam's apple as big as, well, an apple. He went to the first man in line.

"How tall are you?" he asked him.

"Almost six foot," was the reply.

This satisfied the skinny one and he led the man in through the door that everyone eyed with longing. Again we waited, and again the skinny man came out and took the next one of us in line through that door. This went on for the remainder of the morning until there were just a handful of us left.

Then he came out and began to size each one of us. He looked at me, turned away, and then looked back. "You look familiar. What pictures have you been in?" he said to me.

But I was stumped. I never knew the titles of any of the movies I'd been in. "I can't rightly recall," I told him. "I was Morgan Earp in one about that gunfight in Tombstone. Mostly, I rode and fell a lot."

That was all the résumé I needed. The skinny man led me into the building, down a long corridor, and finally, onto an open lot.

"What's your name?" he asked.

"Billy Colter."

"That's a good name," he replied, nodding his approval. Then he told me to wait while he went to talk to a gentleman who I took to be the director. There was something about him that reminded me of Alan Grady, but this man had a much more commanding presence.

I used the moment to look around the set—a make-shift town–as well as search for Grady, Faith, or Toby. There were only strangers, though. And a lot of them. I thought it funny that there were so many people doing the work of what the few of us did in Prescott. *This must be what it means to make a real movie*, I thought to myself.

A moment later the skinny man returned. "Okay, Billy. Here's what you're going to do. You're going to get on that horse there, and you're going to ride out to the end of the street there. Then you'll ride back this way, as fast as you can, and then stop the horse so suddenly that you fall off into that big water trough there. We made it over-sized so that you'll be able to hit it better. You got all that?"

I had it. It was nothing different than I had done for Grady. I got on that horse with confidence. It was a skittish one, what with all the people and activities going on, but it took my commands just fine, and we went down to the end of the street just like we were told.

I waited a moment, set my sights on that over-sized trough, and then kicked my horse into a full run. All the time I was thinking about what Anna Beth had taught me: *Do it the way Charles would do it.* And I did. I must've soared fifteen feet from the saddle to the water-filled trough, my arms and legs flailing. I turned my body at the last moment and hit the water on my back. I sent a tidal wave of a splash up and outward, soaking anything and anyone within ten feet.

"What the hell are you doing?" the skinny man shouted at me.   I stood, as drenched as a drowned calf. "What you told me to do," I answered.

"Yes, but not *when*! The director didn't say action! We weren't ready!"

Alan Grady's yelling had nothing on this fellow's. He may have been skinny but his lungs were mighty.

"Mendoza!" he shouted. Seemingly out of nowhere appeared a young Mexican boy.

"Yes, sir?" he said, like a soldier awaiting orders.

"Take Billy, dry him off and get him a new set of clothes."

As I was hurried away I could hear—hell, everyone in Edendale probably heard—the skinny man shouting, "Get more water in this trough and clear away this mud!"

I was taken to an area behind the sets where there were racks and racks of clothes. The boy had me wait while he went through them. "How long have you been in movies?" he asked. His voice was high and feminine without any hint of "Mexican" to it.

"About a year, I suppose," I replied, "in Prescott."

"Prescott?"

"Arizona."

His lack of response showed him unimpressed. He laid a shirt and pants on a rickety table beside me. "Try these."

I quickly removed my clothes, at which the boy averted his eyes with a short, bashful gasp, and I realized *he was she*, a girl of not more than twelve or thirteen. It was then I could see in her brownish complexion and bright eyes of get-up-and-go and bullishness that she might be quite a pretty young lady if it weren't for her boyish haircut and attire. I apologized and dressed as quickly as I had undressed.

"You did a great fall, Billy," she told me.

"Thanks."

"But you have to follow direction. If it weren't for how good your fall was they would've fired you on the spot."

"I suppose I got a little excited."

She shoved me to hurry back to the set, which was good as everyone was impatiently awaiting my return. "What's your name, again?" I asked her.

"Annie Mendoza."

Her smile instilled me with the confidence that I could do that fall even better than before, which I did, and that I had made my first friend in California.

                                            ಶಿ   ಶಿ   ಶಿ

While I was diving from a horse when I wasn't supposed to, Thomas acquired a little work of his own with Selig

Polyscope. It was an expansive studio that had the look of a Spanish Mission. The job Thomas found there was in the building of sets. If there was one past time he did love it was working with a hammer, wood, and nails. In fact, he didn't really consider it work.

"It's a lot like mending fences," he explained to me. He didn't say much else about his time with Selig because, as he put it, "There isn't much to tell."

Every morning we would go our separate ways. I'd spend the day doing stunts—falling from horses, automobiles, or street cars—and he would build drawing rooms, saloon fronts and barn stalls, among other things.

"One room I built," he explained, "was used in five different pictures, twice as a bedroom, once as a nursery, once as a kitchen, and once as a funeral home. The resourcefulness of that studio is impressive."

Occasionally, Thomas would work through the night. One time, he didn't come home for three days. I had a very bad feeling and took a day off from Sheldon Pictures to go look for him. A gruff man at Selig who reminded me of Mr. McElroy but smaller told me, "He hasn't been here for a couple of days. I haven't fired him yet 'cuz he's good with a hammer. But if you see him, tell him there's plenty of men who want his job."

I checked with some of the other studios in the area,

in case he decided to work somewhere else and not tell anybody. No one admitted to seeing a tall, old cowboy with big hands, though.

So I walked the streets of Edendale and wandered all day until I found Thomas atop a hill, silhouetted against the setting sun. He stood there with his notebook in hand and his clothes covered in grass and dirt, suggesting to me that he'd slept out-of-doors. He gazed upon the Pacific Ocean. He didn't flinch a bit when I stepped up beside him.

"That's where it ends, Billy," he said, not taking his eyes from the water.

"What ends, Thomas?"

"The West."

"Unless you kept on going," I said. "You'd end up in China, I think."

"But, then, you'd be in the Far *East*, wouldn't you?" Thomas replied, finally turning to me with a grin.

"I suppose you would." The both of us turned from the fading sunset and started down the hill. "What happened, Thomas? Did you get lost?"

"I suppose I did, Billy. I suppose I did."

We returned to the hotel to learn we were being evicted. It seems when I didn't go into work I had failed to mention it to anyone there, and they called the hotel looking for me. Our ruse of not being "movies" was uncovered.

For a week, we lived at a nearby boarding house, until Thomas fired off his Colt in the middle of the night, scaring half the residents there. He had shot at something he thought he saw in the dark of his room. The next day we were, again, looking for a place to live. We moved a lot our first few months in Edendale.

Nine

...his spirit lives on

in every hard-working man

of the factories,

of the concrete trails,

of the brick canyons,

to better the rest of us.

L et me say a little about getting paid to fall. That is, doing stunts.

The profession of the stuntman in motion pictures was one that came about inherently, from a desire to entertain the public. With those earliest pie-in-the-face pratfalls, audiences were hooked and yearned for ever greater scenes of daring and danger. Sure, a good story matters, but add an element of peril and you really had something, something that fed and perpetuated an insatiable appetite. You could say that being a movie producer was akin to being a drug-pusher, and the stuntman was the drug.

Those fearless, reckless spirits willing to put themselves in harm's way for a few dollars were not strangers to bodily risk. They came to Hollywood from circuses or the demanding physical comedy of vaudeville or, like me, they were out-of-work cowboys. The work wasn't much different than what we were used to. Instead of jumping from a horse to wrestle a steer, we would jump onto another horse or a stagecoach or a car or a train. The camera would often be cranked slower than normal so that when projected the action came out faster than originally performed, but we still did the stunts at a pretty good pace. And if a plane was involved, well, you can't really fly a plane slowly.

There was no back projection in those days so the stunts were real, with little preparation. A director would say, "Okay you two, Billy you're going to leap from your horse to the train where you'll catch up with Frank on top of that boxcar and you fight." That was all. So we'd do it, usually in one take. If it had to be done again it was because something went wrong, and the more times you did it the greater chance someone would get hurt. Or worse.

Yes, a number of good men died doing these crazy acts. And for what? The money wasn't bad. Falls paid a dollar a foot. If you turned over a horse-drawn wagon you got thirty dollars. Going from a motorcycle to an airplane paid a hundred. But it was about the thrill for many. I can't think of a time I felt more alive, and I can't say I ever did anything particularly dangerous. I just made the actors look good and kept them safe to act another day.

Stars were a studio's greatest commodity. So as audiences demanded characters be put in greater and greater jeopardy, the need for stuntmen (and women) grew. Sure there were the likes of Harold Lloyd or Buster Keaton or Errol Flynn, but even Flynn used a double for the most dangerous stuff. To satisfy this need at Sheldon Pictures, there was me, Frank Dawson, Sam McCutcheon, Clay Smith, Angie Fuller, Martin Fife. (My apologies to the memory of anyone I've forgotten.) And we all had our specialties.

Mine was riding horses, of course. I was certainly no Yakima Canutt, but I did work to be proud of. Frank and Sam were well-seasoned cowboys themselves with a knack for fighting, especially each other. Sam had at one time boxed professionally, and Frank was just a scrapper, not much older than me. They didn't pull any punches when they fought. Their fist-a-cuffs for the camera were the real deal. There was talk of them once being outlaws, having robbed banks and killed lawmen, none of which was ever confirmed. I did, however, see Frank without a shirt and glimpsed a trio of bullet-hole scars along the left side of his body. Both men had physiques that were rough and gnarled from the lives they had led, that much was true.

Clay Smith was a driver, handling automobiles like we did horses. Years later, once I'd moved on from stunt-work, he learned to fly. After shooting his first scene with a plane, which involved him "landing" it between two trees, shearing its wings off in the process, I asked him how long he'd been flying.

"Oh, I learned two days ago," he replied.

Clay had the good looks of a leading man, "all thanks to my mother," he admits, and the nerve of a bullfighter, which he got serving in the Spanish-American War. He also had a cat's nine lives many times over and would be in the business of stunts longer than anyone I'd ever know, nearly losing his life more often than could be counted. He eventually retired to beautiful Santa Barbara and passed away surrounded by his children, grandchildren, and one great-grandchild.

Angie Fuller, our one stuntwoman, was an acrobat and trick-rider from the circus. Her lack of feminine features allowed her to double for men as well as women. It also made for an awkward meeting between the two of us. She was doing a leap from a runaway wagon to the back of Sam's horse when she hesitated just slightly, causing her to miss and fall to the ground. I joked with her after, saying, "You made that jump like a girl. Now do it like a man!"

She clocked me harder than an ornery mule's kick. My jaw ached for days after. As I lay in the dirt, she leaned over me, took off her hat and let her long hair fall and soften the features of her face enough for me to see my mistake, and she said, "Man enough for ya?" I laughed so hard I forgot about my near-broken jaw. She helped me up and we were good friends then on.

Martin Fife was another acrobat, from the vaudeville stage. He performed with the grace of a ballet dancer, and he taught the lot of us a few things about falling without getting too hurt. His career was a short one, however. Doing a fall from an unusually high water tower, his foot snagged a nail at the onset, which sent him into an uncontrollable tumble. His fall looked more like a roll down the side of the tower, hitting every beam and rail along the way. He was crippled by the time he landed and spent the rest of his life in a wheelchair.

As I mentioned, I didn't do anything especially dangerous, but I got pretty banged up a few times. One in particular comes to mind:

It was a scene that involved a number of us, which added to its risk. There was me, Sam, Frank, Clay, Angie, and a few men whose names I can't recall. (Again, I apologize.) More than ten of us in all. It also involved a train, two cars, two horses, a horse and wagon, and a horse-drawn firetruck with a ladder. Oh, and a cow.

The premise was, a drunken engineer falls from his train and chases it as it rolls down the track. While he's doing that, emergency men try to get all the passengers off by having them climb onto the ladder of the firetruck. Some of the gutsier passengers jump from the train to horses or wagons. Further down the line a farmer couple struggles to get their stubborn cow off the track. It was a stupid premise, I know, but Hollywood's logic is most often based on the nonsense of entertainment .

I played the engineer. The fall from the engine was easy enough. But then, oddly, the director had me run to catch the train instead of ride a horse, my specialty. So I did a lot of running. Then, as I climbed upon the rear of the caboose, my suspenders were to get caught on the railing and I'd lose my balance and fall back. Those suspenders were supposed to stretch to a length that allowed me to, well, suspend there, horizontally, my legs locked, above the moving tracks beneath. They were also to have enough elasticity that I would then be pulled back to an upright position.

But that's not what happened. The suspenders had no elasticity and I fell all the way back. My head hit a railroad tie, my body did a flip and a turn, and I was drug along the back of the caboose. Fortunately, the train was not moving too fast since I had to be able to run to catch it. I grabbed onto the "suspenders" and pulled myself to the caboose where I could grab the railing. There my hand slipped and I was drug some more. If the ground had been just dirt and gravel that would have been one thing. But those railroad ties had me bouncing along like a rag doll in the clutches of a small child.

Finally, someone had the wherewithal to stop the train. I was limp from exhaustion as they unhooked and untangled me and carried me to the back of the horse and wagon so I could be hurried to an emergency room. Annie Mendoza had witnessed the whole thing and was with me in the wagon, holding my raw hands and repeating, "You're okay. You're going to be fine." She gave me a reassuring wink as I winced and groaned with each bump and jostle. Every inch of me below my shoulders was bruised. Luckily, I had no broken bones, and no concussion, just a knot the size of an orange on the back of my head. They reshot the scene with another stuntman and it worked perfectly, to great comic effect. I stayed in the hospital for a couple of days, Annie by my bedside. It was the first time, but not the last, that she would be there to help me heal.

Annie was mature far beyond her twelve years, more mature than most adults, and she worked harder than many a cowboy I'd known. We all knew her as "Annie-get-it-done." Whatever was needed–a prop, a location, a piece of costume, a fact of information (she read a lot!)–she was the person to fetch it for you. And if she couldn't, she knew someone who could. Heck, she knew enough about everything in the studio that she could have run it herself. She was especially attentive to us stunt-folk, or anyone who worked behind the camera. She was fine with the bit-players, too. It was the stars she didn't hold a very high opinion of.

From the very beginning, Hollywood's star system was nothing more than a dog-and-pony show meant to milk the public's attention just long enough before the next thing came along. The system didn't make full steam until the 1930's, yet it had been around before the movies, before vaudeville and circuses. As soon as the public was willing to pay to see a performer do whatever they did best, that's when it began. I don't know who the first "star" ever was—a caveman who could grunt and beat a rock better than the other cavemen, perhaps—but there has always been and always will be someone who garners more attention than the rest of us.

"Most of them don't even deserve it," was Annie's opinion. "They're just pretty faces."

We both knew there was a little more to it than that. But only a little. The biggest stars had a certain quality. "It" they would call it. Clara Bow may have been dubbed the "It Girl" in 1927, but Pickford, Brooks, Swanson, and scores of others, had *it* before her. In the earliest movies, actors were not always given credit, either because they were ashamed of being part of such a lowly art form, or because the studios feared the potential power a star could wield. As movies and actors gained popularity, though, the public wanted to know who they were so captivated by. And the tabloids wanted to know who they could exploit!

While audiences were caught up with a star's persona—the sweetheart, the hero, the tramp—the newspapers strived to reveal the person, which was not always flattering. The less flattering, in fact, the greater the readership. People don't really want to know a certain celebrity is good with children and loves their mother. If anyone says so, they're lying. People want to read about the drunkard, or the vamp, or the spoiled starlet and her tantrums. Who slept with who, or who beat who, or who died. That's always been the news of the day. Comedy and good feelings entertain. Tragedy sells.

Annie and I used to play a game. During breaks, we would sit off to the side and guess who amongst the actors with Sheldon Pictures had the makings of a real star.

One afternoon, pointing to a woman with dusty-brown hair and ordinary features, someone easy to miss in a crowd, Annie observed, "There's Nora Melville. She was in that atrocious *Forgotten Lover*. It was so boring, and so is she. I'm surprised she still works here after that one."

"I heard she was a distant relative of that writer," I commented.

"Herman Melville? I doubt it. Even if it were true, it makes her none the less boring."

I gestured to a young lady as delicate as a doll with strawberry-blonde hair, faintly freckled skin and shiny blue eyes. "What about her?"

"Silkie Parks? She is very pretty. But meek. A star needs to be gregarious."

"Grega-what?"

"Gregarious. You know, extroverted."

I gave a bewildered shrug.

"Not afraid to talk to people."

"Oh."

"Look at her. She's terrified someone might notice her. She won't last."

Then we saw Victoria Reade, a plump, mature woman with a genuine, boisterous laugh. She was not unpleasant to look at, one of the better actresses with Sheldon Pictures and had a demeanor that complimented her laugh. She had my vote.

"No, I don't think so," Annie said. "She's not flirtatious enough. She's more motherly."

One day, I pointed out Smitty Smith, an ex-circus performer, and a midget. (That's what we used to call them. I believe the appropriate term today is "little person.") I had always found him funny and told Annie so.

"Of course he's funny. He's a midget," she replied. "That doesn't make him a star."

"Did you see *Bigger Than Life*? He was pretty good in it, midget or not."

"Yes, that's true. But I just don't think he'll go very far."

On another day, Smitty caught on to the game we were playing and joined us. "What about him?" he said with a nod to James Kellerman, an Englishman and seasoned actor from the stage, one of those who thought the movies were beneath him. His real name was Bartholomew Nordstrom, but he used an alias for Hollywood. With his jet-black hair, strong features and wry grin, he made women swoon, including Annie.

"He has potential," she commented off-handedly, a poor attempt to contain her swooning.

"I hate him," sneered Smitty. "He calls me Shorty."

"Well, you are short," I said.

"It's *the way* he says it, like he's better than me. And he uses it as my name. 'Good day to you, Shorty Smith.' 'Fetch me a glass of water, Shorty Smith.' Because he's taller doesn't make him better. Everyone's taller than me, nothing special about that."

Kellerman/Nordstrom left Hollywood and returned to England a year later. I never heard about either of them ever again.

It was Smitty who mentioned one of the newer actresses, Henrietta Van Hughes. She was not nearly as stuffy as her name, quite the opposite, actually. She reminded me of Faith Monroe or Thomas's Ellen Marie, two women I knew as having the star qualities we were looking for. Like with them, you couldn't take your eyes from Henrietta, and not just because of her fetching appearance, but also by the way she gestured and laughed and winked and smiled and frowned. Yes, she certainly had "It."

Annie agreed. "But," she added in a hushed tone, "she has a secret." With that, Annie nodded toward another woman, Priscilla Westlake, whose plain looks made her easy to overlook, yet a minute of conversation made her indelible. I once asked her for a date, with no success.

Smitty and I stared blankly.

"They like each other," Annie said.

"Yes, they're friends. That's no secret," I said.

"They like each other…*romantically.*"

As it finally sunk in, Smitty and I said together, "OHHH!"

Homosexuality was no stranger to the movie business. But Hollywood was not the rest of the country, and their secret was soon exposed—thanks to the tabloids. Henrietta and Priscilla never acted in American films again.

They moved to Europe—Paris, I think—and did quite well there, living and loving and acting together for many years. A happy ending, you might say.

As blood-thirsty for scandal as the public can be, they do like their happy endings. My own life at that point could have been the perfect end to a good story. I had found steady work in an unusual and exciting business. I had friendships with Annie, my fellow stuntmen, and Thomas. I enjoyed an occasional fling with a starlet or two and carefree days like I'd never experienced before. I really wanted for nothing more than what I had.

Ten

There is a sound that snow makes
a whisper in the dark
The touch of a thousand flakes
upon the trees and on the ground

A number of things happened that would take me and Thomas in unexpected directions. The first, as Ellen Marie might have said, was highly fortuitous. It was when I met Anthony Sheldon, owner and production head for Sheldon Pictures. Because Mr. Sheldon travelled back and forth from Los Angeles to New York and Chicago where he managed his other business ventures—a newspaper and a railroad—he would be gone weeks at a time, and I had yet to see him, let alone meet him. Eventually he returned, and that day everybody at Sheldon Pictures was very nervous and focused on their job.

I was doing a scene where I was supposed to sneak out an upper story window and drop to a horse that was waiting for me on the street. I had to do more than one take. The first time, I missed my mark and lost my balance. It was one of those few times I fell to the ground when I wasn't supposed to. On the second take, the horse got skittish and moved just as I was about to land in the saddle. The third take was the winner. I was so cocky and proud of myself that I smiled and tipped my hat to a pretty young gal, an extra in the scene, just before I rode off. Mr. Sheldon witnessed my little moment, and the next day I was called to his office.

Mr. Sheldon was the richest man I had ever met, but you wouldn't have known it to look at the small room from where he worked. The door was paper thin and, except for an over-sized leather chair, his throne, its furnishings were humble. He was standing by the room's only window looking upon part of his empire, such as it was, when I entered.

He was a bull dog of a man—squat, with short, muscular arms and legs that bulged at his tight-fitting suit in comical ways. I would not describe him as having a sense of humor, however. No, physically he was a bull dog, but in character he was a fuming, snorting bull. He turned from the window, revealing a scar on his left cheek and a Browning semi-automatic holstered on his right hip. I would come to learn that the scar came from the knife of a jealous Mexican, and the pistol was just in case that Mexican ever appeared again. His mouth curled into what might have been called a smile and he gestured for me to have a seat in one of his office's two wooden chairs.

"Billy Colter, is it?" he said.

"Yes, sir."

"That's a good name. You've done some acting, haven't you, Billy?"

"Some," I said.

"I could tell. How would you like to do some more? I think you're being wasted on just this stunt work. What do you think?"

"I enjoy the stunts," I told him, "but I could enjoy acting, too."

"You'll be doing both, just less stunts. I'll pay you fifty dollars a week. How about it?"

Fifty dollars! I was making more doing stunts, but his offer was almost double what a lot of folk were making, and I wouldn't have to fall so much. I agreed and we shook hands on it. I left his office feeling quite happy. By the end of the day, I also felt lucky—lucky that I hadn't been fired! It turned out Mr. Sheldon was doing a little housecleaning. He was letting people go like he was shooing sheep out to pasture. There were only a few of us that were allowed to stay. One of them was Annie.

"I saw him walking around the sets earlier today," she confided in me. "He was very serious and scrutinizing. Then at one point he stopped, sniffed the air, and said, 'It's gotten stale around here. We need to freshen things up a bit.' Then he went to his office and started calling people in."

"Well, we still have our jobs, don't we?" I assured her. "I wouldn't worry about it much, Annie. You're one of the most valuable people here."

"I appreciate that, Billy," she replied, "but there's not much chance I'll ever lose my job here. I just worry for everyone else, and you. I'm glad you're staying." She gave me a smile that I suspected would corral many a man's heart in the years ahead as she matured to womanhood. But I was confused.

"How it is you'll never lose your job here?" I asked.

"Well, you see, it's that…" she bit her lip as she hesitated to let the words out. "Mr. Sheldon is my father."

I doubt the best of actors could have concealed their surprise, and I was certainly not the best.

"You have to promise you'll never tell anybody, Billy. Nobody knows. It would make things very uncomfortable. Promise?"

"Of course, I promise."

We sat in silence for a moment, her newly shared secret sitting awkwardly between us. Then I asked, "Why?"

"Why what?"

"Why shouldn't anybody know?"

"Because I'm misbegotten. Father didn't even know about me until a couple of years ago. He'd had an affair with a woman, my mother, down in Mexico."

"Oh," I said.

"She was the wife of another man, Billy."

Then for emphasis, Annie slowly ran her finger down the side of her face, like a knife slicing her cheek.

"OHHH!" My eyes and mouth widened as the elephant-sized truth finally sat itself in my lap.

She put her hand over mine and leaned in secretively. "It isn't the kind of thing people need to know about, especially for a man in my father's position."

"Okay. I promise," I said as I placed my other hand over hers.

"Thank you, Billy. I'm so very glad you're not losing your job."

I was glad too. Not just for Annie and our ever-growing friendship, but for myself, as I was entering a new chapter in my life: stuntman to actor.

      ↾   ↾   ↾

I did three, sometimes as many as five, movies a week for Sheldon Pictures. Mostly westerns as they were immensely popular. Even if they weren't a western there would somehow be a horse involved as my riding abilities were becoming my trademark. I'd still do the easier stunts, leaping from horse to car or car to horse. It's funny how I can recall the particular stunts I did, but not a single plot, which usually involved me facing insurmountable odds to save a girl. Like Thomas had told Alan Grady the first time we met him, "not original, but tried and true."

Though Mr. Sheldon knew tried-and-true made him money, he also continued his pretension of having had enough of it. Truth is, I think he just enjoyed firing people. Directors and cameramen came and went through the studio daily as his patience with the staleness he so abhorred dwindled. "I'm going to get some real, creative blood if I have to hire and fire every single motion picture person from here to Chicago," he announced.

One day late in the summer of 1913, I again met, a new director and cameraman that I would be working with. This time, however, they were movie men I recognized. Alan Grady and Toby Greene! We had quite the reunion, shaking hands and smiling, telling each other about the events that led to our meeting once more.

"I can't say what happened to the others," Toby explained. "Except for Faith. Her face got her in the door of the Nestor Motion Picture Company right away. The rest of us quickly went our separate ways. The best work I could find was running a projector in one of the Los Angeles theaters."

Grady said, "I ended up doing what I've done most of my working life–banking."

"How did you get into the movie business in the first place, as a banker?" I had to ask.

"I went to foreclose on a studio back East. They offered me a job at twice the salary, to travel west and make movies along the way, you know, staying one step ahead of the Patents Detectives."

"They caught up to us eventually, didn't they," Toby reminded us, and we all had a good laugh at that.

"Where's Thomas?" Grady asked, looking around.

"He's working over at Selig," I told him. "He's building sets."

"Building sets! What a waste! I was hoping he would be here with you. I owe my success in Arizona to him."

"You'll be fine," Toby assured him.

"I have to be better than 'fine.' I heard Sheldon is putting directors through the grinder here. That's how we got this job. There's nobody left to hire!"

"Mr. Sheldon is looking to be impressed, alright," I said. This certainly didn't calm Grady down.

"You have to get Thomas a job here, doing…oh, anything! I won't make it, otherwise!"

I didn't tell Grady (there was something about watching him sweat that I found cruelly amusing), but I thought he had a good idea. Getting Thomas to work with us was just what Sheldon Pictures needed, and I would be able to keep an eye on him, too. At the end of the day's shooting, I approached Mr. Sheldon with the idea, and he agreed to it with a wary, "I'm not in the charity business, Billy."

"You won't be disappointed," I told him.

And he wasn't.

Thomas had grown tired of building sets, and the idea of working again with Alan Grady was exciting for him. Mr. Sheldon hired Thomas on as a script writer, but he was mostly Grady's creative consultant. Together they made dozens of one-reel westerns (one reel being about twelve minutes). I was in a lot of them, but not all. Sheldon had other plans for me because I was beginning to gain fans. I was soon doing more and more two-reelers.

When I began to work less with Thomas, I would get regular updates from Toby and Annie. "He's certainly in his element here," Toby told me. "At first glance you might think he was the director and Alan was his assistant."

"Does he ever seem lost or confused?" I asked.

"Lost in his work, maybe. He gets very involved."

That involvement included showing actors how to fight, and not just with guns like he taught us in Prescott, but how to box. He taught them how to use a rope and wrestle a calf. He taught the ladies how to behave like whores. He would also advise builders what a saloon should really look like. His sets had a realism that wouldn't be surpassed until the westerns of William S. Hart a few years later.

None of what I heard surprised me. I would've expected nothing less from my friend. What did shock me was something Annie said:

"He's got himself a sweetheart."

"What? Who?"

"Elizabeth Jerome. She takes care of the horses."

I hadn't met Elizabeth, but I had noticed her. You couldn't help it, really. Her apple-red hair glowed like a beacon in a fog, and it must have pierced Thomas's old, lonely heart. When I finally saw them together, I could see how smitten he was.

"She's good company," Thomas told me. "Like you, but much prettier."

"What about Ellen Marie?" I couldn't help asking.

"If she were here, I'd be with her. But she's not." He could see I wasn't understanding in my naïve way. "You don't think she's spending her days and nights all alone, pining away for me, do you?"

"I suppose not."

"So you wouldn't expect me to do the same for her, would you?"

"No, I suppose not."

"That's always been the nature of Ellen Marie's and my relationship, Billy."

"Okay."

"Besides, haven't you seen the figure on that woman?"

He was right. Elizabeth's red hair wasn't the only eye-catching thing about her. She stood almost as tall as Thomas, which was good for him as it was getting difficult for him to bend down. She'd worked outdoors all her life and it gave her skin a healthy, natural coloring. She never needed to paint up her face like the actresses around the studio. The lines revealing her age did nothing to diminish her allure. In fact, I believe they added to it. As far as her age, I guessed her to be somewhere between me and Thomas. She could've been my mother, or his daughter.

I never really got the relationship between Thomas and Ellen Marie, but I did see how she made him feel. It was the same with Elizabeth. He wasn't just happy, he was balanced. In her company Thomas had fewer of his episodes, and he was writing in his notebook again, poetry I assumed. Working with Grady seemed to help, as well. As Toby had said, he got lost in his work. So when he wasn't focused on the details of a cowpoke's attire or demeanor, or how a lady would saunter her way down the street, Thomas's attention was on a particular red-head.

I was most relieved that she was there for him because he and I would soon live in separate accommodations, as well. We were going in different directions—he behind the camera, gaining notoriety as a "story advisor," while I was garnering bigger and bigger roles.

Yes, I was becoming a movie star.

"You're not a star," Annie was quick to tell me. "Not yet, anyway. You're still just an actor."

"What will you think of me, if I become a star?" I asked her.

"I don't know. Will you still be the same Billy?"

"I don't know what else I'd be."

"People change when they become famous. Good people become not so good. Bad people become worse."

"I don't know why I would go and change," I assured her, seeing how concerned she looked. "I'll always be the same old me."

"That may be, but your *life* will change, Billy. It always does," she said as she forlornly leaned her head against my shoulder and took my hand.

❧   ❧   ❧

Then there was one event, years later, that would not only

affect the lives of Thomas and me, but would also change the entire film industry forever.

It was February of 1915. By then Thomas and I each had over a hundred films under our belts. We were practically veterans. We lived in houses larger than any we'd ever seen in our lives. Sheldon Pictures was competing right along with the bigger studios like Vitagraph and Biograph. It was a very lucrative time for everyone in the business. The American public couldn't get enough of the movies.

In a rare moment, to show his appreciation, Mr. Sheldon took a group of us out to Clune's Auditorium for a preview of a new film directed by D.W. Griffith. He was considered a director's director, one of the best in the industry. The name of the movie was *The Clansman*, an adaptation of a play by the same name that had been very popular. I was excited at having a chance to see the film, any film. I was always so busy making movies that it was hard to get out to watch ones that weren't my own. In fact, I rarely ventured out from that quiet little suburb of Edendale. As I've mentioned, I don't like crowds. I like my space. Los Angeles was a buzzing city with a seemingly endless amount of activity. Automobiles crowded the streets like a stream full of fish, and I don't recall a single horse anywhere.

At one time, Clune's was a Baptist Temple, which was apparent from its outside. The auditorium was opened somewhere around 1906. We walked through the foyer that had some eighty feet in length of doors to allow the audience an easy exit. It could seat as many as 2,700 people. A cantilever system supporting the balcony gave the impression of it floating above the people below. It also allowed those in the back rows of the floor to have an unobstructed view of the stage and screen, behind which, I was told, was a 6,000-pipe organ. There were semi-rings framing the proscenium and those were studded with electric lights. Above everything was a sky-light in the domed roof.

"This is magnificent," Thomas said under his breath.

"Oh, my…" was all Elizabeth could say, which was still more than me. I was speechless.

Mr. Clune hired a full orchestra for this special preview. The audience was mostly movie-people. From Sheldon Pictures, there was me and Thomas and Elizabeth, of course. Alan Grady and two more of Sheldon's directors, Arthur Duff and Franklin Langston. Toby and another cameraman, Jake Wilson, were there, too. There were some executive types who I didn't know and their wives, and, of course, Mr. Sheldon, accompanied by the boring actress Nora Melville. I had wanted to bring Annie but she thought it best not to. So I was on my own.

There was a lot of murmuring about D.W. Griffith and the film's production.

"I believe he hired some old veterans from the war as advisors," someone said.

"I'm not surprised," replied another, "Griffith is obsessed with details."

"I heard somebody died during one of the battle scenes," commented someone else.

"Yes, a cameraman was trampled by horses!" came a response.

Those around me were no different than a bunch of cowpokes I once knew, gathered in a bunkhouse, swapping stories. I saw Thomas listening in, learning that the film was about the conflict between the North and the South. He told me once that he had made efforts to avoid "that damn war." But I could see in his face that he hadn't entirely gotten away from it. As he had said, it touched the lives of everyone in the country, no matter how distant they may have been from the battlefields.

Then the lights went dim.

I can't speak for everyone, but I was as anxious with anticipation as a bull rider awaiting his eight-second chance for fame. From right out of the gate, none of us were disappointed. The orchestra thundered! The curtains opened to the title credits, and we were magically transported to another place and time.

It was the story of two aristocratic families–the

Stonemans and the Camerons–divided by the Civil War, each fighting for the opposing army. Like a double-*Romeo and Juliet,* one son from each of the families falls in love with a daughter from the other family. After the war, and Lincoln's assassination, the Confederate son worries that his beloved Dixie won't be given the proper chance to rebuild itself.

Before, when I had gone to the movies, I enjoyed looking around at the audience's reactions. But that night I could not look away from the screen. And I didn't need to. I could sense the feelings of the crowd around me, the joy from the love story, the excitement from the battle, and the hush caused by the title card: WAR'S PEACE, followed by images of dead soldiers fallen across the landscape.

In the film, the Confederate son organizes his fellow Southerners into a band of vigilantes hell-bent on restoring the South's dignity—the Ku Klux Klan, they were called. In a blood-stirring climax, the Klan saves the day! As I think back, I realize that all of us in the audience that night, not only cheered for the ride to rescue the South, but we rooted for what would later inspire a revival of the KKK. We whooped and hollered for what would become our country's greatest symbol of racism and hatred. It wasn't just a spell of movie-magic we were under, it was the *power* of the motion picture industry.

For the public premiere in New York the following

month, Griffith changed the name of the movie to *The Birth of a Nation*. From the beginning, it was a movie full of controversy. In 1915, the war was still fresh in the memory of America's history. In part, this was what made the film so controversial. It had a terrible truth to it. There was right and wrong on both sides.

Something else that was contestable was the portrayal of Blacks, played, of course, by Whites in grease paint. It seemed to me that in the movie they were played as rather brutish and hostile. One scene depicts what Congress would be like if run entirely by slaves. Representatives are shown lounging in their seats, feet up on their desk, sneaking drinks of whiskey and behaving altogether coarse and disrespectful to their positions. As we were leaving the theater later, Thomas commented about it. "From what I could see, they behaved no different than any White politician."

There was a great uproar from the Black community about the shadow which the film cast upon their character, a shadow they had already worked hard to step out from. Also, I recall in 1995 how the showing of a restored print was cancelled because of the O.J. Simpson trial. Eighty years later and it could still rile up so many people!

Eleven

When I lost him, so too went my voice.

His passage through my life, I hope, was God's
choice.

Maddened he is gone, grateful he was here,

I see him, sometimes, on the horizon,

in the blowing sand,

and I am sorrowed by the silence.

The new-found life of the film industry spread like a social disease. Everyone clamored to make the next *Birth of a Nation*. (Only D.W. Griffith himself was able to top his own creation with a giant of a movie called *Intolerance*. I can't rightly say what it was about as I fell asleep both times I tried to watch it.) Before *Birth*, longer films had been slowly becoming popular. After, that's all audiences wanted to see, so that's what the studios made. Call it an art form all you want, but motion pictures have always been, first and foremost, a business. And Anthony Sheldon was not going to miss out on any of it. He pushed his creative people day and night for ideas and scripts to satisfy his bottom line. That element of desperation made for some real flops.

The first was *A Woman Named Joan*, as in Joan of Arc. The production itself was quite epic and impressive, but the actors were all cut of the same over-dramatic swath as Charles Benz, particularly Caroline Langston, the woman chosen to play Joan. She was atrocious. She didn't think so, of course, and no one would dare tell her as she was the daughter of the movie's director, Franklin Langston. It really says something about her performance when you consider that the acting in silent movies, as it was, already leaned toward the melodramatic. She was so bad that most people who saw the film thought it was a comedy. This devastated her and she never made another movie again.

That flop was followed by a series of westerns. (What else?) They were stories "too big for their saddles," as Thomas put it, long, dull plots of the railroads, of settlers crossing the country by wagon train, of the Indian Wars. And, as Thomas relished in pointing out, they were wrought with inaccuracies.

About *To the Promontory*, a movie about the meeting of the Union and Central Pacific railroads, he exclaimed, "Where the hell are the Chinamen? The railroads were built on the backs of thousands of Chinese laborers! There aren't more than three of them in the whole movie!"

With *Trail of Tears* he was the most upset. "Those

dimwitted executives have titled their latest creation [about a wagon train] after the forced movement of Indians from their homeland! And the props-men don't have a clue about the difference between a Conestoga and an ordinary prairie schooner!"

My favorite disaster was *A Man of Mars*. Science-fiction movies weren't unheard of in the silent era, but there weren't very many. "What's the point of plots that could never happen?" Thomas said at its premiere, reminding me of his opinion on the matter.

It was the story of, well, a man from Mars who comes to our planet to study us lowly Earthlings. Naturally, he meets a woman and falls in love. That's the one thing that hasn't changed throughout the history of the movies: the all-important element of romance. Funny though, what I've known of love has never matched the images that have been endlessly poured upon us from the silver screen. Thomas and Ellen Marie, Thomas and Elizabeth—theirs were unique relationships. Then there were my own affairs, all unforgettable but nothing like I've ever seen in any film.

A Man of Mars was apparently full of metaphors and symbolism about the human condition, something I would've expected from one of those heavy-handed German films. All of that was missed, however, with the absurdity of the alien. Another fact you may not know of movies from the silent-era is that they weren't always entirely black-and-white. A film would often be tinted, by hand, one frame at a time, for effect. *Birth of a Nation* had it done for its battle scenes. In the case of *A Man of Mars*, our hero the Martian was colored with an unflattering greenish hue. It gave him the appearance of a Mexican who was sickly-drunk on tequila.

Thomas was not involved in these movies to any extent. They were all produced so frantically that he had little chance to contribute his knowledge and own special skills. Until, that is, Mr. Sheldon decided to gamble on something *really* big.

He had come across a behemoth of a script about Lewis and Clark called *Journey of Discovery*. It was written by a college professor, Wilfred Brownstone, who had dreamy aspirations of being a screenwriter. What made his script so enormous was the fact that Brownstone did not overlook a single detail in his historical exposé. The plot followed every step of the two explorers and their party as they trekked and floated across two-thirds of this country in their search for the Pacific Ocean. If made as originally written, the movie would have been ten hours, or longer.

Thomas insisted on meeting with Mr. Sheldon privately to discuss the pending production. While Thomas admitted to not knowing much about the Lewis and Clark expedition, he did have some strong opinions about the script. I accompanied him to Sheldon's office but didn't go in. I waited outside, making sure to sit close enough to the door so that I could hear every word. Well, almost every word. Their talk began in a low murmur. It wasn't until each man's passion added volume to their opinion that I could hear what they were saying.

"This script is too long, Anthony," Thomas argued. "It's tedious to read and will be even worse to watch."

"It's an epic tale, a great journey. Audiences will expect it to be long," Mr. Sheldon replied. "Besides, I'll be able to charge more per ticket."

"It won't matter. You'll go broke trying to make this thing."

"I want something *big*, Thomas. This studio needs something big."

"Big doesn't have to be dull. And what you've got here is one big, dull story! Have you read this thing?"

I couldn't make out Mr. Sheldon's reply. He probably turned away from Thomas, looked out his window and grumbled under his breath, something he would do when he didn't want to admit he was wrong.

"It doesn't get interesting until they meet the Shoshones and take Sacagawea on as an interpreter," Thomas continued. "We could pick the story up from there.

That's the part people are most familiar with anyway. They don't want a history lesson. They want to see what they know come to life. And you can be the man to bring it to them."

By Mr. Sheldon's silence I could tell Thomas was winning the argument. Then he admitted, "I have read it, Thomas. And you're right. It's too damn long. Also, I don't like that the woman, Sacawagagea…"

"Sacagawea."

"I don't like her being pregnant."

"But…she *was* pregnant."

"I don't like it," Mr. Sheldon stated firmly. "It might upset the sensibilities of our women audience."

"But she was *six-months* pregnant, Anthony," Thomas said, determined not to lose this argument.

"Oh, and how many people are going to know that, Thomas?"

"I know I said we don't need to give a history lesson, but for what we're going to tell, we should be truthful."

"Well, we won't say one way or the other," Mr. Sheldon concluded. "She very well could be pregnant. We just won't let on about it."

"She gave birth and carried the baby with her!"

Mr. Sheldon eventually conceded, in his own way. "Fine! I want you to work with Brownstone on a rewrite. Treat the matter tastefully. And start by changing the name to 'The Great Journey' or 'The Greatest Journey.' Make it unforgettable, Thomas!" he commanded. I pictured him shooing Thomas toward the door while sitting down decisively in his throne of a chair. When Mr. Sheldon decided a meeting was done, it was done.

As Thomas left the office, I could see he didn't want to talk. He was ready to get to work, and to do his damnedest to be truthful while still giving what the man that paid him wanted. Thomas was nothing if not loyal.

As for Mr. Sheldon, he was nothing if not demanding. One way or another, his biggest picture would be made exactly the way he envisioned. He started by giving Alan Grady the task of directing *The Greatest Journey*. I will say that even though I considered Grady a friend, and while his knack for directing had certainly grown, I did not feel that he was the man for the immense responsibility that was bestowed upon him. He was only given the opportunity because, I believe, he would not pose a challenge to Mr. Sheldon. Not like Thomas would have.

Grady chose Toby Greene as his cameraman, of course. Once again the four of us would work together. But, as this new production began, I came to realize that we were a long way from Prescott.

ô∂   ô∂   ô∂

• • •

While the size of *The Greatest Journey*'s cast was nothing compared to the thousands in a Griffith or DeMille extravaganza, there were more of us than any picture I'd ever been in before. In the group of explorers alone there were upwards around thirty, plus all the Indians they met along the way. It was this that led Thomas and Mr. Sheldon to have another one of their "discussions."

Mr. Sheldon expected to shoot the entire movie in the studio or its general vicinity. With Thomas's need for authenticity, he wanted to shoot entirely on location throughout the Northwest–Montana, Idaho, Washington. He argued that it would make for good billing at the theaters. But Mr. Sheldon felt the expense of moving all the actors and crew and equipment halfway across the country wasn't worth it. To him, the idea of saving money *and* fooling the public was greatly appealing.

"Then let's save the location shoot for just the Columbia River," Thomas compromised. "I hear it's quite beautiful, and I don't believe we could recreate it ourselves. Everything else we could shoot in the mountains right around here." And it was settled.

Next, began the casting of *The Greatest Journey*.

First, there were the lead roles of Meriwether Lewis and William Clark. John Beaumont, a seasoned actor with a

Southern accent as deep as the South itself, was given the role of Lewis. "It's fortunate that pictures don't talk," Thomas commented about him, "because I don't think the audience would understand a word he said."

As Clark, Arthur Troy was cast. Or was it Troy Arthur? Anyway, Troy (as I'll call him) was as ordinary a fellow as you'd ever meet, but a fine actor. Anyone who had seen all his films probably never realized it was the same man they were watching. He was all about the make-up and costume. Every day I would seem him transform from ordinary Troy to a real live replication of explorer and Second Lieutenant William Clark.

Toussaint Charbonneau, trapper, interpreter and husband of Sacagawea, was played by character actor Reginald Chesterfield. He was nowhere as noble as his name implied. A coarse old sot, Chesterfield was only sober twice a day—when he first got up in the morning, and when he was asleep right before that. Playing the other interpreter, George Drouillard, was Richard Baleman, who came down with a terrible stomach flu after filming only a couple of scenes. Mr. Sheldon didn't want to reshoot with another actor so he just cut him out of the script after that. With so many other characters, no one much noticed the disappearance of Drouillard from the rest of the movie.

Then there was York, Clark's black servant. Some

contention arose from Mr. Sheldon because Grady, influenced by Thomas, wanted to use a real black man, rather than the widely accepted practice of a white man covered in dark grease paint, or black face, as it was called. Not that Blacks in the movies was unheard of. There was the notable and awkwardly titled *Bert Williams: Lime Kiln Field Day Club* made in 1913. It was cast nearly entirely with Blacks, many of who performed, absurdly enough, in black face.

For York, Henderson P. Watts, a set builder who never acted a day in his life, was found to be perfect for the part. There wasn't much that Watts needed to do in the way of acting. He just needed to stand there and look Black. So, you might say, he was a natural for the role.

Then there were some Sergeants and a bunch of enlisted men, of which I was one. While I was used to star billing by that time, Grady didn't feel I was right for any of the lead roles. Mr. Sheldon didn't object as long as my name was prominently on the marquis. For myself, I enjoyed having only a supporting role. Being in the background with those other men and the way we joked and commiserated like cowhands was like being on a ranch again. It was the first time in years that I had thought about and missed those days.

Finally, there was the part of Sacagawea.

I arrived to the studio one day to find nearly every

male there gathered together, all their attention upon the center of their mass, climbing over each other to get a look at who they encompassed. I snaked my way through them and saw her.

To describe Rebecca Faye as beautiful…well… it wouldn't be enough. Nothing I could write, if I did nothing but write about her for the rest of my life, would ever be enough. Her black hair, hazel eyes, skin as white as a snowdrift all made for a perfectly mesmerizing image meant for those days of black-and-white movies. In person, she stood out like a Mathew Brady portrait, softening the coarse world of harsh colors around her. The delicate features of her face and her elegant, understated figure left both the Gish girls as nothing more than extras in a crowd.

What was most attracting about Rebecca was the manner in which she ignored you. With only the slightest glance, she snagged you with the impression that her attention was on you and only you, and you would forever watch for that look again. Though it never returned, you watched her. Every man watched her. Every man hoped. I know because I was one of them, part of that fawning, childish crowd surrounding her.

Mr. Sheldon soon arrived and parted the group of us like Moses at the Red Sea. "Rebecca, sweetheart, you made it," he greeted her.

"I only just arrived," she replied and gave him a kiss on the cheek.

Oh, how we all wished to be that cheek!

"Come on, boys," barked Mr. Sheldon, "give the lady some room!"

"They've given me a lovely welcome," she said to him as though the rest of us weren't even there.

Mr. Sheldon escorted her away, leaving us men dumbfounded and longing. When I learned (with some disbelief because of her cream complexion) that she was to be the young Indian woman Sacagawea, I had to meet her. I waited outside Mr. Sheldon's office for her to leave.

She and Mr. Sheldon came through the door full of laughter and charm. She kissed him once more upon the cheek, and walked past me without a nod, without a glance. She did nothing to acknowledge my presence as I followed her. I touched her shoulder and introduced myself.

"I'll be working with you in the Lewis and Clark picture," I added.

"My name's Rebecca," she said, a trace of annoyance in her voice. "What part will you be playing, Billy?"

"Oh, I'll just be one of the enlisted soldiers."

She cocked her head slightly to one side with a glare that asked, *Then why are you even speaking to me?* "We've all had to start somewhere," she said.

"Oh, I've been in movies before. Dozens. You must've seen one of them."

My heart sank as she shook her head with pitying denial. Then she turned and left me, the now lowly extra, to wallow in my disgrace.

While my ego was picking itself up from the knock-down Rebecca had given it, Thomas was busy working with Wilfred Brownstone, the screenwriter, rewriting the professor's tome of a script. There was a great deal of reluctance on Brownstone's part, however. It was difficult and painful to trim down—or "butcher," as he put it—his life's work. Thomas made a valiant attempt to convince him of what was best.

The movie would begin with the tense meeting of a Teton Sioux tribe. The Indians demand the expedition hand over one of their boats before they are allowed passage upriver. The Chief, Black Buffalo, fortunately settles the dispute and a fight is avoided.

"The journey may have started before that," Thomas explained to Brownstone, "but we'll pick up the story from where the adventure truly begins, with a scene of tension and drama."

Wilfred was never fully convinced. "I'll just take my screenplay to another studio," he threatened. Thomas warned of that not being a good idea. And when Wilfred proposed the same threat to Mr. Sheldon, he was immediately fired.

"Read your contract," Mr. Sheldon told him. "I bought your script outright, with or without you."

That was the last anyone ever heard of Wilfred Brownstone, screenwriter.

&ed;   &ed;   &ed;

Alan Grady's directing style had once involved a lot of yelling. With the Lewis and Clark epic, he was all about rehearsing. "All the best directors rehearse before shooting," he said, in hopes of becoming one of them. He also rehearsed because there were key scenes that would benefit from a little planning: the confrontation with the Sioux right at the beginning; the meeting of Charbonneau and his wife, Sacagawea; the killing of a never-before-seen grizzly bear by Lewis; the discovery of a Shoshone village, and Sacagawea's brother Chief Cameahwait. Also, we were shooting "on location"–away from the comfort and security of the studio, that is.

As we rehearsed the first of those scenes, all eyes were on Rebecca, although her role wasn't in the scene. She was just idly watching. Even some of the other ladies couldn't help themselves. Rebecca was an immense distraction.

"She's so pretty," commented Annie, who was assisting with the rehearsals but would move on to another project once shooting started. "And she's so nice."

"You think she's nice?" I asked her.

"We've only spoke once or twice, but she was very sweet."

"She has 'It', doesn't she?" I said.

"She's got something, that's for sure." There was a kind of envious awe to Annie's tone, which left me a little disappointed. It seemed Rebecca Faye was the first actor, beside me, that Annie liked.

"Eyes this way, everyone!" Grady shouted, breaking our trance and effectively reverting back to one of his old habits. "We're here to rehearse, not look at pretty girls!"

As I'd mentioned earlier, I doubted the choice of Grady as the director. I had always had trouble describing him as a director. Yet, he had come a long way, and he was standing up to the challenge Mr. Sheldon had given him. Thomas was by his side with advice only, hardly speaking to the actors and crew. He knew that was Grady's job. The two of us enjoyed watching the nervous fellow we met in Prescott take charge and guide a full-scale production. Grady was the first to the set in the morning and the last to leave every day. As we went from rehearsals to the first day of shooting he began to look like a cowhand at the end of a long day's riding. But it didn't slow him down. He was dedicated to proving himself and become one of those "best directors" he aspired to be.

The first scene we shot was of the explorers meeting the trapper Toussaint Charbonneau and the *pregnant* Sacagawea. According to Brownstone's script Charbonneau was a disreputable character. "He was a rapist, a brute of a husband, and an incompetent boatman," Brownstone wrote. Reginald Chesterfield portrayed him quite believably because, I felt, he possessed many of the same ill-qualities. He was a boisterous drunkard, whose humor came at the expense of others. Strutting about the set in full trapper costume, his beard as furry and unkempt as his coon-skin cap, he was chums with the men and flirtatious with the women.

In a moment when he was supposed to command Rebecca-as-Sacagawea to fetch him something to eat, Reginald improvised the act of pushing her, fake baby-belly and all, hard to the ground. I half-expected Thomas to go after him. Grady praised the scene's realism and drama, and Rebecca took it in a very professional manner, as well. "That kind of commitment to authenticity helps me be better in my role," I heard her telling another actor. Personally, I don't think it had anything to do with Reginald's commitment. I think he was just an ass.

● ● ●

"That gal playing the squaw," he once said to a few of us supporting men.

"Rebecca," I interrupted. "Her name's Rebecca."

"Is that right? Well, I'd sure like to wash that make-up off her and see what's underneath." He was crassly referring to the reddish-brown grease-paint that covered most of her body in an attempt to make her appear more Indian. Unfortunately, her features were all White. There was no hiding that fact.

Reginald's comment made me want to put him to the dirt. But he was bigger than me. That old sot was lucky I was not the fighter Thomas was. As for Rebecca, though my opinion of her was not the highest, she was still a curiosity. Exactly where she had come from no one knew.

"I've never seen her in any movie," admitted Troy Arthur. A few of us had gathered after the first day's shooting. We all agreed with his statement. "We'd remember if we'd seen her before, right?"

We affirmed that with vigorous nods.

"She must've done some kind of acting," said one of my fellow enlisted men. "She ain't half bad."

"She's a natural," drawled John Beaumont.

"Maybe Mr. Sheldon discovered her on a street corner," I joked.

"Maybe she's one of his 'starlets'," Henderson P.

Watts added with a wink.

The rest of them quietly laughed at the thought of that while my comment made me feel a little like Reginald myself.

Then Thomas joined our group. "You men best be careful what you speculate about," he told us.

I then had the idea to learn a little about her directly. As the evening faded to night, I found her warming herself by one of a few campfires. Although our set was only a couple of hours from Edendale, Grady thought it would be good for the actors to connect to their characters by spending a little time sleeping in the out-of-doors. Thus, a few nights a week were spent in tents and under the stars.

"May I join you?" I asked Rebecca.

She looked up and squinted at me, her eyes a little red from the fire's smoke. "Billy, isn't it?"

"Yes." I settled down beside her even though she hadn't yet responded to my request.

"Go ahead. There's plenty of fire." She gave me a sideways glance that told me maybe I was sitting a little too close. "How's the life of an enlisted man?"

"So far not much different than being a cowboy, I guess."

"It doesn't sound like you've put much thought into your role. What's your character's name?"

"I don't know," I mumbled. I'm sure that in Wilfred

Brownstone's script he had gone into great detail about each and every person in the story, even the lowly enlisted men. But for the movie, my part was so small I never gave it any consideration.

"You don't seem to have much conviction to your craft, Billy," Rebecca replied. "It's just a job to you, isn't it? Well, it isn't for me. It's in my blood, acting and performing. It's my life. My mother was an actress. She performed on some of the finest stages in San Francisco. And my father was a singer with a haunting voice."

"Are they still there, acting and singing in San Francisco?"

"No," she said flatly. "They live on within me, and I aim to make them proud."

Not knowing what to make of that comment I asked, "How many movies have you done, Rebecca?"

"This is my first," she answered. Then, with a glare as sharp as a rattler's bite, she added, "Didn't you hear? Mr. Sheldon discovered me on a street corner."

I swallowed hard, choking down what had been my own crude humor, and I knew it was time for me to leave her be. As I walked away, I was angry with myself and somehow sorrowful for her at the same time.

ॐ　ॐ　ॐ

Historically, the meeting of Lewis, Clark and Sacagawea took place at Fort Mandan–built by the exploring party in 1805– in present-day Central North Dakota. The fort burned down before the party's return trip in 1806. A replica was constructed in 1972. It was actually the second replication. The set for our film was the first, built not far from Edendale, in the Angeles National Forest which was part of the San Gabriel Mountains. In the lower elevations, the rolling hills were dense with chaparrals. Pine and fir trees were in the higher slopes.

Since I'd never been to North Dakota, I trusted Thomas when he said our chosen location was acceptable. Actually, what he said, after looking over the lay of the land, was simply, "This'll work." Again, this comforted Grady as he didn't have to be too far from the studio. With every passing day our director looked more and more weary, the weight of the production pressing down on him. A few of us, in fact, were getting a bit under the weather. But on we worked.

Like the original, our fort was triangle-shaped, and it had tall walls made of lumber. But ours was much smaller it turned out, something I learned many years later on a visit to the 1972 replica. In any case, Thomas in particular was pleased with the small touch of authenticity it gave to our picture.

He also insisted on sticking to the fact that a dozen of the men were sent back downriver, carrying maps and artifacts back to Thomas Jefferson, while the rest of the party continued west. This left a dozen of the actors cussing about suddenly being out of work because, like myself, they hadn't read the script. I got the impression from Rebecca that she wished I was one of those leaving the movie. Mr. Sheldon held the opposite opinion. "I want Billy in more scenes," he told Grady. "He doesn't have to do anything. Just have him there in the background."

So, there I could be seen, the enlisted man who was strangely a part of all the most noted events in the historical journey. I was there when Lewis shot the never before seen grizzly bear. (Henderson P. Watts wearing a matted bear suit. He was the only one big enough to fit inside the over-sized costume.) I was also with Lewis when he scouted ahead of the rest of the party and came across the Great Falls of the Missouri. And when the expedition meets Shoshone chief Cameahwait, Sacagawea's brother, there I am standing right next to Clark, for no apparent reason other than to be in the scene.

It was all quite silly, and it drove Thomas crazy. In response, he looked for any opportunity he could for authentic elements. He insisted on accurate costumes and historically detailed tools and guns. Also, Thomas insisted *real* Indians be cast, not merely Whites-as-Indians. "It's embarrassing," he stated, "for both parties." Mr. Sheldon did not share the same opinion. He wanted nothing to do with Indians on his payroll. Thomas convinced him to allow for one, however, on the condition Thomas pay the Indian's wage out of his own pocket. So, for the role of Old Toby, a Shoshone guide, Thomas contacted an old friend.

His name was Eagle Heart, though sometimes he introduced himself as Edward Hart, depending on who he was talking to. "I'm not ashamed of my name," he once explained to me. "In fact, I'm very proud of it, and of my people. So much so that I protect both my name and my people against those who would not understand and appreciate them. I do not have time for those kinds. They do not deserve to know my real name."

As we waited for Eagle Heart's arrival from Oklahoma, Grady filmed incidental scenes—mostly of the expedition party marching through forest and over hills. In one scene we were trekking North Dakota, in others we marched through upper Montana and Idaho, all the while never leaving the San Gabriels. By that time, historically, Sacawagea had given birth to her son Jean Baptiste, so Rebecca walked with a prop-baby wrapped in a papoose. She insisted the Indian child carrier be constructed authentically and that the "baby" have weight to it. After a day of marching, she would nearly drop from exhaustion. Yet, even with the day's shooting complete, she kept the baby close to her, cradling it lovingly to her chest, cooing and singing to it. I couldn't help admire her dedication to her role.

A few of the other actors, namely John Beaumont and Troy Arthur, used the marching scenes to connect deeper with their characters, as well. The rest of the cast just complained, Reginald Chesterfield being the most vocal.

"How long did their journey take?" he stated loudly, a boozy slurring to his words. "Two, three years? We've been walking twice that long!"

For me, I found the movie-making process still as interesting as ever. Toby was there cranking away his camera to his spoken rhythm, "101-101-101." As he filmed, Grady constantly directed the actors:

"Clark. Here's where you name the Judith River to honor the girl you hope to someday marry. Think of her. Long for her."

"You men have reached a fork in the river, and you must make a decision. Do you take the south fork or do you head north?"

"Sacagawea, you see the valley of your people! You're overwhelmed with joy!"

As shooting went on, I couldn't help notice how sick

Grady was becoming.

"Maybe you should rest," I told him. "If we didn't film for a day, Mr. Sheldon would be none the wiser."

"No, no. I'll be fine," he said wearily. "I just need to keep warm." He wrapped himself in two heavy blankets and continued working.

When Eagle Heart finally arrived, he was a welcome sight. Not only because most of us had never before seen an Indian, but also because now we'd get to do something besides walking. He was as tall as Thomas, about the same age, though he looked younger. He was Osage, out of the Mid-west, who had ancestors that had marched the Trail of Tears. I recalled the story Thomas had told me on that train ride to Denver so many years before, the one of how Eagle Heart had rescued him from a flash flood. Thomas owed him his life.

True to his nature, Reginald was not too cordial about the Osage's commanding presence. "My God! He's the biggest redskin I've ever seen!" he said.

"Just how many have you seen, Reggie?" I asked him.

"Just him. But he's a giant!"

Thomas greeted his old friend in his Osage language. They spoke for some time together while the rest of us blankly listened to the strange dialect. I can't even begin to recreate it here, so I'll just say the words were melodic and sing-song. I could've listened to it for hours, and Thomas spoke it as though it were his own. Finally, he turned to the rest of us and said, "This is Eagle Heart. I don't know how old Old Toby was, or if he was very tall. But my friend here is exactly what this picture needs."

We were all surprised at how well Eagle Heart spoke English. He introduced himself in a polite, confident manner. The men took to him right away. The ladies, however, he made a bit timid.

Reginald Chesterfield took a step forward, and straightened up to make himself taller than he was. "What did you say your name was again, Chief?"

"Edward. Edward Hart."

ఞ   ఞ   ఞ

We knew little about the Indian referred to as Old Toby. According to Brownstone's script he was Lemhi-Shoshone and guided the expedition through the Bitterroots. "Without Old Toby," Brownstone wrote, "Lewis and Clark's journey would have ended in the Rocky Mountains, as they would have surely perished."

That was it.

Not that knowing more would have mattered to Eagle Heart, really. He was no actor. Like Henderson, he did what came natural, which in his case was be Indian. He spent most of the film standing, being Indian, and pointing. He pointed a lot because it was the silent movies and how else would someone wordlessly convey the act of guiding.

It was good having Eagle Heart on set in other ways besides being Indian. In the same way Old Toby aided the Lewis and Clark team, he helped us through our own difficult situation. He had a strange and profound effect upon cast and crew alike, especially Thomas, who became more lucid and vibrant in the presence of his old friend. When he wasn't on camera, pointing, Eagle Heart would captivate (and educate) us with stories. This would happen at the end of the day, cast and crew gathered around a fire, Eagle Heart presiding over us.

"My people once ruled much of what is now your country. From Colorado to Pennsylvania, Iowa to Louisiana," he said. Smoke from the fire seemed to circle around him but not touch him. His eyes never flinched at the stinging swirls of gray and black. "Now we live in a small corner of the state of Oklahoma."

He told us of the First Delegation, when a small group of Osage met with President Thomas Jefferson. "The President promised my ancestors many things, things that would benefit both our peoples. In the Second Delegation, one Osage chief spoke the truth about The President's failure to keep his promises. He predicted the Osage's demise at the hand of those false promises."

One thing he said struck me a bit close.

"I rode a train to join you here in California. You people have made many a great invention to ease your way through life. But, I think, this ease makes you forget the ground under your feet and the sky above your head. I hear there are machines that can fly like a bird. Soon you will forget the earth.

"On the train, passengers asked me if I was part of a Wild West Show and where would I be performing. That's how they think of their history, as a show, as entertainment. As long as they remember, that is good, I think. It is good that you are making this moving picture. Maybe it will help your people remember my people and our place in your history."

Some of us, well, *one* of us, didn't take as kindly to Eagle Heart's campfire stories as the rest of us. Reginald would stir and fidget and make impatient sounds while we listened. One night he spoke up.

"Tell me, Chief...people all over the world, throughout history, have been conquered, just like—I'm sorry to say—your people have been. It's a hard fact, I know, but a real one nonetheless." Eagle Heart calmly waited as Reginald paused and collected his drunken thoughts. "So tell me why," he continued, "you think I owe you something. You lost, my friend. Let's move on."

"When Genghis Kahn attacked a village," Eagle Heart replied in a calculated and deliberate manner, "there was no question what his intentions were. He did not say one thing and then do another. The people he conquered knew exactly what he had come to them to do. Not so with my people. Time and again we were lied to. Time and again we foolishly trusted false words. If we had known the truth, we would have fought back. Perhaps we would have lost and things would be as they are. Or, perhaps we would have won." Eagle Heart stopped to smile at the thought of that. "Either way, we would have fought knowing what is true. And that is a good fight. No one wins a war of lies."

Reginald looked at the rest of us and saw it was best that he say nothing else.

∂⊘ ∂⊘ ∂⊘

One night there was a torrential rain. It was loud against the ground and my tent, but in the distance I could hear a voice shouting something indistinguishable. It was Thomas's voice. And just outside my tent, I heard Eagle Heart. He first spoke in his own language, like he was singing. Then I heard him say, "This is not good. Not good at all." His words faded into the storm and toward what seemed to be the direction of Thomas's shouts.

I went into the rain and followed the Osage into the drenched night. Water ran over the dry ground, forming quickly flowing streams. I slipped a couple of times. Though disoriented by the downpour and the dark, I kept following the voices of Eagle Heart and Thomas. Other crew members joined me.

"What's going on, Billy?" Troy asked.

"It's Thomas, isn't it, Billy?" came Toby's voice. It sounded like he was right next to me but I could barely make out his silhouette. I didn't answer him because we both knew. I wished Elizabeth Jerome was with us, but she had been needed for a movie that required a lot more horses than ours. We weren't far from Edendale so Thomas had been able to spend time with her on occasion and give his mind a rest. It hadn't been enough, though.

The group of us trudged along in the cold, wet dark, some sniffling, some coughing, all looking for our companion. Even Grady, the sickest of any of us, joined the search. He gave me a start as he came up beside me. His paled face glowed, as if he just rolled out of his own grave.

"Alan, you shouldn't be out here," I told him. "We can do this. Get back to your tent."

Grady had no strength to argue. Toby took him by his

shoulders and led him back to the camp while the rest of us plodded onward.

We crested a hill as the rain let up. It had been one of those sudden cloud-bursts, the kind that comes and goes like a herd of wild horses stirring up dust that quickly settles as they rush past. We were able then to hear Thomas better. His voice came from below, down the slope from us.

"Belle! Belle!" His calls became clear. "Belle!"

I could see a pair of shadows moving further down the hill. I took them to be Thomas and Eagle Heart because there couldn't have been another pair of men as tall and lanky as those two in the middle of the forest with us. I moved closer until I could make out that they stood in a swift yet shallow stream. Thomas faced the darkness, crying out that name again and again.

Eagle Heart turned his old friend around and spoke to him in Osage. The Indian's strange words began to calm Thomas, and before long he was being led back through the maze of brush to our soggy camp. I finally got close enough to see his face. He appeared older than ever, but in his eyes was the look of a fearful youth.

With the bit of dry wood we had left, we started a fire to warm ourselves. Those of us from the search party huddled together and watched as Thomas returned from wherever he had gone, brought back by Eagle Heart's gentle, trance-like voice. In whispers, we all made our guesses about who "Belle" was.

"A long lost sister, maybe," said one of the supporting men.

"He's never mentioned having any sisters or brothers, to me," I replied.

"Belle could have been his mother" said Rebecca. She was standing outside the group of us, holding her prop-baby, with a sincere look of concern for my friend.

"He's raving mad about his poor dead mother," stated Reginald with finality.

"There's nothing mad about missing your mother," she said with a displeased look to Reginald. Then she turned and went back to her tent.

"She's an old sweetheart," offered John Beaumont. He spoke very little and his thick drawl always came as a surprise. "Perhaps, it's a nickname, like sweethearts give each other."

The others concurred, but I didn't. Ellen Marie was the only woman he had ever spoken about, and he never referred to her as Belle. I kept my doubt to myself, however, as I didn't think it appropriate for me to say anything about her. Then I began to think about how little I really knew about Thomas. Even after all the stories he'd told me, I didn't feel that connection with him that he had with Mr.

McElroy or Eagle Heart. What I knew of Thomas Andrew Benton were only small scenes of a much bigger picture. I wondered if I would ever truly know him.

Finally in English, Eagle Heart said to Thomas, "You should go lie down. You need rest."

Thomas stood without a word to any of us and made his way, tipsy from fatigue, back to his tent. Eagle Heart turned to the rest of us. "Bell was a horse he once had," he said. "Bell Ringer, Thomas called him, for a bell he was wearing around his neck when Thomas found him. He was just a young man then. He rode that horse for many years."

"He lost him in a storm, didn't he, a flash flood?" I said.

"He told you that story, huh?"

"Yes. It was how the two of you met, wasn't it?"

"Thomas must think well of you to share that story with you," he said with a respectful nod. "He loved that horse as much as he loved anything." Then with a look toward Thomas's tent, he asked. "Does he have these…spells…often?"

"Yes," I answered, "a lot more than he used to. And they've gotten worse."

Eagle Heart shook his head. The crackle of the fire filled the quiet.

"The Osage," he then said, "we carry the honor of

our past in our hearts, and we practice our traditions so that we may carry them into the future. We try not to forget. At the same time, we know we must adapt to live on. For example, we've chosen to govern ourselves in the way the White Man does. We know we must move forward to survive. Thomas, he remembers everything, maybe too well. He lives in his past, and there he stays."

Eagle Heart was the only Indian I've ever met. I don't know if his opinions of the world represented that of all his people, or any other Indians, but what he said made sense to me. It explained a lot about Thomas.

With another disheartened shake of his head toward our friend's tent, he added, "That is not good."

❧   ❧   ❧

I had just fallen asleep when Toby came into my tent the next morning. He looked to have not slept at all.

"Billy, it's Grady," he said.

I followed Toby in a rush back to their tent. Inside, Grady lay still, and very pale. "He's freezing!" I said with my hand upon his face.

"He's dead," replied Toby.

"What?" I left my hand touching him, as though that might have somehow brought him back to life. But he just stayed dead. "He must've been sicker than we all thought."

"What do we do?"

It was then that it occurred to me how many of the rest us were feeling ill, as well. "We need to get back to town. We need to get to a doctor."

Thomas was his old self by then. He agreed with me and took charge, calming folk down, getting everyone organized to break the camp and get back to Edendale. Reginald made a fuss about having to work so hard and fast.

"We'll be coming back, right?" he stated clearly and soberly. "Someone can just stay here with the camp. Like Chief there. He's used to sleeping outdoors anyway, right?"

Thomas got within inches of Reginald's face and said, "That's a good idea. But you'll be the one staying."

"I'm not staying out here all by myself."

"Then you can pack up this camp all by yourself. Either way, the rest of us are leaving right now."

"I refuse."

"Then we'll be taking back *two* dead bodies."

"You can't threaten me with your Wild West manners."

"I wouldn't bet on what I can or cannot do."

Reginald backed down and agreed to stay. His idea *was* a good one, since it allowed for the rest of us to leave sooner and Reginald was the best choice to stay with the camp because he showed no signs of sickness. All that alcohol he drank must have kept whatever germs there were at bay. At one point, I heard Eagle Heart say to him with a grin, "I sure do love sleeping in hotels."

The rest of us were in Edendale and at the doctor's before midday, all sick with the flu, some worse than others, but no one as bad as Grady had been. Throughout the whole world at that time, 1918, there was a terrible pandemic of influenza. A lot of people, millions, succumbed to it. Alan Grady happened to be one of them.

ʠ   ʠ   ʠ

Mr. Sheldon paid for a nice, respectable funeral for Grady. The turnout was small, just those of us who worked closely with him. He had never been well-known in the industry. The *Los Angeles Times* printed an obituary that said simply, "Film director Alan Grady dies of influenza." No listing of the dozens of movies he directed. No next of kin. Nothing else.

As we walked from the gravesite, Mr. Sheldon wasted no time getting back to business. "Thomas, you'll be taking over directing the rest of the Lewis and Clark picture."

"I think you can find any number of men more qualified to director a motion picture than me," Thomas replied.

"I disagree. I've seen you work. You're practically directing already."

I agreed with Mr. Sheldon, but Thomas hemmed-and-hawed a bit. I could tell he was interested in the idea, however something didn't sit right with him. Finally, he said, "I'll do it. But you have to give Grady full credit as director. I don't want my name on it as anything but a consultant, just like always."

"Fine," said Mr. Sheldon as he climbed into his limousine. "Come to my office when you get back. I want to go over how we're going to wrap up this project."

While I wasn't surprised by Thomas's gesture to honor Grady, I could tell by his face that it wasn't the only reason he didn't want his name as the picture's director. He knew Grady never really had any control, and Thomas would have even less due to his lack of experience.

It turned out Reginald was wrong about us returning to the San Gabriel Mountains. (Thomas sent a crew of men to break down the camp as soon we had arrived to the hospital, though I personally felt Reginald should have been left out there indefinitely.) "Thomas, you're going to take your crew to the Northwest," Mr. Sheldon instructed. Toby Greene was there in his office with Thomas, and I was there, too, for no other reason than my own curiosity.

"I've seen the footage so far," Mr. Sheldon continued. "It's boring. Pretty, but boring. I don't want either. I want spectacular and adventurous! You suggested we shoot up north and that's what we'll do. You want it to be authentic and so we'll film where it all took place."

I could see Thomas liked the sound of that.

"But take only the most essential people. Lewis, Clark, and Sagawa…Rebecca. And Billy, take Billy."

Thomas *did not* like the sound of *that*. "What about Reginald? Charbonneau was with the expedition to the end."

"He quit. Something about working with an intolerable tyrant. I let him go. Never liked him, anyway, and it's too late in the game to replace him. This project has had enough delays."

"How about Toby? Can I take him?"

Mr. Sheldon's brow furrowed. He did not get Thomas's sarcasm. "Of course, Thomas! Don't be silly!"

"I need Henderson there, too. I'd like to salvage some kind of historical accuracy."

Mr. Sheldon's opinion of all non-white people was expressed clearer than ever in his silence. His lips puckered as though the taste of something bitter and sour had touched them. With great effort, he choked back his true feelings with a curt, "Fine."

I wished Eagle Heart could have gone with us. Having

actually read the entire script by then, I knew Old Toby did not accompany the expedition to the Pacific Ocean. I just wanted Thomas to have his old friend by his side. It didn't matter, anyway. The Osage had gone back to Oklahoma to be part of yet another treaty his people were working on. This time with President Wilson.

Since I knew that having Eagle Heart around was good for him, I got another idea, so I stayed in Mr. Sheldon's office as the others left.

"What is it, Billy?" Mr. Sheldon asked without looking up from the papers on his desk.

"I'd like to suggest one other person to go with us to the Northwest," I said and didn't wait for him to respond. "Elizabeth Jerome."

He looked up at me with that furrowed look of his. "The horse trainer?"

"Yes."

"What the hell for? There won't be any horses. And I don't think the canoes will need much training." He grinned at his joke, but only briefly.

"She's good for Thomas. You've most likely heard about his spells, his lapses of memory, daydreams, or whatever they are. Well, she helps him keep his mind on what he's doing. We could have her go as his assistant or something. She knows a lot about the outdoors."

I spoke quickly, wanting to present my case before he could disregard it. Instead, he leaned back in his chair and thought a moment.

"My mother went forgetful like that," he said eventually. His voice and brow softened. "She'd get lost on the street. We'd often find her wandering far away from home. Before long she couldn't even remember our names. She'd forgotten her own children's names."

He stirred himself from the memories he didn't want to revisit and went back to the stack of papers before him. "That's fine, Billy. I'll send her along, as well."

"Thank you, Mr. Sheldon. Thomas will appreciate it."

"I'm sure he will. Have you seen the figure on that woman?"

❧   ❧   ❧

Once again, I found myself within the torturous confines of a train as we made our way north to Oregon. We went as far as Portland, where we borrowed a pair of cars and drove to The Dalles along the Columbia River Highway, a beautiful, curvy road, paved most of the way but rough in parts. I remember stopping at the Vista House at Crown Point. It was a rest stop as fancy as any Hollywood mansion with unforgettable views of the Columbia River, where we would soon be shooting.

In The Dalles we stayed at the Umatilla House. Mr. Sheldon chose it for our lodgings as he had memories of it being quite luxurious. It may have been something at one time with its spacious dining room and finely carved wood furniture and sculptures, yet the luxury of Mr. Sheldon's younger days would not be our experience. We found the once grand hotel well into its decline (I think it closed down shortly after our stay). All in all, it really didn't matter as we spent little time in our musty rooms. We were there to do a job.

Not but a stone's throw away from the hotel was the Columbia River, our first destination. Lewis and Clark had canoed the white-peaked swirls, and so would we. In fact, there was so much history around The Dalles involving the exploring party that it made me wish we had filmed the whole movie there. Sure, we got away with using the San Gabriels for the most part. But us actors, and the film, would have been better with the landscape of the Northwest surrounding us.

There's a moment I remember, just after a rain, when the sun broke through a clearing of clouds behind us. The sunlight hit a hillside of firs and undergrowth before us, revealing more shades of glistening green than I ever thought there could be. Behind those trees, it was dark as coal from the storm that had just passed overhead. That stark contrast is what I never forgot about the Northwest. Sure, it was gray a lot, stirring gloomy thoughts, and although I'd seen a lot of different kinds of land in my young lifetime–mountains, desert, and plains–experiencing that contrast made me truly appreciate the staggering beauty of nature. Though Toby was a skilled photographer, it was a shame his camera could only capture it in black-and-white.

It was also a shame that he never really enjoyed our adventure there. He was more concerned with keeping his equipment clean and dry than anything else. He fretted constantly about the conditions he had to work in. "If it's not the dust of the desert, it's all this damned wet. It's a wonder I can ever film at all," he griped.

He complained a lot more without Grady around for the simple fact that Grady, his friend, was no longer around. Thomas was not patient or receptive to Toby's troubles, however. Thomas was still a cowboy at heart. When there was work to be done, he believed in getting it done. Problems were just an inevitable part of all work and he didn't see much point in complaining. "Do what you got to do," he'd tell Toby, and any of the others who would have an issue with one thing or another.

"This damp air is not being kind to my sinuses," moaned Troy Arthur.

"All that campfire smoke has damaged my voice," groaned John Beaumont, the nonsense of which was not lost upon the rest of us.

Elizabeth was Thomas's rock. Having grown up in the Northwest, she was happy to be home and had no complaints about the conditions, which in turn helped him stay steady and balanced. Her presence helped the rest of us, too. She did the work of an entire film crew, assisting Toby and the actors, hauling equipment and props.

Someone else who didn't complain, surprisingly, was Rebecca. She was so awe-struck by our surroundings that I wondered if she had ever been anywhere outside the cities of San Francisco and Los Angeles. She was like a child at the circus, living in a happy daze. Rebecca, out of all of us, was most appreciative of those things that made the Northwest unique–the ruggedness of the gorge, the grandeur of Mt. Hood in the distance, the delicate purple of the lupine.

"If movie-making never took me anywhere else in the world," I heard her tell Elizabeth one night, "I would be satisfied with this."

This made a positive impression of her upon me. The first, in fact. To her, though, I was still a simple cowpoke.

The morning after our arrival, we all gathered by the river's edge and listened to Thomas explain the day's shooting, which would involve long camera angles of us floating downstream and over rapids. He made it sound as simple and commonplace as gathering a herd and leading it back to the corral. All in a day's work it would be. I made an innocent comment about how there would be nothing routine for me as I had never spent much time around water.

"I suppose now you're going to say you don't know how to swim," Rebecca said with a glare.

I shrugged.

"You've never gone into a lake or the ocean?"

"That's what boats are for, ain't it?"

"I said *into* the water, not *on it*."

"Never had much call to."

"Sometimes to experience something new is call enough."

"I don't see how I missed anything but getting all wet," I said dismissively. While I was not a fan of water, none of what I was saying was true. I'd spent time in the water, and I could swim well enough. I just never grew a liking to it. I didn't tell Rebecca those things because I enjoyed goading her until she rolled her eyes or shook her head with a judgmental sigh. There was something in her impatience for me that I found quite tickling.

"Well, let's hope you don't go tumbling from the canoe," she said with finality.

"You wouldn't rescue me if I fell in?"

With a glimmer in her eye that I was unsure how to interpret, she replied, "Who knows what I would do if something so tragic were to happen."

Truth was, I had never been on the water in something as small as a canoe. Getting into it was as jittery as mounting a bucking bronco, and my unsteadiness elicited laughter from Rebecca and the others. I felt very unbalanced and silly as we floated from the bank. Rebecca, Beaumont, and I were in one canoe. Troy and Watts were in another.

I think I should mention here that Rebecca no longer carried the prop-baby with her. As part of the explanation for Charbonneau—that is, Reginald—no longer being part of the expedition—that is, the film—it was decided that Sacawagea's child stay behind for its own safety. It couldn't have been more historically inaccurate, yet the infractions of truth had so piled up by then that it no longer seemed to matter. At first, Rebecca was quite distraught, as a mother would be at leaving her child, but before long she became relieved at not having to carry the realistically heavy baby wherever she went.

Now, the plan for the day's shooting was for Thomas and Toby to be downstream and film us as we floated by. This would be done more than once so that Toby could get different angles. Over the rough water we would go. Then we'd pull to the shore, haul our canoes out, and traverse back upstream to our original launch point. This was to be the climax of the adventure, Thomas told us, the most dangerous challenge that would sum up the entire journey. And Toby explained that shooting it from a variety of angles and cutting them together would help accentuate the danger and determination to get through.

Thomas's only direction for us was that he wanted to see that determination in our faces. This was not difficult for me. I was not in control. Horses are powerful creatures with minds of their own, yet I knew how to get them to do what I needed. That canoe, and the three of us in it, was at the bidding of the tumultuous water. It wasn't until you were actually a part of the rapids that you felt just how rapid they were.

We did as many as ten takes, I recall. The first few were erratic and out of control. We weren't paddling or steering so much as flailing to keep from capsizing. At one point, we somehow ended up floating backwards down the river. And when I say 'we,' I mean the canoe with me, Rebecca, and Beaumont. The other two navigated their craft like seasoned river men. It was my crew that would give Thomas and Toby very little to work with in the editing studio.

By the seventh take we were getting more confident and adept at guiding ourselves over the foamy crests. With the tenth take, the three of us were complimenting each other on our teamwork, and I was feeling pretty full of myself. So much so that I took to trying to stand up in the canoe, thinking it might make a good visual for the movie. Then, as you can guess, a turbulent swell sent me from the canoe into the swift moving water! Rebecca reached out for me as I bobbed past her, but the unpredictable current sent her head first into the river, as well.

"Take my hand!" we shouted at one another. Each of us, with an arm outstretched toward the other, bobbed and swirled about, helplessly being carried downstream. I caught a glimpse of Beaumont's desperation at keeping the canoe upright. The last thing on his mind was trying to help us. He could only help himself.

The current took me under a number of times. I felt like I was swallowing half the Columbia River. When I'd come up, I would see Rebecca reaching for me through the spraying mist. She'd call to me but the roar of the water was too much to hear her. I could also see she was tiring. The river was wearing down whatever skill she had as a swimmer. I called to her and took in yet another mouth-full of water.

Then, by sheer dumb luck, the current thrust Rebecca into me and I was able to take hold of her. I held on as much for my own salvation as I did hers. With the strength she had left, she kept me afloat while I veered us toward the shore where we careened into the branches of a fallen tree. It was not a pretty rescue, nor long lived, because upon impact with the tree, my hold on her broke and she continued downstream.

I freed myself from the tangle of branches and went after her. She did what she could to tread upstream and slow herself so that I could catch up. When I reached her, Rebecca had exhausted all her reserves. She clasped her hands together around my shoulders and hung there, floating limp as I steered us to a bend in the river where the water slowed. There, I got us onto the soft earth of the riverbank.

We were on the other side of the Columbia from Thomas and the others. It was some time before Toby made it to the nearest crossing and back to us. Rebecca and I huddled together for warmth, much too tired to care how long it took.

      ෨   ෨   ෨

The days that followed were spent shooting all of us floating calmly down the river. And scenery, lots of scenery. The mouth of the Columbia. Cape Disappointment. The Pacific Ocean. Toby shot every inch of film he had.

I wouldn't say Rebecca and I had become friends, but

since our shared experience, we were friendlier. We spent a good deal of the train ride back to Edendale talking. This new found rapport seemed to relax the others, too, and camaraderie developed amongst us all. I enjoyed it the most because it was a welcome distraction from our mode of travel.

"We're like an acting troupe of days passed," mused John Beaumont, "traversing across the land, village to village, to entertain the peasants." His accent gave the statement a certain authenticity. I think John Beaumont and Charles Benz would have gotten along well.

Back in Edendale and the Sheldon studios, Thomas was called into Mr. Sheldon's office for yet another meeting. (Again, I listened through the door.) Having seen all of the footage from the Northwest, Mr. Sheldon was especially excited about my and Rebecca's swimming adventure. Toby had been filming the whole time. The two of us were near to drowning, and Toby and Thomas went diligently about their business!

"That's exactly what this picture is missing," Mr. Sheldon expressed to Thomas with great inspiration. "A love story!" He then explained how he wanted Thomas to shoot scenes of me and Rebecca–Sacagawea and the lowly enlisted man, that is–falling in love. "Our movie will be about the triumph of the heart as well as the spirit! It will not only be a great journey to discover the Northwest Passage, but one where two people find each other against insurmountable odds!"

It was sappy, melodramatic, and absurd. But I'd never heard Mr. Sheldon more excited about anything, before or since.

From Thomas, I didn't hear a thing. I couldn't make out words, I mean, which was not good. When Thomas was most upset, he would speak in such low tones that it would sound more like the growl of a bear. I'm sure he was giving Mr. Sheldon a history lesson, illustrating how ridiculous his idea was, and flat out refusing to continue anymore work on this picture.

"Fine! I'll finish the damn thing myself!" was Mr. Sheldon's response.

So, the back lot of Sheldon Pictures became the banks of the Columbia River and the forests of the Northwest. Rebecca and I were filmed looking into each other's starry eyes, Charbonneau and her child be damned! We sat close by campfires, and we held hands. Pretty racy stuff. When it came time for the kiss, Toby slowly closed the iris of his camera and created one of those common fades where the image, encircled by black, shrinks until it is gone. The intimacy and the romance of such moments were always best left to the imagination of the audience. (And what an imagination they would prove to have.)

∾   ∾   ∾

As it turned out, the movie-going public knew the facts around the Lewis and Clark expedition better than Anthony Sheldon had given them credit for. They knew Sacagawea was pregnant and that she gave birth to a son—Toussaint Charbonneau's son!—three months after joining the group. They knew about how she carried little Jean-Baptiste on her back for over half the journey. Hell, statues built in her honor as early as 1904 depict exactly that. They especially knew how absurd the romance between her and my character was. All kinds of reviews and editorials were written exposing the flagrant inaccuracies of *The Greatest Journey*.

And yet, it didn't matter.

People flocked to see our movie, and Mr. Sheldon got double the return on his investment. Why? Because all audiences care about is a good story, the heck with facts and truth. This has been proven time and again.

In 1955 another film about Lewis and Clark was made called *The Far Horizons*. In that equally absurd version William Clark and Sacagawea (played by the very White Donna Reed) fall in love while confronting hostile Indians and a *villainous* Toussaint Charbonneau!

And what about that famous shootout in Tombstone? Many reenactments have been made since our one-reeler in Prescott. One of the most ridiculous was *Gunfight at O.K Corral* in 1957. It starred Burt Lancaster as Wyatt Earp and Kirk Douglas as Doc Holliday, both fine actors but miscast in those roles. Douglas was far too fit and strapping to play the dying Holliday, and Lancaster, like all the Earps in the film, didn't even have a mustache. That's right, no mustaches! Worse of all was how horribly the gunfight was staged. It took place all around the corral and lasted several minutes, much longer than the actual fight's thirty seconds. Yet, with all its fabrications, it was a very popular film.

This is all because, I think, the movie-going audience was primarily plain people looking to escape their plain lives. Thomas and I had been just like them once, nothing but hard-working cowboys looking for good work. That was what led us to the picture business in the first place. I wasn't looking to be a movie star. Thomas never looked to be a director. But there we were, making the stories other folk watched to forget their troubles and their plainness. We were living lives they envied.

One day, I would long to live that plainness again.

Twelve

By his possibilities, a man's wealth is measured,
The less he has, the more it's treasured,

L et me say a little about Los Angeles and Hollywood in the 1920's. Actually, I could say a lot about it with just one word: shameful. Not just by the likes of us movie-folk, but by businessmen, newspapermen, city officials, and even the police. We were afflicted with the sickness of make-a-buck-at-any-cost, and have as much carefree and careless fun as possible. Gatsby and his kind had nothing on us.

Prohibition did nothing to slow us down. What was funny about that law was that it only prohibited the making and selling of liquor. It wasn't against the law to buy it or drink it! A thin distinction I know, but we fools bought and drank what other fools were making illegally in their basement stills and bathtubs. Not all of it, mind you. Much of that rotgut would leave you with a headache that made you wish you were dead. Some of it just left you dead. Poor Reginald Chesterfield, who would imbibe in anything that was put in front of him, drank himself to death one Sunday in 1923. Even I found myself indulging like I never had before.

Part of what made it so easy was the corruption of the politicians and the police. Paying them off with a little (or sometimes, a lot) of protection money is what made the wildest of parties possible. I don't mean one of those stylish affairs thrown by Fairbanks and Pickford that hosted foreign dignitaries and the like. I mean a gathering that exhibited nothing but rowdiness and sordid behavior, a party that could easily go on for days and leave you going home with feelings of disgrace and indignity. I frequented those raucous get-togethers as much as anyone. I'm not saying this with pride, but I learned how to drive a car during one of those parties, nearly careening myself and my equally drunken passengers off the road and down a hillside. (Not unlike Thomas in Arizona.) I never thought of where I lived as "home" because I was so rarely there. If I wasn't out at one of those wanton parties, I was working.

It was awhile before I did another movie with Thomas after *Journey*. Mr. Sheldon's intention was to use my and Rebecca's on-screen romance to its fullest profitability. For years we did dozens of short, throwaway pictures that centered strictly on me saving her from some perilous situation—a speeding, out-of-control automobile, or hanging from a cliff, or anything else you can imagine—and that all-important kiss at the end. It was really the same plot told over and over again with different scenery, but audiences willingly handed over their hard earned money to see the two of us go through our romantic routine.

Mr. Sheldon did his best to promote our off-screen affections, as well, of which there weren't any. As I said, Rebecca and I were friendlier, yet she nurtured a certain indifference toward me, which she was good at masking when the public and tabloid reporters were watching. In more private situations, Rebecca would talk—and talk!—typically about herself, or with disdainful tones about the baseness of Los Angeles compared to the grandeur of her birth-city, San Francisco.

"Everywhere you look it's like a picture-postcard," she said to me, dreamily, almost too dreamily, of the bay city. "Those beautiful Victorian homes. The hilly streets and the cable-cars. And the fog, I love the chill of the fog. And what's here? Sunny. And dry. All the time. Always the same. Have you seen that 'Hollywoodland' sign they put up? Dreadful."

I had never been to San Francisco, myself. I knew many movie-people who used the foggy city as a weekend getaway. But I also knew of how Fatty Arbuckle got himself into a load of trouble up there.

"Why do you stay here, then?" I asked her. "You seem to miss home so much."

"This is where the movies are. And there's no better opportunity for a young actress like myself than the movies," she stated with confidence. Like Faith in Prescott, Rebecca had it all figured out.

"Of course," she continued, "it is the stage where any actor should truly be. My mother is a wonderful actress. Her Ophelia, you know, Shakespeare, was chilling. The critics loved her. She objected to me coming down here, even after I explained that success here could open doors for me elsewhere, like Chicago or New York. She thinks I'm taking the easy road. She thinks I should sacrifice through hard work like she did. But I'm sacrificing just as much as she did. I'm working hard, and getting better."

"You're a fine actress," I told her, because whatever my opinion of her, it was true.

"Yes. And I'm getting better."

Her mother's criticism of movie-people wasn't any different than the country's moral majority at that time. *Leisure without effort* was how we were labeled, condemned for our cavalier lifestyle. We were viewed as all play and no work there in Southern California, and the newspapers were the greatest culprits in perpetuating that view. From the Arbuckle scandal to murdered directors to promiscuous starlets, our immorality was great fodder for selling papers.

Like I said, I was as irresponsible as anyone. Those wild parties and promiscuous starlets were not strangers to me. I had also gone to some lengths to avoid going off to the war in Europe. Thomas had strong opinions against fighting someone else's battles, so he instructed me to lie about my age. Since I was never quite sure about my date of birth, it was an easy thing to do. It didn't feel like a lie. And when the draft age went up to forty-five, Thomas fabricated how I was his grandson and only surviving kin and how I needed to stay home to care for my senile, old grandfather. Again, not entirely untrue.

"What does your father think about you coming here?" I asked Rebecca.

"He has always been encouraging, and has the loveliest of manners. And what a singing voice he has! His rendition of 'O Sole Mio' is unforgettable!"

"It sounds like you miss them," I said, and surprising to the both of us, reached out and patted her hand. She looked away at my gesture, though she was not entirely uncomfortable. "You know," I then added, "San Francisco's not that far from here. You should pay them a visit."

"Oh, I saw them just last weekend," she replied with a hesitant thought.

The predictable, routine plots of our movies made for

a routine working life, like a nine-to-five kind of job. Similar, I imagine, to what doing a television series decades later would have been like. Much of the day's shooting happened at the studio, only some of it in areas outside Edendale, depending on what kind of peril I was saving Rebecca from that day. Our little films were the bread-and-butter of Sheldon Pictures, while the pictures Thomas worked on could be considered the meat. My movies paid the bills. Thomas's made Mr. Sheldon's fortune.

Like *The Promised Land*. An epic picture of settlers crossing our great continent to new homes and new lives. It was made for a relatively small amount of money because it didn't require immense, costly sets to be built, like the Babylonian palace of Griffith's *Intolerance* or the castle in Fairbanks's *Robin Hood*. The backdrop for *The Promised Land* was the great outdoors. Mountainous landscapes, rolling plains and desert were all within a day's drive of the Sheldon Pictures studio. For a small percentage of the profits from *The Greatest Journey*, Mr. Sheldon made *The Promised Land* into one of his largest grossing films.

The story, about a husband and wife with sordid pasts who take their son out West to find a fresh start, deeply struck the population of immigrants that had been pouring into our country for decades. That was the greatest thing about the silent movies: their universal appeal. Although titling was commonly used, it wasn't nearly as important as the pantomime of the actors or the shooting by the director and his cameraman for the telling of the story. In the hands of the best filmmakers the audience didn't need to be able to read English to know what was happening.

"Think of those stories you've enjoyed the most," Thomas once said, "they all have something in them that you recognize from your own life. And if those stories are as accessible as your local theater? Young, old, foreigners right off the boat. Hell, you could be a dim-witted mute and still enjoy a movie."

You couldn't have a movie completely without titling, however. (An attempt was made, without success.) The best movies used them minimally, yet artfully. It wasn't just a matter of using the fewest words, but they had to be the right words, to best explain what was happening and move the story along. Like poetry.

For *The Promised Land*, Thomas used lines from his own poetry as titles. With THE SETTLER, WHO FORGED A PATH FOR THE REST OF US we meet the main character, Charles W. Lowell, or "Charlie" as his wife affectionately calls him, the simple man who dreams only of a small plot of land to farm and raise his family with his darling Isabel, or "Izzy," as he affectionately calls her, and their two-year old son, William.

HIS YIPS AND SHOUTS ECHO OVER THE PLAIN, HIS SPIRIT LIVES ON IN EVERY HARD-WORKING MAN OF THE FACTORIES TODAY introduces us to Jack Morgan, the cowboy. We are also introduced to the legacy which we owe to the early settlers and cowboys, a connection to them we often forget. Morgan takes a liking to the Lowell's son, calling him "Little Friend," which brings a grin to the child's face. When Charles and Isabel are killed in an Indian raid, Jack takes William into his care, saying to him WILL WE WORK AND RIDE 'TIL THE TRAIL'S DONE?

Captain Thompson of the cavalry, WHOSE LIFE OF VIOLENCE TAMED A LAND DETERMINED TO BE WILD, comes on the scene to bring justice against the murderous Indian warrior, Red Hawk. To some criticism, Thomas showed sympathy to the Indian, the western film's common "villain," with titling like ROAMING A FOREIGN PLACE HE ONCE CALLED HIS OWN, IMPRISONED UPON HIS CHERISHED HOME, and punctuated Red Hawk's death with: HIS TOMBSTONE—THE MOUNTAINS. HIS HEAVEN—THE EARTH.

The movie opens with: THOSE DREAMERS AND FORTUNE SEEKERS, THEIR WAGON WHEELS'S RUTS CRISS-CROSSING THE LAND. MEN AND WOMEN WHO LEFT THEIR MARKS—INDELIBLE, REMEMBERED. And then we see the wagon train crawling across the landscape, silhouetted against the horizon. Striking images like that opening shot appeared throughout the film, which received high praise from the likes of directors Allan Dwan and Henry King. Even Griffith himself commented on its "visual lyricism."

I doubt Thomas ever knew of such compliments. He kept a distance from the goings-on of the film community. Movie-making was his work, a job that he did. If he wasn't on set, whether in the studio or out on location, he couldn't be found. There was a period of time that I never saw him outside of the lot. I knew he and Elizabeth kept a private little bungalow somewhere, but most of what I knew of Thomas during then I only heard from Toby and Annie.

I often saw Annie buzzing around the studio, too busy to stop and talk for long. When she did, it was either to tease me about my fabricated love affair with Rebecca or update me about Thomas's condition.

"I saw him directing the other day," she once told me, taking me aside. "He was so caught up in the scene we all wondered if he weren't living it right then and there. It was a little eerie."

"What was the scene?" I asked.

"The leading man had to say goodbye to the woman he loves, a prostitute he rescued from savages, I think, and the actor, Troy Arthur, you know him, well, he wasn't doing it to Thomas's satisfaction. He kept telling Troy, 'No, like this!' or 'That's not right! Like this!' and then he would do it for him like he were actually living the moment without any of the rest of us around. It was eerie."

Then, as always, Annie would give me a wink and say, "Hurry off to Rebecca now, mustn't keep your sweetheart waiting."

Another time, Toby confided in me, "He's never without Elizabeth. She's called his 'assistant,' but I know she's there to keep him...um...focused."

"So, his spells have gotten worse," I said.

"People who have never worked with him think that she's his nursemaid, from the way she dotes on him and soothes him. Next thing, I imagine, she'll be pushing him around in a wheelchair."

"How does he get any work done?"

"That's just it. Once she gets him focused he becomes quite effective and commanding. But..."

"But what, Toby?"

"Even then, when he's directing, he doesn't seem to be entirely there, as though he were in a trance of some kind."

I knew exactly what Toby was talking about. I'd seen that look many times before in Thomas. He just hadn't been what I would call 'functional' during those times. Yet, Thomas directed some of his most successful films in that trance-like state. Along with *The Promised Land*, there was *The Peacemaker* and *The Scout*.

The first, about a lawman who gives up his star to avenge his wife's killing, was as rough and gritty a western as I'd seen anywhere. When asked why he gave up his oath as sheriff, the ex-lawman, Matthew Bell, answers: I PLAN TO BRING THE MEN RESPONSIBLE TO JUSTICE. IT JUST WON'T BE A LAWFUL JUSTICE. And in *The Scout*, a half-breed cavalry soldier searches for a woman, A SOILED DOVE, who other men would never give a second thought to, kidnapped by renegade Indians. It ends with a line from another of Thomas's poems, one about him and Ellen Marie: TOGETHER, THEY ARE NOT RUINED, BUT AS PEACEFUL AND AGLOW AS THE SETTING SUN. I don't know when the first time was that movie-goers saw a hero ride off into the sunset, but I don't think it was done any better than at the end of *The Scout*.

Like many of those pioneering directors, Thomas borrowed from his own experiences, from what he knew of the world, in the making of his motion pictures. For Thomas, though, I think it was more than just to add color and authenticity to his storytelling. As Eagle Heart had said, "he lives in his past, and there he stays." Yet what I couldn't figure out was whether Thomas wanted to be there or not. I always thought of my friend as fearless, but was he afraid of what the present-day offered? Or was he only trapped within his aging mind, longing to come out?

ॐ   ॐ   ॐ

As I mentioned, Annie used to tease me about my relationship with Rebecca. Yet, there were others, *many* others, who took our affair quite seriously. If scandal was fodder for the papers, gossip of romance was the dessert.

The first to perpetuate our romantic façade was Mr. Sheldon. He knew it was a lie. Yet, he also knew it sold pictures, and that was the business he was in, after all. "Whatever affairs you two partake in outside this studio is your own concern," he explained to us, "but you're under contract to me, and you're obligations to that contract are my concerns."

What became quickly clear to Rebecca and me, however, was that the obligations of our contract, and being in the picture business, went beyond the confines of the studio. We were under the ever-scrutinizing public eye. Since our salaries were paid by their ticket purchasing, then, it seemed, they had part ownership of us. We were as obligated to the movie-going audience as much as we were to Mr. Sheldon. If they wanted to see the two of us in love on-screen *and* off, so it would be.

It was simple and innocent enough. We would accompany each other for lunch or dinner, or I would join her for one of her many shopping sprees. We would be photographed, strolling arm-in-arm and smiling. For the most part, my smiles were genuine. Rebecca, as I said, was certainly pleasant to look at and, when she wanted to, could display a charm of personality that rivaled even that of Clara Bow. Playful, teasing, seducing onlookers with a mere wink, yet never vulgar. Reporters and the public loved talking to her, and what photographer could resist the glow on her face as she beamed at all the attention?

The Sunset Inn, Café Montmartre and the Pig-'n-Whistle were some of the places we went to regularly that I can still remember the names of. And wherever we went, so went the journalists and the photographers. I never did understand how two people having a meal or being out for a walk could be so newsworthy, but it seemed even a couple of small celebrities like us sold papers, which in turn, sold movie tickets.

"Audiences want to see the couple beyond the adventures," Mr. Sheldon explained. "The more they see you as real people, the more exciting those adventures will be."

Rebecca easily understood and accepted Mr. Sheldon's intentions, but I didn't get it. Rebecca illustrated it in a different way. "Think of it as advertising, Billy. We're like walking, talking movie posters. Do you notice how I try to mention our newest picture when answering reporters' questions? It's all about promotion. All the stars do it."

Like whores standing on the stoops of their brothels in Denver, I thought to myself.

At one point I asked Rebecca, "What happens when the public finds out we're not really in love?"

She paused to answer, a confusing kind of pause, perhaps considering a thoughtful reply. Eventually, she said, "It would be a different kind of publicity, but publicity nonetheless." Then she said something that made *me* stop to ponder. "I guess it would all depend on who broke who's heart."

In many of those newspaper photographs, we're kissing. Or rather, Rebecca is kissing me, usually on the cheek, flirtatiously playing-up our affair to the cameras. With all those intimate moments, all those "dates" of dining, shopping, walking on the sand, captured for all the public to see, it's not surprising that the two of us began to fall for the very charade we were weaving.

One time, a reporter asked Rebecca (they much preferred talking to her than me), "When did you fall in love with Billy? Was it after he rescued you from the waters of the Columbia River?"

"Well," Rebecca answered coyly, "you might say we rescued each other that day." She looked at me with a knowing wink. The comment garnered some "ooohs" and "aaahs" from the group around us, and then she went on,

"Yes, for me it was as we huddled on the shore waiting for the others to come get us."

"What about you, Billy? Was that the same moment for you?" the reporter asked.

I hesitated slightly and replied, "I thought we were only huddling to keep warm."

The group laughed. Then another reporter said to me, "Maybe in your next movie, you should have a twist—she rescues you!"

Again, everyone laughed, Rebecca especially. "Oh, Billy, that would be a hoot! Let's do it!" she said.

So that's where the idea for our next, and what would be our most popular, movie came from. It would be a movie directly made to appease the public, one strictly borne of publicity, you might say. We took the suggestion to Mr. Sheldon and he became quite excited. "Audiences love it when stars poke fun at themselves! You'll endear yourselves to them forever! It's a great idea!" he said.

With *Marigold and the Tenderfoot*, directed by Anthony Sheldon himself, the public's perception of us is turned upside-down. In it, I play a city boy, dressed in an ill-fitting suit and ignorant in the ways of farm life, and Rebecca is the rough-and-tumble farmer's daughter. She wore a blonde wig in her portrayal of Marigold, partly because it better suited the character's name than her own raven-black hair, and partly to replicate the look of Mary Pickford, Hollywood's biggest star of that time.

As Jimmy, the tenderfoot, I'm determined to "make it on my own" and leave the comforts of my family's home. But I make it only as far as rural Los Angeles before my junky automobile breaks down, a car I had proudly purchased from a shyster the day before. Rebecca comes to my aid and tows the car with her horse to the farm where her father can repair it. HE'S A WHIZ AT FIX'N MOTORS AND SUCH, she exclaims. But what she doesn't say is that he's very slow at his "fix'n." What is promised to take a few days turns into weeks.

The father was played by a Sheldon Pictures stock-actor Barry Thompson. He was as tall and shaky as an aspen, and nearly as old. A joke around the lot was that Sheldon's studio was built around old Barry.

Having little money, it is agreed that the tenderfoot will earn the cost of the repairs by doing work on the farm. Thus ensues a series of shticks with Jimmy learning the ways of rural life—milking a cow, slopping the pigs, feeding the chickens, moving bales of hay. Pretty cliché, even in those earliest days of motion pictures. Also, we learn of the father's ruse to find a man to wed his daughter.

WE DON'T GET YOUR KIND 'ROUND HERE TOO OFTEN, he tells me.

WHAT KIND IS THAT? I ask him.

ELIGIBLE BACHELORS!

The "peril" from which Rebecca-as-Marigold would rescue me involved a tractor and a cliff, which is humorous in itself knowing that one of those old John Deere's ran about as fast as a person could walk. It begins with me plowing a field, until the tractor gets stuck in gear. Also, I can't figure out how to turn off the motor, being a tenderfoot and all, so the tractor rolls slowly along with me frantically trying to shut it down. At one point I climb off the tractor and walk along with it as I attempt to figure out what to do. Fortunately, the comedy was in the situation rather than my performance. My skills at slapstick could never be lumped together with those of Chaplin, Keaton, or Lloyd.

While walking beside the tractor, my character then realizes it is heading for a cliff—absurd, again, knowing the scarcity of cliffs in rural Los Angeles. I climb back on the lumbering piece of machinery, now even more frantic. It is there that Marigold shows up on horseback, a scene we had to shoot several times as Rebecca was not a rider. She looked as uncomfortable in the saddle as I once did inside of a canoe. Stuntwoman Angie Fuller was used for longer angles. (I don't think Angie would be offended if I said *very* long angles.) Marigold tries to instruct Jimmy to no avail, and the tractor creeps dangerously along toward the precipice.

To pull the tenderfoot off the tractor as it's about to careen over the edge, Marigold lassos his chest and arms and yanks him free. Rebecca didn't lasso me, of course, that was done by Angie off camera. But Rebecca was on the horse as it pulled me off the tractor. Tractor seats are hard enough to set into let alone be yanked from, and my trouser got caught and ripped as I was pulled, thus causing me to lose control over my fall. I came down hard upon my tailbone. It made for a perfectly comical moment, however the stunt nearly crippled me, again. I sat motionless in the dirt, the rope taut around me, as that old John Deere tumbled off the ledge to a quarry of rocks below.

The audience at the premiere roared with laughter and cheers at my rescue. What they didn't know was that I was near tears from the pain. It felt as though my lower spine had been fractured to pieces. When Rebecca came down from the horse she was supposed to wrap her arms around me with a thankful embrace. But as she saw me there in such agony she nearly came to tears herself, and a flood of genuine feelings washed over her. She wasn't acting as she ran her hands over me in a panic, looking for other injuries.

She wasn't acting, either, when she said, "I'm so sorry, Billy. Are you okay? You have to be okay! I don't know what I'd do if you weren't! Please, darling, tell me you're okay!"

"I'm okay," I strained to tell her. "Don't worry. I'm

fine."

Audiences of silent movies got to be quite good at reading lips and were swept up in the tenderness and intimacy of our moment. I heard that many of them came to tears, as well, when Rebecca took my face in her hands and kissed me. The censors had the kiss cut long before it actually ended, but it was on screen long enough for anyone to see that, in that kiss, neither Rebecca nor I were acting.

Thirteen

And the song she sings
weighs upon my heart until
I've sunken down beside her.

It's funny how your perception of someone changes when you fall in love with them. I had once looked upon my time with Rebecca with annoyance. Our "dates" were nothing more than an inconvenient part of my job. Then I found I didn't want to be anywhere else but with her. Our hand-holding and longing gazes, our smiles and our kisses were no longer just show for the press. We became a necessary part of each other's lives.

Rebecca was no longer judgmental of me. Well, let's say her view of me was much less harsh, more endearing than critical. Where I had once been a dull-witted cowpoke to her, I was now quaint, even charming. She didn't always understand my indifference to matters she considered important—the arts, the adoration of a metropolitan lifestyle—but she came to appreciate my down-to-earth, common manners. About my looks, she liked to tell me I was "as handsome as a movie star" and give me a demure wink.

To me, Rebecca became not so snobbish but, rather, proud and confident. I had earlier wrote about how she could hook an on-looker with a gaze that left them wanting more. Well, I was learning what it was like to get that *more* for which so many others longed. In the same way my common words could never justly describe her beauty, I'm at a loss here to share how it was being the recipient of her affection. Rebecca was a woman who, once deciding to give you her full attention, and her love, was very generous. There was no more hope of stemming the waves of emotion and joy that she washed upon you than there would be of stopping the ocean's tides—you could either be drowned or swept away. Or, loving Rebecca could be compared to facing a stampede of horses—you could be crushed trying to slow it, or you could jump on for one hell of a ride. However I illustrate it, I think you get the point.

Regarding the press, I had begun to tire of them. Since our relationship was no longer just for show, I felt the photographers and reporters had served their purpose and had become an intrusion. But with the success of *Marigold and the Tenderfoot* it seemed Rebecca and I were more newsworthy than ever. Our only respite from the attention was to take long drives in the countryside. Even then, the more insistent photographers would learn of our route and appear from behind some bushes or a rock for a "candid" picture. I never confirmed it, but I suspected Mr. Sheldon himself was paying off those less than discriminant newsmen as part of his publicity plan for the two of us.

That gave Rebecca the idea of a long weekend getaway to her hometown of San Francisco. We told no one, especially Mr. Sheldon, of our plans. Once again, I was subjected to the confines of a train. This time I didn't mind.

I can't say I've ever been to someplace as romantic as Paris, but I can say I've been to San Francisco. I don't know if it's the close proximity to the ocean and all the musing imaginations that go with it, or how the cityscape rests upon the hills like a fine piece of cloth draped over a woman's curves, but even with all its bustling activity, that bayside city left me with a blissful sense I will never forget.

Like many movie-people, we stayed at the St. Francis. It stood stately and imposing there in the middle of the city, as though the grand structure had been built first and then the rest of the city grew around it. It is still there, of course, but history and progress have diminished it somewhat. Its marble floors and columns, intricate and flowery railings, cornices, and chandeliers made us feel like royalty. The Oxford in Denver had been a nice hotel, but the St. Francis was a palace. Our room overlooked Union Square, a welcoming public plaza named after a plot of dirt where Union-supporters had once gathered at the dawn of the Civil

War. An interesting bit of history, I thought, and later shared it with Thomas. "The effects of that awful event reached to every corner of the country," was his reply, of course, along with a weary shake of his head.

I feel fortunate to have seen the city at a time before it was infected by tourism. Chinatown was a neighborhood where Chinese people lived, not where you went to buy cheap, gaudy trinkets. Cable cars were what you rode to help traverse those steep hills, not merely a way to see the sights. During the day, Rebecca took me all over, from the top of Nob Hill down to the piers and the water. At night, we went to the theater. The St. Francis was not far from auditoriums like the Wilkes.

"My mother performed here," Rebecca recalled as we stood before yet another building of statuesque design, "back when it was the Columbia. She was a wonderful Ophelia."

"Yes, you've told me," I said. "I would like to meet her. And your father."

"Oh," she replied with a faraway gaze to the marquee above us, "they're out of town right now. New York, I think."

We saw a play with Pauline Frederick. I don't recall much else. Not because the production was unmemorable but because afterwards we visited a speakeasy or two, and nothing will disintegrate memory faster than bathtub gin. It's a wonder I remember anything about our time there because between every building or down every alleyway was a heavy door that led to one of those clandestine places where you imbibed to your heart's content (and your liver's regret). It was as though the Anti-Saloon League had never set foot in San Francisco. And, strangely, Rebecca knew exactly where to find every one of those dark holes.

My favorite of the illegal saloons was in the basement of the St. Francis itself because it was a mere elevator ride back to the room once the indulging was over. Rebecca knew which of the three elevators would take us all the way down. "Chewing gum," she told the operator. At one of those heavy doors, she confidently recited the password again, "chewing gum," and we were allowed inside.

It was a small, unglamorous room, the kind that made you feel as though you were partaking in something illegal. The liquor smelled of turpentine and the air was thick with smoke from cigarettes and cigars. Even in that dingy place, though, Rebecca glowed. She was having the time of her life, and her pleasure was contagious. I also appreciated that, while we were recognized from our movies, we weren't treated with any special preference. All of us there were equal conspirators.

At one point, a voice came from behind us. "Well,

Little Becky," it said and we turned to see an elderly fellow behind the wood plank bar. He was thin but muscular. The tautness of his neck, face, and hands revealed many years of hard physical labor. His long, dark hair, streaked with gray, was slicked back in a poor attempt to be stylish. Rebecca lit up even more at the sight of him.

"Bobby!" she squealed and wrapped her arms around his powerful shoulders. He laughed and smiled a semi-toothless smile.

"You're so grown up," he said, "and a movie star!" When Rebecca turned to introduce me, the old man quickly took my hand with an enthusiastic, crushing grip. "And I know you. It's an honor to meet you Mr. Colter, a real honor. Can't say that I've seen all your pictures, but I've seen a lot of them, and enjoyed every one."

"Billy, this is Bobby Smithers. He used to work for my family, since before I was born."

"Oh, I still do, Becky. I'm there every day, stocking shelves like always, and at night I serve up drinks here or at the Drake."

"You're a busy man, Bobby," I told him, thinking he was someone I'd like to know.

"Yes, sir, I like to keep busy," he replied with his gaping grin. Then the grin faded as he said to Rebecca, "The market isn't the same without you, Becky. Especially the way you up and left like that. Your mother's doing better. I know it's hard, but you should try to see her, too."

Rebecca's jovial mood soured slightly. Her eyes wavered from Bobby and me. "I suppose," she finally said, hesitantly. Then her face brightened again and she put her arms around the old man once more. "It was so good to see you, Bobby. I've missed you."

The old man embraced her as though it were the last time. Then he took my hand and said, "You two take care of each other."

"We will," I replied and followed Rebecca as she led me back to our room.

On our last day there she showed me parts of the city where she had grown up, like the Tenderloin District, particularly around Market Street, one of the busiest streets I've ever seen. There was a time when the sight of all the pedestrians, the automobiles and the street cars in a hurry to get to wherever they were going would have left me flabbergasted. Yet, there I was right in the mix of it. My dusty, worn cowboy attire had long been traded for double-breasted vests and single-breasted jackets, my battered leather hat replaced by a felt homburg, my checkered bandana now a silk handkerchief. With a woman like Rebecca by my side, I was the picture of sophisticated city living. Almost.

The only things I hadn't given up were my boots. Whatever fashionable men were wearing on their feet then, Oxfords I think, they pinched and hurt my toes. But my boots, their once stiff leather softened by years and miles, were as comfortable and forgiving as a pair of old bunk mates. We had travelled a long way together, and I wasn't about to give them up for anything as odd to me as fashion. Though long gone were the days of the prairie, they were not forgotten.

We ended up at the Crystal Palace Market, a huge indoor bazaar of stands selling fruit, meat, produce, and appliances. I remember a man with teary, swollen eyes selling fresh horseradish that he grated right there. You could have your fortune told by a woman in a gypsy costume and her parakeet that snatched cards from a deck. There were musicians who strolled the crowded aisles between the endless rows of booths, and an organ grinder with a monkey. It was standing-room only in some spots, appearing that all those people I had seen hurrying along the streets moments before had now congregated together in that one place. For a moment, I thought I might see Maxwell Jackson from the Triple-T. He had talked about opening a store in San Francisco, and it certainly looked as though every businessman in the city had set up shop at the Crystal Palace.

"Here it is," Rebecca said, squeezing my arm, "my

father's stand."

She gestured to a booth that looked like all the other booths around, except this one sat beneath a sign that read "Faye's Emporium" and was packed full of anything and everything for the home: toasters, shoe polish, cookware and silverware, those infamous Fuller brushes, and even a refrigerator. There must have been hundreds of items. The busy stand's customers were being served by a pair of women, one of whose gracious enthusiasm alone made me want to purchase something from her. The sheen of her black hair in contrast to the cream-white of her complexion was quite becoming, and the way it was pulled back in a bun accentuated a pair of wide, expressive eyes that misled the truth to her actual age. Only a dusting of gray in her hair, a few subtle lines around her eyes and mouth, and the gentle sagging of her full figure revealed her advanced years. She was such an attractive woman that, without knowing better, I would've guessed that she was Rebecca's—

"Mother!" Rebecca's voice pierced through the commotion of shoppers.

In an equally piercing tone the woman exclaimed, "Becky! Oh, my God! Becky, Becky, Becky!" and hurried out from the stand and into the aisle. The woman's elation at seeing Rebecca caused such a stir of communal joy from the crowd that we all laughed. The woman embraced Rebecca with such fervor that I thought she might suffocate her, but then she let go and wiped away a stream of tears, all the while chattering, "Becky! Oh, my God, look how beautiful you are! I didn't think I would ever see you again! Are you here to stay? Oh, sweetheart, I've been so worried. How have you been?"

"What are *you* doing here, Mother?" was Rebecca's response. "When Bobby said I should visit you, I didn't think he meant you would be *here*. When were you released?"

"When did you see Bobby? He didn't tell me," her mother replied.

"I saw him last night."

Her mother gasped and whispered, "You didn't see him in one of those saloons, did you? I don't want you going to those places, Becky! It can't be safe!"

Rebecca ignored her mother's concerns. "Is everything alright with you? What did the physicians say?"

Her mother shooed the questions and turned her attention upon me. "Oh, I know who this is! The movie camera doesn't do justice to your handsomeness at all. And you're so much taller!" she said, all the while with a comely grip on my arm. It was such that it became a bit awkward there in that public place, her daughter watching. I tried to take her flirtatious manner in stride.

"It's a pleasure to finally meet you, Mrs. Faye," I said.

"My name is Margaret. But you can call me Maggie, dear."

"Mother, where's Father?" interjected Rebecca.

"Oh, God only knows where he's gone off to this time. As soon as I returned he left me the work of running things."

"He's probably gone off to find products to sell. It's always been that way, Mother, you know that. You manage the shop and he procures inventory."

Rebecca's curt and chastising demeanor toward her mother reminded me of the way she used to treat me. I felt a little uncomfortable for Maggie. I also felt as though I were intruding somewhat. Maggie seemed to think nothing of it, however, as she took my hand and asked, "Have you seen the sights?"

"Rebecca's been showing me around, yes," I replied.

"But," said Maggie with a squeeze of my hand, "did she show you *everything*?"

"We don't have a lot of time, Mother. We're heading back to Los Angeles today," said Rebecca, taking my free arm with a firm tug.

"So soon, Becky? Oh, but this won't take long. Do you drive, Billy?"

No sooner than I told her I did the three of us were in Maggie's flivver making our way up the Twin Peaks. That old Model-T had seen better days, but it chugged dutifully along and soon we made it to a spot where the entire city could be viewed. Since neither of the bay's bridges had yet been built it was a view few people, if any, would remember today. It was an unusually clear day. The narrow, tall Victorian homes glowed brilliantly under the sun. The hills of the city in the foreground framed by a backdrop of trees and rolling landscape made for a perfect picture-postcard image. As Maggie had promised, you could see everything.

On the way down, just as on the way up, Maggie sat in the front, talking non-stop, while Rebecca was in the back, quietly seething. I couldn't tell you much of what Maggie went on about because Rebecca's manner had me concerned. Was she angry? Embarrassed? Perhaps some of both. At the first lull in Maggie's ramblings I took the opportunity to interject conversation of my own.

"Rebecca has told me you're quite an actress," I said.

"She has?" Maggie replied, with genuine surprise. "I have had my moments on the theatrical stage, I suppose. It's a wonder she remembers that. She was very young."

"She's gone on about your role as Ophelia on more than one occasion."

"Oh, that? Oh, I was just an understudy. I only really had two lines."

Then, as though a stage spotlight suddenly lit her up,

Maggie struck a pose. She stuttered to speak, fell silent with a bemused look, and then said, "Oh, I can't remember what those lines were. But it was a wondrous time. It's comforting to know I made such an impression upon my little Becky. She's become such the actress herself, hasn't she? I'm so proud of her."

I recalled something Rebecca had told me, about how her mother was critical of her being a movie-actress rather than a stage-actress. That didn't seem to be the case, however. I glanced back at Rebecca who was glaring out the window. "We have a train to catch," she said dryly.

We returned to the Crystal Palace to find a crowd of people cluttering the sidewalk and blocking its main entrance. They didn't appear to be there to shop. It turned out they were there to see Rebecca and me. Heading up the group was a reporter from the Chronicle. He fired questions at us as the mob surrounded our car.

"Miss Faye, Billy, are you in town to shoot a movie? Is this a romantic getaway? Where are you staying? Are there wedding bells in your future?"

Normally, Rebecca would have happily responded to the eager newsman, but this time she remained despondent, unwilling to put on her public face. I did my best to answer him as I helped her from the car while her mother quickly mingled with the crowd.

"We're just here..." I began, almost telling the reporter we were there to get away from reporters. Instead, I said, "We came up to see this fine city. Rebecca was born and raised here."

"Is that true, Miss Faye? You were homesick?"

"She came up to spend time with her mother," Maggie announced to the whole crowd. She squirmed in between and took the both of us tightly in her arms. "Now she has to return to Hollywood and make those wonderful movies you all love so much!"

"Is that right? You're *Mrs.* Faye?" asked the reporter.

"Yes. Yes, I am Becky's mother, and I couldn't be more proud of her."

"Can I get a picture of the three of you together?"

Maggie pulled us closer, intertwined her arm with mine and squeezed Rebecca's hand firmly at her side. Her face was radiant with pride and joy, while Rebecca and I were a pair of bookends—I, sullen and concerned about Rebecca's pensiveness, and she, unsuccessfully feigning a look of sentimental longing. It was not the best acting of her career. Behind us and the dusty Model-T, star-struck on-lookers squashed together for a closer view. Years later I would spend endless hours staring at that picture.

Our train ride home began in silence, until I noticed the glisten of a tear outlining the gentle curve of Rebecca's cheek. I took her hand and she turned to me.

"Billy. I'm sorry, but I have not been entirely truthful with you."

"I suspected as much," I told her.

"I'm ashamed about some of the stories I've told you."

"We all have parts of our lives we'd rather not be honest about, don't we?"

"I guess you're right...still." She gazed back out at the slow passing countryside.

"What was your mother in the hospital for? She seemed perfectly fit to me."

"My mother ails up here," Rebecca replied and tapped a finger to her forehead. "It's hard to see what's wrong. In some ways, she's like Thomas. But his mind is being affected by age. It just happens when you get old. My mother on the other hand, well, she's always...Father committed her to the Stanford State Mental Hospital in hopes they could help her."

"But now she's out. Maybe she's better."

"It's hard to say. It'll take time to know. She'll go on for a while, seeing only as far as what she imagines in her head to be true. Eventually, there comes a time when her imaginings and what is real clash together, sort of like waking suddenly from a dream, a gentle, pleasant dream, to the brash, often cruel ways the world can be. It can make her feel quite lost and confused."

"Kind of like when a movie ends, and you leave the darkened theater to the bright sunlight and crowded street?"

Rebecca smiled, and the gloom of the moment lifted slightly. "Yes. Yes, Billy, that's exactly what it's like."

We sat quietly for a spell. It was the first time I ever enjoyed the lulling, clacking rhythm of a train. I felt closer to her than I ever had with the commonality we now shared–I had Thomas, she had her mother. Then I asked her, "Is it true your father was out surveying inventory?"

"Oh, yes, that was true," she answered brightly. "Well, partially. He uses it as an excuse to get time away from my mother. I'm sure he's out doing other things, as well. He's quite versatile."

"He sounds like an interesting man."

"Oh, he is, Billy. He's very interesting. I wish you could have met him. You two would get along just fine."

"I imagine there will be another opportunity in the future."

Rebecca gazed at me with a look of wonder and said, "The future." And then she kissed me with such emotion that I was awash with great hopefulness for what was ahead for the two of us.

Fourteen

...roaming a foreign place
he once called his own,
imprisoned upon his cherished home,
forgotten long before that,
dead years before the burial,
the reservation—his grave...

I
t seems I've strayed a bit from the topic of Thomas. As I said, after *The Greatest Journey* I didn't make any films with him for a while because Mr. Sheldon wanted to market Rebecca and me.

While Sheldon Pictures was enjoying steady financial success and some artistic notoriety, Anthony Sheldon felt he hadn't yet produced that one film, one that would stir a lasting impression–his own *Birth of a Nation*–and carry him and his studio into infamy. In 1922, he had yet another opportunity, this time in the subject of General George Armstrong Custer. The idea came from old Barry Thompson, the character-actor who played Rebecca's father in *Marigold and the Tenderfoot*. Old Barry was so old that no one at Sheldon Pictures could remember him being young. He was older than Thomas. There were all sorts of guesses to just how long he'd been around.

"He was in the Civil War, and old even then," one person stated with questionable authority.

"On which side?" I asked.

"The North. No, the South. Or one of the other ones. I don't remember. But I heard he was an officer."

Another person surmised that he was a boy-soldier in the Revolutionary War, while someone else had the more realistic idea that he had driven a wagon train across the plains of Oklahoma, or Nebraska, or Kansas, while yet another guessed that he had come out to California in the 1850's in search of gold and never left. But, they were all just guesses. Barry himself never spoke of such things. He was an authority on only one subject—being enlisted in the U.S. Cavalry in the war against the American Indians.

His own opinion of the experience was mixed. "There was many a time when we had to defend our lives, and the lives of others, from some very savage attacks. It was either us or them, and I don't regret the things I had to sometimes do. But there were other times when innocent lives were taken for no reason. I don't have much pride in that. Warring, killing and dying should be left strictly to soldiers. That's their duty."

And, he knew General Custer.

"A braver man I never did meet—nor more foolhardy. His brashness in battle what made him famous would prove to be the very cause of his untimely end."

It was a subject Thomas knew little about but was especially interested in. He and Barry spent a good deal of time together talking. That is, Barry talked, Thomas listened. When Mr. Sheldon got wind of their conversations, he urged the two of them to write a screenplay about it. Specifically, Custer's defeat at Little Big Horn.

"Can't say I'm much of an expert on that massacre," was Barry's response to the idea. "I wasn't there, of course. If I had been, I wouldn't be here."

There was enough written about Custer's final battle to satisfy Thomas. And fortunately for him (and what would prove to be *unfortunate* for Mr. Sheldon) he was given, oh, what do they call it, *carte blanche*? At that point in their relationship, Thomas was the only person Mr. Sheldon fully trusted professionally. He knew, no matter what, Thomas would make a solid motion picture. What he didn't know was that Thomas had no intention of making a picture about Custer. The story Thomas wanted to tell was that of the Indians—the Sioux, the Cheyenne, and the Arapaho, and, especially, Crazy Horse.

For that, Thomas didn't rely only on what he read

because it was all written by White Men. He went directly to the source, to where it all happened—Southeast Montana—and met with members of the Cheyenne and Sioux tribes. He went alone, so I can't say what all transpired during the two weeks he was there. When he returned, Thomas was as determined as ever to make the movie he wanted to make.

The movie's working title was *Crazy Horse*. Only the actors and the crew knew that. Mr. Sheldon never would have approved it. Neither would he have approved Thomas shooting much of the film south of Los Angeles, on one of the reservations there. Thomas swore his cast and crew to secrecy. Mr. Sheldon trusted Thomas, so he didn't question him, but that didn't keep him from snooping for information. Everyone was instructed to say Thomas and his crew were off shooting in the foothills, or just somewhere other than a reservation.

I don't know if the countryside of Southern California looked in any way like that of Montana, but I was getting the idea from rumors that those kinds of details no longer mattered to Thomas. It was the stories he wanted to tell that took precedence, and the small things became less important. Some of the big things, too. At the movie's premiere, I remember how Toby sat with his head down, embarrassed by such scenes as the Indian camp populated by an array of Mexicans, in local clothing, who had snuck onto the set searching for work or food. He told me later that Thomas had never given them a second thought, saw them but went right on filming.

"Mexicans kind of look like Indians," Toby rationalized with a shrug. "But not really. Especially when they're dressed like...um…"

"Like modern-day Mexicans?" I said.

"Exactly."

"And Thomas didn't notice?"

"No, it's not that so much. He didn't seem to care. I mean, look at the Indians themselves. They don't look like Cheyenne or Sioux. Some of them aren't even dressed in historic attire."

I didn't admit to Toby that all Indians looked the same to me. But I did agree there was something 1920's about the appearance of the Kumeyaay used for the film.

Barry, Thomas's co-writer for *Crazy Horse*, had a complaint of his own. "He sure sleeps a lot," he griped about Thomas. Even at his advanced age, Barry was one of those who rested lightly, with one eye open all the time. Perhaps something learned from his soldiering days. "Sometimes he sleeps right through the best parts of the day, making us shoot at odd hours of the night."

Toby had expressed a similar concern. "We had to get creative with lighting, shooting around campfires a lot. Very big campfires! It made for some extraordinary footage, as you'll see, but a royal pain in the rear to accomplish."

Annie, then in her twenties, had worked her way up to production assistant for the movie. She shared some of her own observations. "He's mostly become forgetful. He repeats directions over and over. Or he has us set up a scene that we've already completed days ago. But some other things are more worrying. The other day he was interacting with the actors as though they were the characters they were portraying."

"Maybe he was trying to help them," I said, "you know, to make their acting more convincing by keeping them in character."

"But we were done shooting for the day. And for some of the actors, their work was done for the movie. They wouldn't be coming back. Like Robert Bowman. He played the scout George Herendeen who only appears near the beginning of the picture. Well, I overheard Thomas saying to him, 'You have a safe return to the Montana Column, sir.'"

"What did Bowman say?"

"He laughed, thinking it was a joke, and told Thomas how honored he was to be in one of his movies. But nothing about Thomas looked to be like he was joking, and he said to Bowman, 'Thank you for your service, and give my best to General Terry.' The moment became awkward for Robert, and the rest of us who were watching."

She paused for a moment and shook her head before going on. "And…now I don't speak any Indian or anything, but I know it's not all the same language…when he spoke to those from the reservation in some kind of Indian, they didn't seem to understand him. They all stared blankly. It wasn't until he started gesturing with his hands, making signs to illustrate what he saying, that they began to get what he wanted them to do. It was very tedious. When I suggested to Thomas we find a translator, he thought I was being funny and shooed me from the set."

Toby and Annie's concern for Thomas began to rub off on me. The more I heard, the more I wondered if there wasn't something else going on with Thomas beyond just not caring. So I decided to pay my friend a visit, something I hadn't done in a long while.

The bungalow he and Elizabeth Jerome shared was on a private lane just outside of Hollywood, in Pasadena. The house was secluded. Even looking for it, you could easily drive past its hedge-lined lot. As soon as I parked and got out of my car I could see why Thomas had picked the place. It was quiet. The kind of quiet you find being out on the open range.

Elizabeth met me at the front door. It had been some

time since I'd last seen her and I'd forgotten how well she wore her age. Silver streaks highlighted her flowing red hair like snow blowing across a plain, and the lines on her face served more to frame the beauty of her youth than reveal the years passed. She greeted me with a down-to-earth graciousness that I'd come to forget. So much of the Hollywood manner was just for show, as though a camera was always nearby, and you had to play your part just right to be convincing. Elizabeth was just herself, and it was refreshing. This, I'm sure, came from working with animals, especially horses. A horse has to trust you. It's easy to lie to people. But lying to a horse will get you nowhere.

Their house was modest. Humbly decorated, which showed Elizabeth's preferences, and very neat, which showed Thomas's. It was nothing like where I was living at the time. When once I'd been happy with a bunk in a room with five other cowboys, I then resided in a stately house with features part Spanish-Mediterranean, part American Colonial, and part grand hotel. It was white, as many of the houses were then. It had five bedrooms that I knew of and countless other rooms—including a study, within which I never studied, and a leisure room where I never leisured. Most of the house was empty of furnishings, making the echoes of the marble-tiled floors all the more sharp. I think it also had a swimming pool, which was nonsense because we all know how I feel about water. Looking back, it really was a ridiculous way to live and never a place I ever called home.

Elizabeth led me to the back of the house, through a pair of French doors, onto a stone patio. It was covered by a fine mesh screen that softened the harsh Southern California sun. Thomas was not there. He was, instead, out in the yard, sitting beneath a tree with his leather-bound notebook, the same one that he used to write in under the skies of Utah and the Triple-T Ranch. A breeze went through the patio, stirring a set of chimes that hung there. Before I approached, I watched a moment and wondered what events of his life he was putting to words now.

He looked up as I walked toward him. He didn't recognize me. Sure, it had been a bit of time since I'd last seen him, and the sun was in his face, and I was several steps away, but I could tell he didn't know who I was.

"Hello, Thomas," I said. "It's Billy."

His face lit up finally. "Billy!"

He didn't stand, which was a good thing. His legs, once lengthy and strong, were now spindly and wasted. I don't know that he would have been able to stand without great effort. I went and sat beside him.

"We're almost done here, Billy," Thomas said.

"Yes?" I replied. "Are you satisfied with how it's

turning out?"

"It looks good. Some of the best work I've seen."

I nodded to let him know I was happy for him. At the same time, I was concerned. From what I'd been hearing, *Crazy Horse* was not something to be proud of. Another breeze swirled around us and set the chimes to ringing, louder this time. Thomas's gaze went away from me to somewhere distant. I braced myself for one of his episodes, thinking he might chase off after his long lost horse again.

Instead, he returned his gaze upon me with an air of surprise. "Billy! We're almost done, you know."

"Yes. You said."

"Did I?"

"You said it's some of your best work."

"Yes, it is." The sun had moved ever so slightly, as did the shadow of the tree, exposing Thomas to the bright, morning light and showing his advanced years more clearly. He was somewhere in his nineties at that point. "Thanks to you, Billy."

"How's that?"

"I'd never gotten far on these fences on my own," he explained. "We've got less than an acre to go."

It was then I realized that in his mind we were out on the Triple-T, mending fences, not talking about his current picture.

"I always have to check the work of the others," he went on, "especially Stoud. Leaving him to wrangle a calf or bust a bronco is one thing. But if I need something constructed that will stand straight and true, well, that's a whole 'nother matter. Likewise with the Johnston brothers. Jamie's got his mind on that girl of his instead of the task at hand, and Frank's always thinking about the future rather than the present. No, if I want something built to last, you're my man, son."

On the one hand, I enjoyed being reminded of those fellows we knew in Utah. I had often missed them, and that life, but was always too busy to give it much thought. On the other hand, listening to Thomas talk as though he were somewhere else started me to feeling a little queasy.

We both went quiet. He returned to his notebook, and me, I didn't know what else to say. I sat with him a time and tried to enjoy the calm of the morning. Eventually, Elizabeth came to my rescue, gesturing from the patio for me to join her.

"The trick is to keep him engaged in the moment," she explained as we returned to the house. "It's easier for me, I think, because we don't have as much history together. He has a lot more memories with you."

"I suppose that's true," I said. "Around here I've known him longer than anybody. I can only wonder what he'd be like if he was with Mr. McElroy."

"McElroy," she said with a thought, "Is he the 'Mac' I hear Thomas talk about sometimes?"

"Yes. They go way back, back further than before I was born."

"I think we all have someone like that, Billy, a person that's been a part of our whole life. Even if they haven't always been around, they're still there." She smiled, thinking, I guess, of that someone who's been that in her own life. I would never get to know her well enough to know who that was, however.

"I suppose Thomas would be that person to me," I said. "I moved around too much to get to really know anyone." I looked out through the French doors to that old man sitting on the grass, fully drenched in the morning sun, his hands as gnarled as the branches of the tree he sat beneath. I had the feeling I wouldn't have him in my life much longer.

"Thomas has more than just one person in his life like that, doesn't he, Billy? Do you know who Ellen Marie is?"

I hadn't heard that name in so long, and the question took me by such surprise that I had to stop a moment. "She's a prostitute in Denver," I replied, very matter-of-factly. "He had known her mother, and her mother's family. I only met her briefly. Does he often talk about her?"

"No. Never." Elizabeth seemed disappointed that I didn't know more. "He's received a number of letters from her of late. I don't read them, I only see the envelopes. He doesn't talk about them and I don't pry. I only see that they have a powerful effect on him. I just thought…if I knew more, I could do more to help him."

"It seems to me you do plenty for him. He's very lucky to have you in his life," I told her. Then, in hopes of lightening the mood, I deliberately gave her fine figure a looking over, from head-to-toe, and added, "In more ways than one."

She gave me a sideways glance, and a wry but approving smile, and said, "Save it for the starlets, young man." We shared a laugh, and she offered me coffee. Then she asked, "Speaking of starlets, how's that little one of yours?"

"Splendid." I said. "I'm thinking of asking her for her hand in marriage."

I had been thinking about it for some time, but that was the first I'd said it out loud. I was filled with nervous excitement at the sound of those words, and hoped that it wasn't too apparent to Elizabeth. She reached out and took my hand.

"Congratulations, Billy," she said. "I'm very happy for you. I've never been married myself, but I think I would've quite enjoyed it."

We were sitting at the breakfast table. Sunlight crept toward our feet through the French doors and the generous windows on either side of them. Elizabeth and I spent the remainder of the morning there, talking.

I knew she was from Seattle, Washington, but that was all. She told me she was born of a retired lawyer, and when she was only five, her mother died of pneumonia. She spent much of her childhood inside a casino her father owned, which she hated. As long as she could remember, she wanted to live on a farm like her mother had always talked about. She ran away to Montana and found work on a ranch by pretending to be a boy. She quickly discovered she had a knack for horses.

Her story made me feel a kinship toward her. She confessed to catching the wandering bug, like me, and crisscrossing the country for many years, working many jobs before ending up in Los Angeles. What most surprised me was to learn that she wasn't but maybe ten years older than me. (I was nearing forty then.) I had always thought she just carried her age well. But, instead, the silver in her hair, the lines on her face, and the roughness of her hands were from having lived a full, hard-working life, rather than simply a long one.

"My relationship with Thomas isn't what people think

it is," she explained. "Not that it's anybody's business."

"People here like to make everything their business. Or at least talk about it like it is," I said.

She took a sip of coffee and gazed out to the old man under the tree. "He reminds me of my father. When I'd left home, my father was strapping and tall. But years later when I returned he'd become so frail I nearly didn't recognize him. His mind was still sharp but he had trouble getting around. It was heartbreaking. He eventually needed help doing everything. He was ashamed and wanted me to leave him alone, but I knew he wouldn't be able to get by without me, or anyone. What else could I do but stay with him?" She took another, longer sip. "Thomas spends a lot of time inside his memories, forgetful of everything around him. Pretty soon, I think, he won't ever leave them."

"You sound like Eagle Heart," I told her.

She gave me a quizzical look and smiled that wry smile of hers. "So now I'm a wise, old Indian?"

We spent a little time comfortably in silence before I had to leave. As she escorted me out, I thought only about how much I didn't want to go. I still look back at that morning with her as one of the most pleasant of all my time spent in California.

   ૏ ૏ ૏

Long gone were the days when I could sit outside Mr. Sheldon's office and listen through the door. I eventually came to rely on Annie's accounts of what was happening behind closed doors at Sheldon Pictures. One day, Annie took me aside and told me of an explosive argument she'd overheard between Thomas and Mr. Sheldon. The entire studio had heard it, and the ripple of whispers had long reached me before Annie had.

"Sheldon threatened to shoot him," someone said.

"I heard they came to blows!" said another.

"Mr. Sheldon fired Thomas!"

But Annie knew the truth. "Father had demanded to see Thomas's picture about Custer." Only when things were serious did she refer to Mr. Sheldon as *Father*. "He saw it without Thomas's knowledge."

"And your father didn't like it, did he?" I said.

"Christ, Billy, he hated it! He hated it like I've never seen him hate anything before! 'Where's the movie I paid for?' he kept shouting. Can you imagine? I mean, the only thing he hates more than Indians is Mexicans! And Thomas's movie is stock-full of both!"

Mr. Sheldon re-filmed more than half of *Crazy Horse*, cutting, you might guess, as many of the Indians and Mexicans from the picture as he could. He replaced them with scores of White cavalrymen dying at the hands of the **RED SCOURGE OF THE PLAINS**, as one of his title cards put it. He also re-named the picture *Custer*.

Fifteen

I am so small, but I matter

Because I have to.

You cannot live in my city

Without living

N o, Mr. Sheldon did not fire Thomas. When the dust settled between them he realized, per contract, the old man owed him two more movies.

Custer experienced mild success, due only to the free publicity of gossip. Newspapers and magazines, like Photoplay and Motion Picture Story, could make or break a movie. The drama behind the production of *Custer* became the talk of Hollywood and was much more interesting to the public than the movie itself.

If there's one thing about the movie business I always found most bewildering, it is how the very product it creates is often less important than how it was made, or who made it, or how they lived their lives while making it, or not making it. They are like children playing, entertaining only themselves, and the parents are the public, watching without interfering because, of course, children will be children.

Because *Custer* did not garner the attention he'd hoped for, Mr. Sheldon put Rebecca and me in Thomas's latest project. Our star-appeal was such that we could guarantee success for even the greatest dud of a movie. Mr. Sheldon had lost faith in Thomas and would not take any more chances. He even put Annie in charge of production so she could keep tabs on him, which was good because I had my own distraction—Rebecca's mother.

Not long after our visit to San Francisco, Maggie Faye began to surprise us with visits of her own. They were frequent and short. At first. Soon they became planned stays lasting a week, or longer.

"I can't say no to her," Rebecca said. "I worry what that would do to her state-of-mind. Besides, it's not too horrible having her around, is it?"

"She's fun. She can stay as long as she wants," I replied naïvely.

"She is a hoot, isn't she?" Rebecca said with the biggest of smiles. Then she embraced my neck and kissed me, making any inconveniences from her mother worthwhile. Whatever rocky history the two of them had had due to Maggie's "state-of-mind," Rebecca loved her mother very much.

It was true, though, Maggie wasn't bad company to

have around. She did her best not to be underfoot and even kept Rebecca's house clean and orderly. Having her there made Rebecca's too large a place feel cozier. She cleaned my house once, as well, and was shocked, and interested, at finding my pistol in my room. I entertained her with stories of the West I once knew. "Oh, how exciting!" she'd remark about even the most boring events of my life. The length of her stays grew enough that she moved into one of Rebecca's extra rooms, and the three of us became a regular site around the Hollywood community in the summer of 1927.

Her favorite place was Hollywood Boulevard, full of cars, shops, hotels, restaurants, and celebrities, lots of celebrities. We frequented The Blue Front, where stars could be seen enjoying a meal, and the recently opened Chinese Grauman Theater. Maggie was enamored by the hand-prints of stars like Mary Pickford, Norma Talmadge, Douglas Fairbanks and Norma Shearer imprinted there in the concrete.

The three of us became darlings of the tabloids. At any given time we could be seen in multiple publications. We'd pose for pictures and answer questions everywhere we went. The photographs were always the same: me in the middle with the ladies on either side, which was Maggie's doing, even if it meant her frantically circling around to be on one side of me or the other. And she always feigned surprise.

"Oh, I must look frightful enough to scare a ghost," she'd exclaim. "I can't have my picture taken like this!"

To which reporters would reply, "Nonsense, Maggie! You look great!" (She did, because she'd spent so much time primping before leaving the house.)

Newsmen were very familiar with us, approaching like they were dear, close friends. Judy McDonald, an unscrupulous gossip columnist with the *Times* wrote, "Ms. Faye and Mr. Colter are the sweetest of couples, brought together by a ruthless, unforgiving industry, but not so jaded by fame as to forget the precious mother-daughter bond."

Not all our interactions were so agreeable, however. There was one evening, as we were dining, that I noticed a man pacing outside the restaurant's front window. He was portly, wearing a fine suit that didn't quite fit him, and he never stopped staring at us with the wildest of eyes. It was concerning enough that I asked the maître d to investigate.

I watched as their interaction played out with silent bravado like a scene from one of my own movies. The portly man became greatly animated as he objected to the maître d's requests to move along. The maître d's own manner went from composed and professional to irate when the man gave him a firm shove, all the while the man's crazy eyes darting back-and-forth between the maître d and the three of us.

The antics outside eventually got the attention of the entire restaurant. "Billy, what's happening?" Rebecca asked.

"Oh, dear," said Maggie, more intrigued than shocked.

The maître d had waved over a police officer from across the street by then and the two of them were attempting to physically move the man away from the restaurant, but his size and frenzied flailing made it a near impossible task. He broke free from their hold and ran to the restaurant's entrance, making it just inside before another officer arrived. With great effort the three of them managed to subdue the large, now hysterical man, but not before he shouted "I love you!" multiple times, his eyes fixed in our direction. As he was wrestled away from the premises I caught sight of one of the officers removing a pistol from the man's back pocket.

A photographer, who had been lying in wait for us, showed himself to capture the strange moment. He then turned his camera upon the three of us. The next day we were in the paper beneath the simple headline: **CRAZED FAN!**

Maggie couldn't get enough of seeing our printed pictures. She quietly collected publications, sometimes multiple copies of a single issue, and neatly stacked them in a corner of her room. Rebecca or I often found her sitting on the bed, a pile of magazines in her lap, whispering to herself while delicately turning each page, like a child enraptured of a storybook. I once asked her what she was doing. Her manner was calm and peaceful as she turned to me, but in her eyes was desperation...and panic?

"I cherish our time together," she replied.

"We've enjoyed having you here, too, Maggie," I told her. "You'll always be welcome."

She smiled, yet remained sadly distant.

I told Rebecca about that moment and she responded with a bit of panic of her own. "I know that look. We need to be careful."

"Why? What's happening?"

"She's conflicted, confused about whatever's in her head. Oh, I knew we shouldn't have let her stay here. She should be home, with her friends, busy at work. I just..."

"What can we do?" I asked, taking her hand. Rebecca only shook her head. Then I said, "How about she spend tomorrow with me. We'll relax. I'll take her on a drive. We'll see the ocean. Then we won't invite her back for a while. We'll explain how busy we are with work, and insist she get back home to her own life."

I'll never forget the sweet smile Rebecca gave me. "That's something my father would do."

"Would it work?"

"Sometimes."

❧   ❧   ❧

The next day I told Maggie that Rebecca needed to prepare for the following day's shoot, and that it would just be the two of us. I had it in my head that I would engage Maggie in the way Elizabeth or Eagle Heart would Thomas, helping him to get back to himself.

We began that day early with a drive to Santa Barbara, taking the Pacific Highway north. It had been awhile since I'd gotten out of the city. The countryside of hills and trees were as therapeutic for me as I hoped they would be for Maggie. I drove a Chrysler Tourer in those days, and with the ragtop down we enjoyed the air and the sun like we were riding horseback across the plains.

What I liked about Santa Barbara was that you felt like you were somewhere important without paying the price of crowds and space. In some parts, there was the bustle you might find in an industrious, big city, but not too big. In others, there was the quiet of a small town...like Prescott.

Prescott.

So often would my memory take a peek back there, inspired by the sight of a cluster of pines or the rare caress of a dry breeze. I could never say what it was that I'd left there, but I always had a feeling I would go back one day to find it. Perhaps, I thought, I could take Rebecca and she would love it as much as I.

What you may not know about Santa Barbara is that more than a thousand silent movies had been produced in that little coastal city. One of the world's largest studios of the era, Flying A, had been located there until around 1922. Like much of the industry, however, it moved to Hollywood, the rapidly growing epicenter of entertainment.

The Flying A couldn't have left at a better time as a severe earthquake struck the area in 1925. There was still a bit of reconstruction going on when Maggie and I drove through a couple of years later. Buildings were taking on a Mediterranean transformation of white walls, tiled roofs and iron embellishments, all making for a striking image against the green of the hills and the blue of the coast.

"I could live here," Maggie commented in a breathy, faraway tone, "for the rest of my life." Then she turned to me. "That would be lovely, wouldn't it, Billy?"

"Yes," I said. "I think you could be quite happy here."

She took my hand and squeezed as though she had come to an important decision. I caught the glimpse of a tear in her eye, a happy tear, and I felt I'd accomplished what I had set out to do that day—bring Rebecca's lost mother back.

We returned to Los Angeles for lunch. We ate at the

original Brown Derby café on Wilshire Boulevard, not to be confused with the more famous version which opened a few years later on Hollywood and Vine. I thought Maggie would find a restaurant shaped like a hat whimsical, which she did and couldn't stop talking about it, saying things like, "Can you imagine the size of the gentleman who would wear this?"

To which I replied, "It certainly would be a mess for us to try and eat while he walked about!"

We didn't stop talking and laughing the entire meal. Even the presence of gossip queen Judy McDonald couldn't dim the glow of the moment.

To describe Ms. McDonald as a snake is an insult to all reptiles of the world. But her pale, tight skinned complexion, her narrow, lipless mouth, and her venomous manner left me with no other image than that of a slithering rattler, waiting to strike from under the rocks upon her next unsuspecting prey. No, I cannot muster an opinion of her any higher than that.

She spied us across the diner, having just lunched herself, and came to the table obviously looking for some kind of tidbit to feed into her typewriter back at the office.

"Oh, Billy and Rebecca," she said, "how lovely to see the happy couple enjoying time together." Then she stopped with faux-surprise. "Oh, I'm so sorry, Billy. I only assumed you were with Rebecca."

"This is Rebecca's mother. You've met," I said.

"Oh, yes. Margaret, isn't it?"

"Yes. But please call me Maggie," she responded, aglow from the attention.

"How darling of you, Billy, to entertain your sweetheart's mother while she's doing who knows what without you! Where is she, playing a romantic scene with another handsome actor, or traipsing the town, garnering the interests of other producers? There's talk she's had enough of stodgy, old Anthony Sheldon."

"We have a big day of shooting tomorrow," I told her, ignoring the snake's prodding. "She's resting."

"Of course she is. The life of a star can be so demanding. What's the picture you're working right now? I forget."

"You'll be invited to the premiere like everyone else."

"I'd better be. It was a treat to see you again, Maggie. I hope you'll forgive my mistake, I really thought you were your daughter. The apple has not fallen very far here. And the way you two were enjoying your lunch together! How could I not guess you were Hollywood sweethearts?"

Maggie blushed as red as a tomato and Judy sauntered away with a carefree goodbye.

"She's delightful, isn't she?" Maggie gushed.

"Yes," I said. "Delightful."

The main reason Rebecca and I had a day off from shooting was because the set builders for *The Last Roundup* were behind schedule, due to Thomas's insistence on detail. The set was to be the main street of a Wild West boomtown, and Thomas wanted sturdy, solid structures, not the typical stage flats of canvas walls and plaster-of-Paris molding.

"There's going to be a hundred head of cattle moving through here," Thomas explained. "I don't want the saloon or the mercantile or any building to go toppling over." Then he added with a rare chuckle, "It might deter from the realism a bit."

The Last Roundup was the story of an aging rancher, Silas Hickery, making his final cattle drive before selling his spread to land barons and retiring to a remote cabin in the hills. I'VE WRANGLED MY LAST STEER, he tells his men. I'M TIRED TO MY BONES, AND IT'S TIME I GAVE THEM A REST. The part of Silas was played brilliantly by old Barry Thompson. It was his first and only leading role.

The drive does not go without a hitch, of course. No, the journey is befouled with trials and tribulations: cattle rustlers, Apaches, a flash flood and a dust storm. When the drovers finally reach their destination, the herd is startled and a stampede tears through the middle of town. A tragic end to a tragic story.

Since there was no shooting during my day with Maggie I thought I would conclude our afternoon with a tour of the studio. Sheldon Pictures was never as grand looking as other studios, a fact that did not escape Rebecca's mother. "It's so dreary," she noted as we approached and went inside.

The first person we met was Annie. She was especially busy with trying to keep the production of *The Last Roundup* from falling even farther behind, but she took a minute to give Maggie a gracious welcome.

"It's a pleasure to meet you, Mrs. Faye," she said. "Billy's told me much about you, but he didn't tell me how beautiful you are." Annie put her hand on my shoulder in the friendly way that she has been known to do. I watched Maggie's eyes narrow in disapproval of this gesture.

"And did he not tell you that I am Rebecca's mother. Perhaps a little decorum would be appropriate."

"I'm sorry. I don't understand."

"I'm sure you don't."

Annie and I looked at each other dumbfounded as Maggie turned to leave. I thought it best for Annie to get back to her work and let the matter alone. It was Maggie who chose to stir it up further.

"I don't think it was appropriate for that girl to be so familiar with you," she said to me.

"We're old friends, Maggie," I explained.

"You're more than friends, Billy. To her."

"I think you're exaggerating."

"Men and men, and women and women can be friends. Not men and women."

"You and I are friends, aren't we?"

The silent, piercing glare she gave me at that moment left me at a loss. She became a stranger, judgmental, looking right through me. And when she finally spoke, saying, "Of course," I wasn't sure if it was me she was answering.

I moved her along, continuing our tour. We took in all the sights and activities that is a motion picture studio, making our way to the backlot. Maggie stared aghast at the chaos of people and equipment. "It is no simple thing, is it, making a movie?" she said.

"No. No, it isn't," I said. Then, spying Thomas, I pointed and added, "It's men like him who keep it all together."

"Oh, who is he?"

"He's one of the finest directors you'll ever meet, and my dear friend, Thomas Andrew Benton."

With all the commotion around us, he still heard his name and looked our way. His face lit up, and I knew he was presently enjoying a coherent demeanor. Elizabeth was with him and followed as he came our way. Introductions were formal and this seemed to relax Maggie from our encounter with Annie. In fact, Maggie was taken with Elizabeth, either because they were closer in age or because Elizabeth kept calling her "Ma'am" or because she showed no inappropriate "friendliness" toward me, I can't say for sure. I was just happy the awkwardness from earlier was gone.

Elizabeth showed Maggie the town set for *The Last Roundup* a little more closely, leaving Thomas and me to ourselves.

"What do you think?" he said, gesturing to the set.

"It's impressive, Thomas. It reminds me of many a town I've ridden into in my life."

"It does, doesn't it? Tomorrow we'll have a hundred head running through here."

The set stretched for what could've been two city blocks. A canvas backdrop of mountains and forest hung behind buildings of immense detail and a street of dirt and rock went between them. I stepped onto he set, the crunch of earth beneath my steps, the sun in my face, and was transported to another time. The tingle of movie magic crept up my back.

"A hundred head you say?" I mused.

"As many as I can get," said Thomas. "I'm going to do this one right, Billy."

On one hand, I was glad to see my friend committing himself once more to such detail and accuracy. But, *a hundred head of cattle?*

"Elizabeth tells me you're going to ask that gal of yours to marry you."

"Yes. I've come to the decision, but have yet the nerve to ask."

Maggie and Elizabeth were with us again by then. Maggie's eyes were as wide as a little girl's in a doll store. "Billy? What's this? Marriage?" she gasped.

"I didn't intend for you to find out this way, Maggie," I told her, "but, yes, I'm going to ask Rebecca for her hand in marriage. With your blessing, of course."

"And the blessing of her father," Thomas added.

"Yes, of course, I should go meet with your husband as well."

Maggie moved to speak but the words strained to leave her throat. She smiled and a tear ran down her cheek. "No. That won't be necessary, Billy," she managed to say. "He's a very busy man. I'm sure he would give you his blessing. Just as I do."

She wrapped her arms around my neck and cried and laughed and squeezed until I couldn't breathe.

Maggie was flushed with excitement as I drove her back to Rebecca's. "It's been a most wonderful day, Billy. Thank you," she said. Her eyes glistened with joy.

"It's been my pleasure, Maggie."

"I'm going back to San Francisco tomorrow. There

are so many things I need to do. I have a wedding to prepare for. A honeymoon in Paris would be lovely, wouldn't it? That's where artists go."

"Yes, well, remember Rebecca doesn't know, yet. Please don't say anything to her."

"Of course! It's news too wonderful to spoil! I'll just tell her I've got to get home. She'll understand."

Not only did Rebecca understand, she was overjoyed. "You did it, Billy!" she said to me once we were alone. "Mother's going home. And she's so happy!"

"We had a good day," I said, doing a bit of acting. "She came to realize it was time to go."

❧   ❧   ❧

In *The Last Roundup*, Rebecca and I did not have roles our audience had become accustomed to. I played a cowpoke with a nefarious past using the cattle drive and a false name to hide from the law, or whatever it was he was running from. It was never made clear. Something to add to his mystique, I suppose. Rebecca played the young wife of the aging chuck wagon cook who had won her in a card game. Her past was murky, as well.

"Who these people *were* isn't as important as who they are now," is the way Thomas explained it.

Early in the film, the cook is killed in a raid by rustlers. Rebecca must take on the responsibilities of the chuck wagon though she's never prepared a meal in her life. My character comes to her aid by showing her a thing or two about handling a wagon and fixing up grub for famished cowboys. A romance blossoms between them, of course, but it plays only a minor element to the bigger story—the drive.

By the time Silas Hickery has gotten his cattle and men to their destination, his herd has dwindled and the men are ragged and threadbare. Tensions between man and beast are thick. Thomas showed this through lots of close-ups, not of just the faces of the cowboys, but also in their calloused, bleeding hands, their wide, tired eyes, and the sweat on the sinewy muscles of the cattle. Considering what all had happened, the audience was equally fatigued and wanting for it to be over by the time the drive rides into the small boomtown of Aspen Flats.

When Rebecca and I arrived on set that morning of the stampede shoot, there were nearly seventy head of cattle packed into a narrow corral, calmly awaiting their cue. It wasn't the hundred Thomas had hoped for, but the number of them in such a small space was enough to stir one's nerves. A pair of stuntmen, old cowpokes themselves, was there to keep the herd unruffled. This proved a challenge. As actors and extras began to fill the soundstage and equipment was moved and adjusted, the cows began to stir.

One thing I noticed that was not typical for a Thomas Andrew Benton shoot was the number of cameras and cameraman that were being positioned about the set. There were a lot more, more than I could readily count, than just Toby and an assistant. When I questioned Thomas about it, he simply replied, "For authenticity."

So I asked Toby.

His attention was taken up by getting the cameras and operators coordinated. As he hurried from one end of the set to the other, he was able to answer me with a breathless and stressful, "He wants to do it in one take!"

"Do what?"

"The stampede."

"The stampede? What do you mean?"

Toby stopped, impatient with my not getting it. "He wants to shoot the stampede in one take, as it happens. No cutting."

He left me there dumbfounded. I understood what he was telling me. There would be no movie magic here. No shooting the action in pieces, from different angles, safely and controlled, and editing it later into an exciting sequence. No, Thomas wanted to document a true-to-life cattle stampede. What I didn't understand was why.

For authenticity, he'd said.

I'd been in only one cattle stampede in my life. It was in Wyoming, on an open range, not in the confines of a canyon or a town's main street, and that was hair-curling enough. I could only imagine what it would be like to be in the middle of a raging herd with no way to escape. And I didn't like what I was imagining.

Annie made the call for actors to take their places, and I ran to find Rebecca. She was to drive the chuck wagon into town closely behind the cattle, and I was to ride a horse beside her. Instead, I climbed aboard and sat with her.

"Billy, what are you doing?" Rebecca asked.

"There's been a change," I told her. "I'll steer the wagon."

It was then Thomas called, "Action!"

I urged the horses forward so we would be ahead of the cattle. Actors and extras went about their rehearsed roles of townspeople. I called out to deaf ears to stop the action and cameras! The herd of cattle was more than agitated as one of the stuntmen opened the gate to the corral.

But the cows barely moved. They mooed and cried out their displeasure, only a few wandered from their confines and mingled in the street.

Until Thomas stood upon a rung at the back of the corral, in his hand a pistol. He raised it above his head and fired three shots.

The herd exploded from the corral! They tore through the gate and burst down the fence, splintering rungs and posts like a tornado of flesh and muscle and horns tearing across the land.

I whipped the horses to get us out of there. I could see the panicked faces of the actors as they ran for safety. This had not been rehearsed. Some of the cameramen abandoned their posts just before their equipment was shattered. No one expected the rampage. No one except Thomas.

Our horses became unnerved, overcome by the crazed steers running pell-mell all around them. Rebecca gripped my belt with one hand and the wagon seat with the other. It felt as though we were back on the raging Columbia River, our small boat at the mercy of its violent water. I did all I could do to keep the wagon steadily moving forward.

On either side of us, actors and extras broke down doors and jumped through windows to escape pummeling horns and hooves. A few leapt onto the back of our wagon, hanging for their lives to the canvas and railings. One poor soul caught his foot in the spokes of a turning wheel and was dragged beneath the trampling frenzy. A number of people were scooped up and thrown to the backs of cattle, holding on for their lives. Shouts and cries were engulfed by the shattering of glass and splintering of wood for the most jarring of noise. The whole scene was an avalanche of madness.

As I tried to steer the wagon from the set, it leaned enough that some of the cattle caught one side under their horns and flipped it over. Rebecca screamed and I cursed as I let go of the reins and took her into my arms. I didn't have a plan other than to keep her close to me—we were at the mercy of gravity and the stampede! A pair of extras who had been clinging on were crushed as the wagon landed and slid, while a third was flung over the top of us, tumbling safely to a stack of hay bales.

Our fall to the dirt was broken by the canvas cover tangling around the two of us, and the overturned wagon served as a barricade from the crazed cows. It also slowed the stampede by milling the cattle back onto itself. Not to say we were out of harm's way. Though slowed, the steers were still jittery. I stood between them and Rebecca, shooing them with slaps of my hat and shouts. As soon as I felt they were settling I scooped Rebecca into my arms and carried her from the set, her face pressed against my chest. All I wanted was to get her away.

Once more, our escape from danger was caught on film—the entire tragic scene was! Just as Thomas had envisioned it, and it was edited into one the most exciting action sequences ever made. Every destructive, harrowing moment preserved forever. Twenty-some people were injured, four killed. Unfortunately, this was nothing new. Films like *Ben Hur* and *Noah's Ark* suffered loss of life during their production. But it had never happened in one of my movies. Because of that, I've only watched *The Last Roundup* once.

If there was one thing to be grateful for it was that the cameras were not on me as I carried Rebecca off the set. As I said, all I wanted was to get her away. Not only for that moment, I knew then I wanted her with me for the rest of my life. That want overcame me, and Rebecca could see it in my eyes as I put her down.

"Billy? Everything is fine. I'm okay," she said. "What's the matter?"

"Nothing's the matter," I told her. And then I dropped to one knee. "In fact, nothing would be better, Rebecca Faye, if you would do one thing for this dim-witted cowpoke."

Her eyes went as bright and blue as a full moon and her voice quivered to speak. "What's that, Billy?"

"Marry me!"

Before the words could leave my lips, Rebecca fell upon me, her arms clenched my neck and together we went to the ground, crying, kissing and laughing. "Yes, yes, yes," she said between elated breaths.

Although cameras were not on us, my proposal did not go unwitnessed and word spread like, well, a stampede of cattle.

The aftermath of the mayhem was not lost upon the two of us. I went to work helping calm and clear cattle while Rebecca did what she could to aid the injured. As we worked, people congratulated us on our engagement. There was an air of bitter-sweet about it all.

Annie found me amidst the activity and wrapped her arms around me. "I'm so happy for you," she said. "And I'm glad you're okay. I'm sorry. I should have seen this coming." She looked around at the wreckage of the set.

"How could you?" I replied.

"I'm in charge of production. It's my job. I just never expected Thomas would…"

Her voice trailed off and I thought to myself, *Thomas!*

I left her to find him.

He was at the far end of the set, near what was left of the corral, directing workmen in the repair of the fencing and others in the gathering of cows. I approached him with a tight fist. It was the first and only time I wanted to hit my friend.

"What were you thinking?" I shouted at him instead.

"We need to fix these posts and get these cows contained," he answered.

"I could've been killed! Or Rebeccca!"

"Rebecca! Is she alright?"

"Yes, yes. She's fine. Thomas, look at this!" I took a good look at the destruction myself, and for the first time, saw the lifeless bodies in the street. "What the hell were you thinking, you crazy old man!"

Thomas stared blankly all around. A wash of confusion went down his face, and he stammered incoherent thoughts and explanations. My anger teetered with pity. It was then someone put a hand on my shoulder. There couldn't have been a worse time for Mr. Sheldon to call me into his office.

He was pacing behind his desk when I walked in.

"I heard about what happened down there, Billy. Is it true?" he snapped.

"Yes. The cattle got out of control. A lot of people got hurt, some pretty badly."

"Is it true you proposed to Rebecca?"

"Um…yes. Yes I did."

"What the hell were you thinking? How long have you been planning this?" He came around his desk to within inches of me.

"I'd been thinking about it for some time. But it just sort of happened today," I replied. "Mr. Sheldon, I think someone was killed down there."

"Yes, that is unfortunate," he said, stepping away. "Was a camera on you when you proposed?"

"No, we were off the set."

Wheels were turning in his head and it made me nervous. "You and Rebecca stay in costume. We'll set up a camera once they get the set cleaned up."

I knew what he had in mind, and I quickly said, "No."

"No?" He stopped. *No* was not something Mr. Sheldon was used to being told. "You're right. We should do it now while there are extras and cows still milling around."

"No, Mr. Sheldon–"

"They've cleared out all the cows already?"

"No, it's not that. I don't want my proposal to be in a movie."

He stopped again, and then sat in his chair—the throne from where any decisions made were final.

I stood my ground. "That moment was between Rebecca and me. If I could, I would do it again some place faraway from here. Just the two of us. But as it is, it happened the way it did, and it's done."

"What if it had been written in the script that your character proposes to her character?" he asked, coolly.

"Well, I suppose that would be different."

"Then I'm doing a last minute rewrite to *The Last Roundup*. You'll propose to her. The end."

I took a deep breath. "No. It's done. The movie can end with me carrying her off. People can think what they want after that. Anyway, it'll all be in the papers tomorrow."

"All the more reason to put it in the movie. Audiences will storm theaters to see it."

"It's done, Mr. Sheldon. You can't rewrite real life."

As I gave him a respectful nod before turning to leave, I could swear he felt he had the power to do exactly that. *Which just may be*, I thought to myself, *but he wasn't going to rewrite my life.*

Sixteen

Who knows what a storm will bring?

The breeze whispers of its coming,

But is it welcoming or foreboding?

A s it turned out, *The Last Roundup* was Sheldon Pictures's most successful movie ever. I think the film would have done well without all the publicity of the tragic shoot and my engagement to Rebecca. It was a very good film. I'd like to say all was forgotten between me and Mr. Sheldon because of that, but as he was one to hold a grudge, there remained a cautious rapport with us.

I've mentioned that Hollywood is nothing more than a playground for spoiled children. They entertain themselves with publicity, and awards. (There weren't so many in my day. I would leave the industry before the first Oscars. But, oh, how they love to give themselves awards!) And parties, we mustn't forget the parties. To celebrate *The Last Roundup's* success, Mr. Sheldon threw one such party.

He wasn't known for events that let people into his home. But when he did have one, it was always extravagant. His mansion was deceiving. It did not reflect the Mr.

Sheldon that we all knew, or even popular Hollywood, for that matter. The furnishings were elegant, not showy or excessive. Rather than an over-sized chandelier looming in the foyer, guests were greeted with understated lighting of delicate design. Picture windows allowed sunlight to drench the main rooms, and the floors were of warm, inviting woods covered by European rugs rather than cold marble. For this particular event, Mr. Sheldon turned his spacious garden of manicured, exotic flowering plants into a ballroom of sorts. A banquet of food was laid out at one end, an orchestra arranged at the other. Between was a dance floor.

His latest success was only one reason for the celebration, however. Mr. Sheldon also used his soirees to woo talent. He was soon to lose his best director (Thomas owed him only one more film, per contract), and he was always on the lookout for the next Clara Bow or Louise Brooks. So everyone in Hollywood was invited to the party, not just those under contract to Sheldon Pictures. For that reason, Rebecca insisted we arrive early.

"Isn't that unfashionable?" I asked her.

"Applesauce!" she replied. "I don't care about that. Not tonight. You never know who might show up. Oh, Billy, do you think Chaplin will be there?"

"Maybe," I said, though I could never imagine Charlie Chaplin would associate with Anthony Sheldon.

We arrived to the party two hours late because, well, that was Rebecca. She really did care about being fashionable. No matter how hard I tried to get her out the door, she wasn't happy with her clothes or makeup. After considerable deliberation with herself (she never asked me for my opinion because I always thought she looked perfect) she decided she was ready by replacing a particular hat with a particular tiara.

In the end, it was much more fun to see who was in attendance by mingling. Many of the guests were as "fashionable" as we were, arriving late right along with us. Rebecca took immediately to prowling, for not only who was there but what they were wearing, something completely lost on me. Where she oohed and aahed the silk crepes, velveteen fur edgings, tasteful embroideries and rhinestone buckles, I only saw one straight, flat gown after another. One thing I was grateful for was that Rebecca never chose the short flapper hairdo for herself. I was partial to her long, dark curls, and she was always creative about how she wore it, sometimes down and flirty, sometimes up and stylishly exotic. I may not have noticed what other women were wearing, but I did notice how happy I was with Rebecca.

"Oh, look," she said as she took my arm and drew me close to whisper, "isn't that Marceline Day? She was wonderful in *The Beloved Rogue*. Remember, with John

Barrymore?"

I was at a loss to recall the woman with the sad eyes from across the room. Rebecca jabbed an elbow into my ribs and laughed.

"Oh, that's right. You fell asleep, as usual," she said.

It was true. I had a propensity for dozing off in movie theaters due to my hectic shooting schedule. Where once I couldn't wait to sit in a darkened theater for hours at a time, I now grew weary after the first reel.

"And isn't that Snitz Edwards?" Rebecca went on.

I did recognize the mature gentleman strolling toward us. It was hard not to remember his unusual, hang-dog face. He often worked with Buster Keaton, of whom I was a fan.

Then it was my turn to point out someone, a robust fellow known for many westerns. "That's Jack Hoxie."

Through the growing crowd of guests Rebecca spotted Helen Gibson, saying, "I thought she left Hollywood for the rodeo. She was much better than Helen Holmes in the *Hazards of Helen* serials, don't you think?"

I agreed. I also thought how she was considered the first stuntwoman, known for her trick-riding, and how my friend Angie Fuller might object to that title.

As Rebecca and I made our way out to the garden-turned-ballroom, I noticed an actress by the name of Edna Purviance, who had been in a number of Charlie Chaplin's films. I pointed her out to Rebecca and said, "There's the next best thing to Chaplin himself."

Rebecca was elated.

The orchestra played popular tunes of the day like "If You See Sally" and "Leonora" as we helped ourselves to the lavish buffet. It was then I saw Mr. Sheldon himself. He seemed as mesmerized by the lush beauty of his garden as any of us, as though he rarely spent time there. He mingled aimlessly, unusually melancholy, seemingly oblivious to the throng of guests around him. Until he saw Rebecca and me.

He blurted our names and his face lit up like a theater marquee. With his bulldog arms around us he said, "I never congratulated the two of you on the happy news!" (It had been weeks since my proposal.)

"Yes. Thank you, Anthony," Rebecca chimed. She remained the only person I knew who got away with calling him by his first name.

"Thank you, Mr. Sheldon," I said and shook his hand. "You might say we owe our engagement to you. If you hadn't made us work together, well..."

"I never intended for the two of you to get married!" he said with a humorless laugh tinged with nerves. "All I saw were profits, Billy. Nothing makes money in this business like love. But marriage? That's a death sentence. To profits, I mean. Love is slippery, you never know where you'll end up, and that's what audiences want. But marriage? Well, marriage is dull. To audiences, I mean. The only thing to cure that dullness is scandal. People will watch a married couple only on the chance that something scandalous will happen. Scandal sells. Scandal and love. Marriage is neither. So we may have to do something scandalous, won't we?"

He laughed again, with even less humor than before.

We left him to enjoy the buffet and sat at a table crowded with an array of Sheldon Pictures employees. Mostly actors. Barry Thompson, Victoria Reade and Smitty Smith are the few I can recall. The only non-performer was my old friend Toby Greene, who I spent most the meal talking with.

At one point, Annie stopped at our table on the arm of a young beau. I don't remember his name. I don't believe he was in the movie business, and I don't recall ever seeing him again after our brief introduction. All I remember was how lovely Annie looked. She was in her mid-twenties then, with the air and confidence of any number of male executives that dominated the industry. She declined our invitation to join us at the table, stating there was no place left to sit. I think, however, it had more to do with her general dislike of actors.

There was a photographer, hired by Mr. Sheldon, roaming about, capturing memories. He stopped by our table and we all squeezed together to get everyone in one shot. What I wouldn't give to see that picture again. It was a playful, childlike moment as we tried to upstage each other, positioning ourselves for the best angle. Rebecca ended up in my lap. We laughed and kissed and smiled at each other, not the camera.

I saw Thomas there, at the far end of the garden, talking with Mr. Sheldon. Their demeanors were business-like, but civil. They spoke briefly then shook hands.

"They're arranging Thomas's last picture," Toby said to me, leaning close.

"What's it going to be about?" I asked.

"I don't know. He's taking some time away to write it, that's all I know."

"How do you know it's his last movie?"

"I heard Sheldon won't be renewing his contract."

"What's he going to do? Find a new studio?"

"I don't know. You'll have to ask him."

I watched Thomas amble amongst the other guests, Elizabeth by his side, and realized how far apart we'd gotten. I hadn't spoken to him since yelling at him for the stampede. There was a time I didn't have to talk to someone else to know what was going on with my friend. Others would come to me for insight. While our time together was just a short interlude in his long life, he was a part of mine more than anyone. He was my best friend. For a time, he was my only friend. I felt that if he went to another studio, or stopped making pictures altogether, I would never see him again. The thought of that left me downhearted.

The touch of Rebecca's hand distracted my pensive musings as she pulled me from my chair and onto the dance floor.

I will never be remembered as a dancer. But, the gaiety of the evening, the music, and the beauty of the ladies swept my feet into such rhythmic steps the like of which I'd never known before or since. My newfound hoofing surprised and delighted Rebecca. We danced to songs like "Nothing Could be Sweeter," "Let's Make Believe," and "I'll Just Go Along." Eyes and smiles were upon us as we glided over the dance floor, drawing everyone else along in the wake of our lightness and joy.

The music slowed to a more romantic tempo, and I pulled Rebecca close. I felt so much—

"Billy! Is that Billy Colter?" a woman's voice, quite loud and exuberant, came from behind us, breaking our blissful spell.

I turned to see Faith Monroe. She danced with a heavy gentleman in an ill-fitting suit who was surprisingly light on his feet. Something in the way he gleefully glared at me and Rebecca was vaguely familiar, but my attention couldn't help but be on Faith. She was as beautiful as ever, now sophisticated and mature. The sequined gown she wore gave her a look of royalty. It all sent me into stunned silence.

"Oh, Billy, don't say you don't remember me! I'd be heartbroken!" she said with a flirtatious pout.

"Billy, who is this?" Rebecca interjected with a wary tone.

Before I could answer, Faith extended a hand and said, "Faith Cassidy, Miss Faye. I do enjoy your work."

Rebecca warmly took the hand of a woman with whom I'd once been intimate. Faith had always had that way about her. She could soften the growl of a grizzly, if only for a moment.

"Cassidy?" I asked her, finally finding my voice.

"Yes. I'm married, again."

"Again?"

"Oh, my, it has been a long time, hasn't it?"

"This is Mr. Cassidy, then?" Rebecca queried with the hint of a vindictive grin, nodding to Faith's portly partner.

Faith laughed. "Oh, no! This is my newest dear friend, Jonathon Cabot. Mr. Cassidy is at home. His rheumatism. He's not up to evenings out these days. Jonathon and I met just the other day. I caught him following me while I shopped, and I was just about to call the police on him when we started talking, and I found him to be so sweet and harmless and as gentlemanly an escort a lady could have."

"And quite a dancer," Rebecca added. She introduced herself to Mr. Cabot, who responded with the high pitched shrill one would expect from an adolescent girl meeting Valentino.

"Would it be rude to ask for an autograph?" he asked.

"Of course it would!" snapped Faith. "An evening like this should be a respite from adoring fans. Leave them be."

Duly reprimanded, Cabot's face folded into the most comical frown, his eyes drooping like a scolded puppy.

"How do you know Billy, Mrs. Cassidy?" asked Rebecca.

"We used to act together. We made small, unimportant movies in the mountains of Arizona. My, that place was horrid!"

"Yes, he's told me about those days," replied Rebecca, "But he didn't mention you."

"What? Oh, Billy," Faith responded with a bit of melodrama.

"In my defense," I said, "I don't believe I've mentioned *anyone* from those days. Except for Thomas, whom you know."

"And Toby. And Mr. Grady," said Rebecca.

"Well, yes. But there were others there, as well."

"How *is* Thomas?" bubbled Faith.

"He's as well as can be expected, I reckon," I answered. "He's here tonight. You should find him. I'm sure he would be delighted to see you."

Faith looked around the garden for a moment, but she did not take my bait to leave us and keep me from further awkwardness. Instead, she let her hands down from Mr. Cabot and said, "Would you mind if we switched?" Then she turned to Rebecca. "Would you mind, dear, if I had a dance with an old friend?"

Cabot could barely contain his excitement as he made a move at me. Faith scolded him again and motioned him toward Rebecca, who obliged Faith by relinquishing her hold upon me. "Of course," she said unconvincingly and gave me a kiss on the cheek before being swept off by the large Mr. Cabot.

Without missing a beat, Faith continued our conversation, now in a quieter, more intimate tone. "How is Thomas…truly? I've read that he's had spells."

"I didn't know that was public knowledge," I said.

"Dear, everything is public here. Perhaps it's some consolation that he's blissfully lost to know about all that goes on in this town."

"I don't believe that's the case with him. I think he's very aware of what's happening to him and around him. It leaves him discouraged and tired."

"It's hard losing someone close to us," she said, "especially when it's slowly." Faith's genuine concern was comforting.

We danced in silence for a moment. I glanced over to Rebecca who feigned a look of interest as Cabot pratted on about who-knows-what.

"I was so saddened about the news of Alan," Faith broke in. "He was a dear man. Maybe not the greatest director, but a dear, sweet man. Did he pass quickly?"

"He died in his sleep after being sick for a long while," I said.

"That's how I would like to go, wouldn't you? Just lie back and fall asleep. Forever."

I asked her if she knew of anything about the others from Prescott.

"That old curmudgeon Charles Benz did some theatrical plays in New York, but who knows after that. And Anna Beth, she used to write me letters. She came into some money a few years back, a dead aunt, I think, and opened a clothing business in Chicago. She never did settle down with a beau last I heard."

"What about Arty?" I asked. "I kind of liked him, though I know he was not so fond of me."

"Oh, that poor man. He tried harder than anybody to

make it in this business. But, I mean, had you seen him in anything?"

"No, I can't say I have."

"The movies didn't need another Arbunkle."

"What happened to him?"

"He went and killed himself."

"I didn't know," I said, thinking somehow that I should have.

"Few people did," Faith replied with a shrug. She looked to Rebecca dancing with her new friend. "Do you love her?"

"I can't say I've ever loved another more," I replied.

"She is very beautiful."

"One of the most beautiful."

Faith snapped her gaze from Rebecca to me. "*One* of the most? If your love is so pure she should be *the* most beautiful woman you've ever seen! That was how you thought of me once, wasn't it? Wasn't I the most beautiful woman you'd ever seen?"

"Well…" I said with a thought, calculating the trap waiting to snare me, "at the time you were. I hadn't much experience around women before meeting you. But since coming to California—"

"Where we're a-dime-a-dozen," she sighed. Then, goading me further, she said, "So, truly, I needn't have been much prettier than a horse and you'd have thought me the most beautiful ever. Simply by comparison."

"I don't know about that. I *had* seen a lot of horses by then in my life, some of them quite beautiful."

She laughed, like the teasing, vivacious Faith I knew.

Then I went on, "What I have learned is that there are a lot of beautiful women in the world. But there's only one Faith. And," I gazed to Rebecca, my bride-to-be, "there is only one Rebecca."

Faith's gaze followed mine. When I turned back to her, I saw something in her face...regret...envy...I wasn't sure. I relaxed my arms to bring our dance to an end but she tightened and held on.

"One more song," she said.

I obliged. Then I asked her about the two Johns whose names I could never remember.

"They opened an art gallery together here in Los Angeles," she replied. "They're lovers, you know. Homosexual." She laughed at my surprise. "It's quite common in our business, you know. Your fiancé is dancing with one right now."

I looked at Rebecca and Cabot. Then he looked at me. There was a *crazed* glare in his eyes, and I realized who he was—the fan in front of the restaurant! I released Faith and hurried across the dance floor. I wrenched Cabot's hands from Rebecca's and pulled her to my side.

"Billy! What's going on?" Rebecca and Faith seemed to say in unison.

"It's time for you to leave," I told Cabot. He hesitated, and I emphasized, "Now!"

I ignored him as he stammered in his defense. I turned first to Rebecca, saying, "He was in front of the restaurant that night. Remember? The police had to drag him away." Then I turned to Faith. "How could you bring him here? You barely know him. You endangered Rebecca."

"What are you talking about?" exclaimed Faith. "He's done no harm."

"I'm sorry, Billy," whined Cabot. "I just wanted to meet you."

He grabbed my arm with such intensity that I reacted with my fist to his jaw and he went down. He was crying as Faith knelt by his side. I moved Rebecca away, and the crowd that had gathered parted.

The orchestra wisely began to play once more. The disruption quickly passed and everyone went back to their gaiety. Rebecca got me to calm by dancing. As I watched Faith lead Cabot from the dance floor, she asked, "Did you enjoy reminiscing with her?"

"I suppose," I answered after a pause. "But they're just memories, and should stay that way. It's good to see she got what she always wanted, though."

"How about you, Billy?' Rebecca teased with the sweetest of smiles. "Have you got everything you've always wanted?"

I looked into Rebecca's blue eyes and was hit with a torrent of thoughts. Yes, Thomas and I had come to California looking for simple work and found wealth beyond our imaginations, but I had wondered at times if I wouldn't have been happier on a ranch somewhere for little pay from a hard day's work. Satisfying work, not frivolous like acting. There had always been something uncomfortable inside of me knowing that men toiled away their lives in factories for pennies a day while I was doing nothing more than posing before a camera for thousands of dollars a week. My work, my life, was shameful.

And yet, without it, I would not have met Rebecca. So at that moment, there with her on Mr. Sheldon's dance floor, I couldn't see my life any better. I couldn't imagine a future without her. I smiled and answered her, "Everything and more."

Seventeen

It can tear across the land like a juggernaut.
It can rest upon the earth, no fury wrought.
But a storm brings change, unwanted or not.

I woke up in a hospital. I had no idea how I got there. Yet another blackout from bathtub-gin. But I knew where I was. Maybe it was the uncomfortable, metal bedframe, or the metal table and chair next to me. Or maybe it was the cold cleanness of the room. Or the quiet. I was either in a hospital room or a morgue. Yes, for the briefest of moments I thought I was dead. But that changed with the unbearable sensation of pain I was feeling in my throat. I assumed a person didn't feel pain when they were dead, so, by the quickest path of realization I could manage in my groggy consciousness, I decided I was in a hospital room, recovering from what could have only been the most raucous of parties. What I couldn't figure out was why my throat hurt so bad.

I lay there for what seemed a whole morning before I thought, *is it morning?* My sense of time was so off-kilter I had no idea if it was early or late. Or what day it was. I only assumed it was the day after the Sheldon Pictures party but really had no idea. I gazed out the window in hopes of determining if the sunlight was that of dawn or dusk or somewhere in between.

Eventually, a nurse came into the room. She had a motherly yet stoic look about her. She didn't smile as she looked at me and said, "You're awake. Good."

I began to ask her the time and about what had happened to me only to find I couldn't speak, and it was extremely painful to try. I tried again and winced. I touched the bandages covering the left side of my neck. She took a small blackboard and piece of chalk from the bedside table and curtly placed them in my hands. Then, just as curtly, she said, "You shouldn't speak until your throat has healed. Write down whatever you have to say here."

The chalk's clicking upon the board reverberated through the quiet of the room as I wrote, "WHAT DAY IS IT?"

"Tuesday," the nurse replied.

So it had been two days since the party, I surmised. "WHAT HAPPENED TO ME?" I scribbled.

The nurse turned sharply away and said as she was leaving, "The doctor will be in shortly to answer your questions."

By her behavior, I couldn't help but guess that

whatever happened couldn't have been very good. I laid my head back, closed my eyes and tried hard to remember the last thing I could remember.

I was dancing with Rebecca. I remembered that. And Faith was there. Did I dance with her, too? Of course, later on I would slowly recall the details, just as I've written about them. But for a time my memories of that night were a shadowy blur. Especially after the dancing and how I came to be in the hospital, which to this day is an incomplete puzzle.

I could see myself shaking hands with lots of people. Directors and stars, friends and strangers. And I could recall music, melodies echoing repetitiously in my head. Then I saw Rebecca and I doing some kind of...pantomime? Finally, I could see me helping her into, or out of, my car, both of us barely able to walk. She took my hand and stumbled to my arms. It was a miracle if I was able to drive a block. Maybe that was it! I had driven us into a tree, or an even more terrible accident!

But, I could remember kissing her. And a sudden burning in my throat.

That was it. I could muster no recollection as to the cause of my injury, or what happened to Rebecca, or anything to fill in the blanks.

After what seemed hours, a doctor came into my

room. He was my height and twice the weight with a calm manner yet tense, serious eyes. He saw that I was awake and asked me how I was feeling. Instinctively, I tried to speak then cringed from the pain.

"You're lucky to be alive, Mr. Colter," the doctor said (he never did introduce himself). He bent over me and examined my bandages. "You could have very easily bled to death with a wound like this. As it is, you'll just be in a fair amount of pain for a while. Don't try to speak. The best chance you have to get your voice back is to keep quiet and let it heal."

He turned to leave but I stopped him with an ache-filled grunt. Upon my chalkboard I drew a question mark and an arrow and pointed it toward my throat.

"You don't remember what happened?" said the doctor.

I nodded and gave him a pleading, confused look.

"It's a gunshot wound, Mr. Colter," he said, as impartially as he could. Then, as he left the room, added, "Apparently self-inflicted."

⇛ ⇛ ⇛

I shot myself? I shot myself. How could that have happened? Was I cleaning my gun, unaware it was loaded? Why would

I have been doing that in such a state of drunkenness? Or was I toying with it, showing off for Rebecca? Yes, I could see myself doing that.

Well, no, I couldn't see myself doing that. I couldn't see myself doing anything. I could only lay there and imagine no more than what I've already recalled above.

There was a clamor of voices outside my door, like a crowd of people in the hall. It sounded as though they would burst through the door. I heard a lot of questions being shouted back and forth. I knew it was the press. No one else would be as loud and insistent with their inquiries. I could also hear an authoritative voice telling the crowd I was not allowed any visitors. *Thank you*, I thought, *whoever you are. A room full of hungry reporters is the last thing I need.*

The door opened just enough for a thin nurse to squeeze through. She took a moment to catch her breath before turning to me. *Funny, she looks remarkably like*—Annie!

She shushed me to stay quiet. I pointed to my throat and gave a comical shrug. She did not respond to the humor in kind, but reached out and tenderly touched my bandages.

"Oh, my God, Billy," she whispered. "It *is* true." She caressed my forehead. "What happened, Billy? Oh, what have you done?"

I grabbed my chalkboard and wrote, "I CAN'T REMEMBER." Then I gestured to her nurse's uniform.

"I borrowed this from the costume department. The police are only allowing hospital personnel in here. There's a crazy big crowd of reporters and fans all around the building wondering what happened."

"I WISH I KNEW," I wrote. "NO ONE WILL TELL ME." And, "MAYBE REBECCA CAN SAY."

I was embarrassed and uneasy that I hadn't considered Rebecca until that moment. Then that uneasiness turned to a knot in my stomach as Annie's complexion paled. And the knot became nausea as her big brown eyes filled with tears.

"You really don't know?" she choked. "No one's told you anything?"

I couldn't write, but only give a fearful stare.

"The police found the two of you at your home. You'd both been shot. You were in a chair. The gun, *your* gun, was lying on the floor next to you." The rest of her words were broken and lost beneath her crying. But I heard enough to understand.

Rebecca was dead.

I was wretchedly sick to my stomach. Too shocked to cry, I looked around the room for some kind of escape. I tried to sit up but was still too weak and painful. I never wanted anything more in my life than to get out of that room and get back to that night, to remember what happened, to get back to Rebecca.

Annie struggled to compose herself, futilely wiping away the tears. "They say you shot her and then shot yourself. But no one knows why. No one knows anything. They're just guessing. That's why I had to sneak in here. I don't believe it! I don't believe you could have done what they say. Only you know, Billy. You have to remember. Oh, God, what happened?"

That's when I began to cry, like I've never cried, ever. What foolish thing did I do that took Rebecca's life? Tears came, but no memories. The injury to my throat was now nothing compared to the agony in my heart. I wanted to die.

Annie gripped my hand. But she didn't say that everything would be okay, and that I would be fine. Not this time, because it wasn't true.

She stayed just long enough for me to calm down. "I have to go," she said. "It'll look suspicious if I'm in here too long."

I held her hand to stay, but I knew she was right.

"I'll come back as often as I can. You need to rest, and heal." She kissed my forehead. "And remember."

The hallway exploded with voices as she left the room. Newsmen bombarded her with questions. I could only hope that her scheme wouldn't be discovered and she would be able to visit me again. At that moment, Annie was my only friend in the world.

∾ ∾ ∾

Real nurses came and went through my room the rest of that first day and into the next morning. I was eventually visited by the police in the rumpled form of Detective Dennis Collier. His rumpled-ness wasn't so much in his clothing but in *him*. In his eyes, his face, his posture he wore the burden of finding unpleasant truths, and it weighed him down such that, after introducing himself, he slumped into my room's only chair. He removed his hat and took a moment to look about the space.

"You're under arrest, Mr. Colter," he said finally, "for the murder of Rebecca Faye, and for your own attempted suicide." He studied me and waited. "Nothing to say about that, huh?"

I sighed, and then pointed at my wound and the chalkboard at my bedside.

"Oh, yeah, that's right." He straightened up in his chair and cleared his throat. "You wanna try and tell me what happened? It would save us both a lot of trouble."

I wrote what I would end up writing many times in the weeks to follow: **I CAN'T REMEMBER.** (I should've had a sign made of it.)

● ● ●

The detective adjusted the hat upon his lap and cleared his throat again. "You don't remember anything?"

"I REMEMBER DANCING WITH REBECCA, AND WAKING UP HERE."

"Well," he replied as he stood, with effort, and put on his hat, "that is inconvenient. I hope you have a good lawyer, Mr. Colter. You're gonna need it."

He shuffled to the door. I stopped him by tapping on my board.

"WHY BOTHER WITH A TRIAL? WHY NOT HANG ME NOW?" I had begun to weary of the guilty-until-proven-innocent notion I was getting from him and others.

The detective responded with an apologetic shrug. "As soon as the doctor says you're ready, we'll be moving you to a jail cell. Until then, if I provided you with pen and paper, could you write down everything you remember?"

I nodded.

"Good day, Mr. Colter." He turned to leave but stopped and added, "About that lawyer. If you don't already have one, I recommend Harvey Wells. He's the best I know."

ॐ   ॐ   ॐ

My short meeting with Detective Collier was the dose of

clarity I needed. On one of Annie's disguised visitations, I asked her to contact Harvey Wells. And then I put all the conscious effort I could into remembering what happened that fateful night.

I closed my eyes and thought hard, and wrote down any detail, no matter how small, that came to me. The tiara Rebecca wore. What we ate, some kind of fish, I recalled. And the faces, so many faces, of the people that were there. Unfortunately, I was so drugged with pain-killers that I would often fall asleep as I meditated, and wake to a nurse or doctor standing over me.

Before long, those small recollections led to bigger ones. The details of Mr. Sheldon's home. His garden. The speech he made to the two of us. Faith, and her escort, Cabot. Most of all, how it felt to dance with Rebecca. I played the images over and over in my head until I finally saw something new.

I saw us with a group of others, in Mr. Sheldon's library or study, play-acting some kind of scene. I heard us arguing, playfully, not in anger. I saw me driving us up to my house. I knew it was after the party and not some random memory of me behind the wheel. It was dark. Rebecca was going on about wedding plans. Something about wanting to go to Europe for the honeymoon. Paris. That's where artists went.

Then I heard a gunshot.

I opened my eyes to a stranger sitting in my room. By the way he smiled at me I thought he was an old friend I couldn't remember, yet there was nothing familiar about him. Except for the streaks of gray in his hair, he looked to be about my age. He held himself in his chair with vigor and confidence, and something about the Brooks Brothers suit he wore said he'd earned it. There was a sincerity in his eyes I took to right away.

As the gunshot I'd dreamt still rang in my head, the handsome stranger seemed to know what I was thinking and said, "A car backfired down the street. It startled you awake. Everything's fine." A faint east coast accent affected his speech. He put his hand out and I took it. "I'm Harvey Wells, Mr. Colter. I heard you could use a lawyer."

He sat back down and his friendly manner became professional and serious.

"Let me begin by saying how sorry I am for your loss. I'd never met Miss Faye, but I've enjoyed her motion pictures. While I believe very little of what's printed in our newspapers, anyone could see by the photographs how much the two of you meant to each other."

He set aside the hat he'd been holding and pulled a leather briefcase into his lap, removing blank paper and a pencil from it.

"I'm going to be honest with you, Billy. It doesn't look good. On the surface, this case is closed before it's opened. But I wouldn't be very good at my job if I left it at that, and my job is to find you innocent, or at the very least, find extenuating circumstances to lessen the charges against you."

"I DIDN'T KILL HER!" I wrote.

"I understand, and I apologize for suggesting otherwise. But we have to *prove* you innocent, and the evidence is stacked against you. That's where I come in. Finding the truth is not always in the best interest of the police. But the truth is always there, beneath the surface, sometimes very deep, and I always find it. You can help me by writing down everything you can remember."

He handed me the paper and pencil. I stopped him and gave him, instead, the pages of notes I had been making for Detective Collier. He took a few minutes to read them.

"This is a good start. I'll take these. Continue writing down anything you can recall. You'll never know what minor detail may save your life."

I wrote down that the notes were for the detective.

He slipped them into his briefcase and said, "I'll be working with Detective Collier—" He stopped at my concern and laughed. "He may not look it, but he's a good detective. One of the few I trust. I wouldn't say we were friends, but we do work well together."

With a confident tip of his hat, he turned to leave. "I'll be in touch. Oh, and don't talk to anybody–*anybody*–about *anything*."

He left me with the reassurance I wasn't alone or crazy. I had Annie, Wells, and even slovenly Detective Collier on my side. I was able to lay back with a grain of peace-of-mind.

❧   ❧   ❧

One morning, a nurse came into my room, which was nothing unusual. But this one skulked about the room, doing non-nurse things for a minute before I noticed her oddness. I tapped my chalkboard to get her attention.

I went sick in my stomach as she turned to me. Those heavily massacred eyes. The layers of makeup covering her snake-like skin. The way she crept across the floor. Judy McDonald!

"Hello, Billy. You look well." Her plastered smile became a fake frown. "Well, no, you don't actually. Does that hurt? Are you in much pain?"

I slapped her hand away as she reached for my bandage. If I could have called for help I would have.

"Oh, how stupid of me," she went on, her voice a hiss

as she tried not to talk too loud, "of course you're in pain, aren't you? I can only imagine how devastated your heart is." She pulled the chair closer to the bed and sat, just out of arm's reach.

I pounded out two words, breaking my chalk. "GET OUT!"

"I'll be leaving soon enough. I wanted to see how you were doing."

I thrusted a finger toward the door.

"I'm here for your fans, Billy. They're worried about you. They want to know how you are."

"ASK THE DOCTOR."

"He'll only tell me how you're doing on the outside. But I...*we*...want to know how you are on the inside, deep down."

My best smoldering glare had no effect upon her.

"There's something else we want to know."

I threw my hands up in resignation.

"Why did you do it, Billy? How could you kill that poor, sweet girl?"

I surprised her, and myself, by flinging my covers off and rolling from the bed. I grabbed her arms and lifted her from the chair, which tumbled with metallic clamor against the wall. She rattled on like a Tommy gun as I pushed her toward the door.

"She was your betrothed! What drove you to do such a heinous thing? Jealousy? Was there another man? Or another woman? You were seen dancing with Faith Cassidy. Was it her? If you didn't kill her, who else was there that night?"

I came very close to putting my fist into that woman's face. Not because of what she was saying, but because of the pleasure she took in saying it. The glint in her eye. I wanted to smash the joy she took in raking muck and stirring untruths.

Instead, I threw open the door loud enough for the police officer down the hall to hear. He stood between my room and a number of reporters and photographers. The hallway went as hush as a library at the sight of me standing there in my disheveled gown, exposing parts unknown, with both hands gripping Judy. She hung there, frozen like an ornery cat by the scruff, until I shoved her at the officer. He took her from me with an embarrassed glance, and a photographer whipped up his camera for a shot. I slammed the door closed before the lot of them could rush my room.

I went to the window in hopes of calming down. I looked out to see a crowd gathered, spilling into the street. They were there for me? It was nothing compared to the crowds that mourned Valentino's death the year before, but there were so many people. Did they despair for me? Or were they a lynch mob? I didn't want to know. I was fearful of either scenario. I stepped away from the window before someone saw me.

As much as I wanted to collapse, I paced my bedside because of something Judy had said. *Who else was there that night?* It provoked a memory, an image of someone in the shadows. It wasn't because that snake had planted an illusion in my head. No, I was remembering something. Something important. Someone had been hiding in my house, and they had waited for Rebecca and me to come home.

When I saw Detective Collier again, I told him.

"Who was it?" he asked.

"I DON'T KNOW. THEY WERE IN THE DARK."

"Do you have any evidence that they were there?"

I pointed to my bandaged throat.

With a laugh he replied, "You're going to make me earn my meager paycheck, aren't you?"

I shrugged and couldn't help but grin. I was beginning to like that sloppy detective. In some ways, he reminded me of Thomas.

Eighteen

A sheet of cold laid out
from crystals gently falling.
They announce a new season's come about.
Nothing else makes that sound.

As Detective Collier had said, I was moved from my cold, white hospital room to a cold, gray jail cell as soon as I was cleared by the doctor. The pain in my throat had subsided, but it would still be some time before I could speak. The doctor was impressed with how quickly I was up and walking around on my own, evident by my physically removing Judy McDonald from my room, and by my late night pacing.

I welcomed my new accommodations. They would be a respite from the "adoring" public and the meddlesome horde of reporters. (My incident with Judy was not the last. One bold photographer managed to climb a tree outside my window. I doubt the picture he got was any good, but I'm sure it made the front page.) At my arraignment, I refused bail. I didn't want to go home, there wasn't anything for me there. I knew the world outside would offer me nothing until

• • •

I was found innocent. My cell became my sanctuary.

I don't know how it was with other suspected murderers, but I was treated well in jail. The guards were courteous and familiar, calling me Billy like we were old friends, and I signed more autographs than I could count. I concluded that the guards saw me as one of their own because in my movies I'd often played characters who were likable, hard-working common-folk. But Hollywood is an industry built on illusions. Mary Pickford wasn't all that innocent, and she was much older and richer than the impoverished waifs she was known to portray. Chaplin was no lovable tramp.

I was allowed many more visitors than the average criminal, too, I think. The guards would kindly tell me who was there to see me, and if I didn't know them, they would be sent away. Annie would visit every day. Elizabeth came to see me once, explaining that Thomas was too engrossed in writing his next movie and it wouldn't have been good to distract him. I told her I'd rather he didn't see me like I was, so it was fine. Like Annie, Elizabeth never questioned my innocence.

"The truth will come out, Billy," she assured me. She squeezed my hands with her strong fingers and nearly brought me to tears. But I had cried so much by then that my despair was exhausted.

I grew weary of thinking about my own situation so I asked her, "HOW'S THOMAS?"

Her posture slumped slightly and I could tell that she had been weathering her own dark clouds. "He never leaves his study," she explained. "He's working on something very important to him."

"THAT'S GOOD, ISN'T IT?"

"Yes, of course. But he found inspiration in things not so good. Like that stampede. It devastated him what happened. He grieved for days. And then you and Rebecca. And…"

She paused, and in that quiet moment, the abundant tangle of feelings she had for him was evident. She once told me their relationship began as romantic, and then settled. But it had not lessened. Anyone could see it had become so much more.

"He received a letter the other day, from Denver," she said. "Ellen Marie passed away. She had been sick for some time, complications from syphilis, and she finally succumbed to it. When he read it, I thought he had died himself. He wouldn't eat or sleep. I couldn't get him to speak to me. Then he started writing, and that's all he's been doing for a week now. He works until he falls asleep in his chair. I have to remind him to eat and use the bathroom. Otherwise he works, and nothing stops him. He writes as though it's going to be the last words he's ever going to write. His epitaph."

We sat in silence, mutually reflecting on that old man.

Elizabeth did not visit me again after that. She would apologize later but I told her there wasn't a need. I could never feel bitter toward her.

I was disappointed, however, that Faith didn't come to see me. I had hoped she would tell something about that night, something that would spark more memories of my own. Mr. Sheldon did not visit, either.

"He's too broken-hearted," Annie told me during one of our talks. "Some days he doesn't even come in to work. She was like a daughter to him, a *real* daughter." Annie was not normally prone to self-pity. It added to my own melancholy to see her like that. "He stopped carrying his pistol," she also said. "I guess that's one thing good to come of this."

How a singular event could have such an effect over so many people! I could only helplessly watch it roll outward like ripples on a cold lake.

And what of Maggie?

I heard nothing from either of Rebecca's parents. Did they even know? I hated to think they would've gotten the news from a front-page headline. Perhaps they did and Maggie hated me, blaming me for Rebecca's death. She was prone to believe everything printed in the papers, and according to Annie, I was being portrayed as guilty beyond a doubt. Hell, until I fully regained my memory, even I couldn't be sure of my innocence.

I'd also considered the thought that if her mother had not gone back to San Francisco, Rebecca would still be alive. It was a thought that spurred a memory: one of Rebecca calling out to her mother. But, without context, it was nothing but a ghost of an image that echoed when I least expected, and then faded away.

❧   ❧   ❧

While visitations from friends left me hopeful, it was my meetings with Harvey Wells and Detective Collier that I most looked forward to. Having investigated the crime scene on his own, Collier made me anxious to hear what he'd found one day as he flipped through his notebook.

"There was a lot of blood in the foyer," he began, then stopped. "Sorry. These details could be a little unsettling. Are you okay with this?"

I nodded.

"There was a gun, a thirty-eight caliber Colt, lying on the floor a few feet from a chair just as you enter the home. Five of the six chambers were discharged. There were smudged fingerprints on the Colt, but enough was lifted to indicate they were yours. Two slugs were found in the wall behind where Ms. Faye is presumed to have been standing. This leads us to believe she was fired upon four times, being shot in the chest twice. You, of course, were hit once in the throat. You were found slumped in the chair."

He paused to see how I was doing before he continued. I listened as best I could, without reacting, to the cold facts he presented. But inside, I was raging with determination. I was going to find Rebecca's killer. Or hang for her death. I didn't want to live otherwise.

"You own a gun, correct?"

I nodded.

"Is this it?" he asked as he showed me a photograph of a pistol lying on the rug in the foyer of my home. It was mine. My left hand was also in the picture, my limp arm dangling from the chair. There was blood on my hand. I looked away and nodded in response to his question.

"Where do you keep your gun?"

"BEDROOM."

"Now, you say you remember seeing someone else there. Can you remember where they were standing, or where they came from?"

"IN THE SHADOWS. FROM IN THE HOUSE."

"So, if there were someone else there that night," he surmised to himself, "they would have gone all the way into the house and to your bedroom to get the gun, then waited in the dark until you got home. It could have been someone you know, who knows you have a gun and where you kept it. Or it could have been a robber who just happened to find the gun, and the two of you caught him in the act."

He stopped to allow his thoughts to settle like stirred up dust. He then asked, "Was anything missing from your home?"

I shrugged.

"Of course you wouldn't know," he quickly said. "You haven't been home since…"

After a moment of his silence, I wrote, "YOU BELIEVE ME."

As though I'd nudged a groggy bear, the detective collected himself and replied, "Frankly, no. I don't." He stood to leave. "But Harvey Wells does, and he's not often wrong."

❧   ❧   ❧

Together, the detective and Harvey Wells had begun the tedious task of locating and interviewing everyone that had attended Mr. Sheldon's party, from Sheldon himself to the guests on down to the caterers and the musicians. While Collier would stop in to see me every day with an update or a question, a number of days went by before I saw Wells again. He was friendly when he showed up, but I appreciated that he didn't muddy our time with pleasantries and got directly to business.

"We've talked to everyone that was there that night," he began. "Everyone we could find, that is, which was nearly everyone." He saw my expression of disbelief and said, "Yes, it was quite an undertaking. I apologize for not keeping you apprised of my activities, but I like to be thorough, and that tends to make me aloof."

He removed an impressive stack of papers from his briefcase and grinned, again, at the look on my face. With a laugh, he said, "Don't worry. I'll summarize. Let me know if you can add anything, or if there's anything amiss."

From there, he went through each page. His idea of summarizing was still fairly detailed and he recounted every moment of that evening of which I've already written, and then some. Apparently, once Rebecca and I had finished dancing, after the incident with Jonathon Cabot, we went into Mr. Sheldon's study for a rousing game of charades.

"After that, there are a number of accounts that say the two of you argued. Do you know what that might have been about?"

I was giddy because a memory came clearly back to me! And then I laughed recalling our argument. "REBECCA

WAS VERY COMPETETIVE," I wrote. "SHE HATED MY CHARADE CLUES."

"So you're saying the argument was nothing to kill her over."

The humor quickly left me and I wrote, "NEVER!" with a snap of my chalk.

"I'm sorry for putting it like that, but the prosecuting attorney is going to look for anything he can to hang guilt upon you."

I shrugged, nodded and calmly wrote, "AND THEN HANG ME."

Wells smiled grimly and continued. "A few people saw you leave a short time later, stumbling to your car and driving away a bit erratically."

"DRUNKENLY."

"And you remember nothing further after that."

I shook my head.

"Except that someone else was in your house when you arrived. Are you still sure about that?"

I nodded, and he could see my frustration with not being able to remember any more details.

"The most important thing right now, Billy, is that we prove that you did not shoot Rebecca, that someone else was there, and that someone else pulled the trigger. Who that person was doesn't matter right now."

"IT MATTERS TO ME!"

"Yes. It matters to me, too. But right now you're innocence matters to me more. I need to show the court that it wasn't you, which I think will be a lot easier than finding the real killer. Once that's done, we'll find whoever did this heinous act."

I resigned. "HOW?"

"Let me begin by asking you: are you right or left handed?"

"RIGHT."

"That's what I thought. Now, trust me. I'll take care of the rest from here."

Nineteen

Trail dust turns to sand on the shore

packed hard by the water,

Coarsened by the wind,

punished into going no farther.

Here the cowboy-journey's done

I won't go into great detail about the trial, frankly because I don't recall much of it. The tedium of the process often frustrated me to distraction. I only remember what mattered.

"Good news," Wells told me one morning, "Richard Kopecky is the prosecuting attorney. Kopecky is an opportunistic publicity hound. I'm sure he knows there's not enough hard evidence to incriminate you. He just wants the attention. Don't be surprised if you see him running for office next year. Winning this case means nothing to him. It might even be better for him if he loses. All that he cares about is being in the limelight, because that's all the mindless voters will remember. It's absurd that we are even going to trial."

This did little to put me at ease. It didn't say anything

good about our justice system, and I wanted nothing to do with being part of the circus that is politics. It did serve as a diversion, however, that kept from me thinking too much about Rebecca.

It's a cruel thing that someone leaves our world but not our heart and mind. The feeling of her presence, when I allowed it, was as powerful as if we were once again warming by a smoky campfire or riding a bumpy train—it was such a wretched ache that I'd wished I could die myself, or suffer greater amnesia and forget her and everything. Anything to make the torment end. And that would make me feel worse because, truly, I wanted to never forget her.

What riled me most was why anyone would want to harm Rebecca. I concluded that it was somehow because of me. I may not have pulled the trigger, but I was in some small part responsible for her death. I, and a madman.

Harvey Wells could see I was in quite the wicked, emotional state. Which is why, I think, he kept telling me, "Don't worry. I'll take care of the rest."

And it didn't help that my throat still hurt. The healing was going slow, and I still relied upon my chalkboard when it came time for the trial.

$$\approx \quad \approx \quad \approx$$

It seemed the whole world was crammed into that courtroom. The crowd flooded the hall and flowed out to the courthouse steps. I could tell by their glares and murmurs that most were looking to see me hang—even if Harvey Wells proved me innocent. I clutched my chalkboard as though it were my only friend.

I got my first look at Kopecky, the prosecuting attorney. At a glance, you'd think he was a dandy. His soft features and delicate hands hinted at a pampered upbringing. His suit was impeccable, and something about his sharp, cutting manner reminded me of a long, finely crafted knife used for filleting fish. He entered the courtroom and proceeded directly to his station. He didn't appear to notice our presence, or was simply choosing to ignore us, and laid out multiple stacks of papers just so on the table before him.

Being on trial is not something I wish upon anyone. It is about being on display in the least flattering manner possible. You are not there to be praised, but drawn and quartered. Kopecky's case, as Wells had predicted, was thin and superficial. But it was also scathing and unforgiving. He began by showing photographs of the murder scene.

"I apologize, ladies and gentlemen of the jury and those here in the courtroom," the prosecutor said. His composed voice and clear tone filled the room like smoke from smoldering embers. "The nature of these images is disturbing and shocking. But the death, *the murder*, of this poor, young girl *is* a shock. To all of us."

You can guess that I couldn't bear to see those images. But I had to, if only a glimpse. Both of us still wore our coats. It seemed we had barely made it through the front door before the shadowed figure appeared. I sat limp in the chair, a mere arm's-length away from Rebecca, helplessly staring down at her as she lay on the floor of my foyer, a pool of black beneath her, a startled look upon her face. I turned away at the sight of her wide, dark eyes.

As the prosecutor spoke, describing the gruesome scene, he made it a point to say her name repeatedly. Sometimes with tenderness, sometimes with sadness, even forcing his voice to crack occasionally.

"He's trying to create sympathy for her," Harvey whispered to me, "and turn the court against you."

Kopecky proceeded to present his case in this dramatic fashion. He didn't merely show my pistol as evidence but held it up high for all to see. "Billy Colter's gun!" he announced. "The murder weapon! One and the same!" Holding it next to the photograph of me in the chair, the Colt on the floor beside me, he said, "See it lay there, five chambers empty: four for…Rebecca…and one for himself, after the realization of the horrible, unforgivable thing that he'd done. Members of the jury, with a verdict of 'guilty' you can help this poor, disturbed man finish what he started. Not to send him to a better place, no, that is reserved for the likes of this poor, innocent girl. Rather, send him to the only place he deserves to be—hell!"

After the photographs and the gun, Kopecky began to call witnesses, half-a-dozen or so people I didn't recognize. They were Mr. Sheldon's domestic staff who had worked the night of the party as servers, and the prosecutor asked each about my behavior that evening.

"He seemed to me he was enjoying himself there like everyone else," said one woman who held herself straight and proud as though overcompensating for her lot in life. "He was high-spirited and gentlemanly."

"And at no time he acted untoward in any way?" Kopecky questioned.

"Well…"

"Yes?"

"He did hit another gentleman. Knocked him right down."

An older gentleman, Mr. Sheldon's groundskeeper, I think, told the court, "He danced with a woman who was not Miss Faye for a time. Quite some time, actually."

"I-I saw him arguing," said a young gal with eyes as big as saucers and a downtrodden posture.

"With whom?" Kopecky asked her.

"Miss Faye."

"Can you tell us what they were arguing about?"

"N-no. Not exactly. They were whispering, s-so as not to attract attention. B-but they were both v-very upset."

And others claimed to have seen me leaving the party and driving off in an "agitated state."

Afterwards, Kopecky held up a bound stack of papers for the entire court to see. "Your Honor," he said, "I have here an affidavit signed, under oath, by forty-seven people who were at Mr. Sheldon's residence the night of the murder and witnessed the same questionable behavior of the defendant, Billy Colter, just as you heard described from our witnesses here: Mr. Colter did have an altercation with said Mr. Cabot that ended with Mr. Colter punching him straight in the jaw and knocking him down; Mr. Colter did spend an unusual portion of the evening in the company of another woman, a Mrs. Cassidy; there was a heated argument between Mr. Colter and Miss Faye, inciting them to leave the premises emotionally inflamed. It would be less than an hour later that the police would arrive to Mr. Colter's residence, responding to a call of shots being fired, and find a horrific scene, images of which you've been shown."

Kopecky then called another witness: Jonathon Cabot.

Cabot was sweating profusely as he sat at the witness

stand. Kopecky offered him some water. Cabot accepted and apologized for his "condition." He dabbed and wiped a handkerchief across his face as he waited for the prosecutor's questions.

"How do know the defendant?"

"Well, really I don't," Cabot said. "I'm just…a fan of his work. I've seen all of his movies."

"So that night was the first time you ever met him?"

"Yes. When I agreed to escort Mrs. Cassidy to the party, I never expected I'd get to meet him."

"That must have been quite special for you," said Kopecky with a genuine interest that was unsettling.

"Yes, it was."

"As well as a chance to dance with *the* Rebecca Faye."

"Yes, yes. That was splendid as well!" Cabot's giddiness all but overwhelmed him.

"How did that once-in-a-lifetime opportunity come about, anyway?"

"Well, Mrs. Cassidy wanted to dance with Billy–er–Mr. Colter. They're friends from way back."

"*Just* friends, were they?"

"Yes–er–as much as I can say, they were."

"They could have had a more intimate relationship, as much as you could say, isn't that true?"

Cabot squirmed and Wells objected to the

prosecutor's question, citing it as speculation. The judge sustained the objection. Kopecky shrugged and continued.

"Why did Mr. Colter hit you?"

Cabot squirmed again. "I…I really can't say. I mean, I don't know. He seemed to take offence to me dancing with Miss Faye."

"So he hit you out of jealous rage!"

"Objection!" Wells called out once again.

Kopecky announced he was finished with his questions before the judge sustained. Confused, Cabot stumbled from the stand and made his way from the courtroom.

Next, Kopecky called Faith as his next witness.

She entered the courtroom, and for once, did not seem comfortable with being the center of attention. She wore little makeup, and she had on as plain a dress as she could find from what I imagined to be a very extravagant collection in her closet.

Kopecky got right into asking about our history together, the movies we made in Arizona and the nature of our relationship, which in those days was a bit promiscuous and unseemly. (Though entirely common for much of the Hollywood community.) In other words, it did not paint me in a very good light.

"Was he in love with you?" the prosecutor asked.

"Yes, I believe he was," answered Faith.

"Did you love him?"

"I was fond of him, and the two of us had a lot of fun together. But, no, I wouldn't say I was in love with him."

"Unrequited love!" Kopecky stated to the court. "Carried, bottled up for all those years! And then to see her– a woman mere mortal men only dream about–to see her after so long. Can you imagine the emotions that could have stirred and raged inside the defendant?"

Wells objected to the prosecutor's speculation once again and the judge sustained it. Faith looked uncomfortable. I tried to read in her face whether she thought I was guilty or not, but I could see in her only the sad desire to be somewhere else. Wells could see it, too. Up to now, he had refrained from cross-examining Kopecky's witnesses because he wanted to unravel the prosecutor's loosely-knit case once it was fully weaved. But he stood and approached the stand when Kopecky acknowledged there were no further questions.

Wells gently put a hand upon the rail of the stand and gave Faith a consoling smile. "May I offer you some water?" he asked her.

"No. But thank you."

"How long had it been since you last saw Billy Colter, before that night the two of you danced?"

She did the math in her head. "Nearly twenty years."

"When you attended Mr. Sheldon's party, did you expect to see him?"

"I suppose I did. I knew he worked for Sheldon Pictures."

"It was fun to see him again, after all those years, wasn't it?" Wells's tone was relaxed and genial.

For the first time since she walked into the courtroom, Faith smiled. "Yes. Yes, it was."

"Had you met Miss Faye before that?"

"No. Before that I'd only seen her in the movies."

"And then Billy asked you to dance."

Here, Faith actually blushed. "Well…no. I was the one who suggested we switch partners. I wanted to visit with an old friend."

"You had been dancing with Mr. Cabot, is that correct?"

"Yes."

"What did you and Billy talk about, if I may ask?"

"We reminisced about our time in Arizona and the friends we knew there."

"You have lot of memories together, don't you?"

"Yes, we do."

"During your time together in Arizona, did Billy ever tell you that he loved you?"

"No…no, I don't believe he did."

Wells's tone was changing from one of casual conversation to that of a lawyer. "Then how do you know he was in love with you?"

Faith's smile turned to a sly smirk. "A woman can tell when a man's in love with her. He doesn't have to say a word."

There were some snickers from the court's audience.

"When the two of you were dancing," Wells quickly continued, "those nearly twenty years later, did Billy tell you that he was still in love with you?"

The smirk went away from Faith's face. "No," she said after a pause.

"So then, could you *see* that Billy was still in love with you?"

"No."

"'*No*' you couldn't see that he was still in love with you, or '*no*' you *could* see that Billy Colter was *not* in love with you, anymore? Because a woman can always tell, can't she, Mrs. Cassidy?"

"No, Billy wasn't…isn't…in love with me anymore."

"Because–you could tell–he was in love with someone else. Isn't that true?"

Faith's voice went sullen. "He looked at her the way he used to look at me. Even more so."

"Rebecca, you mean?"

"Yes. And rightly so. She was a lovely girl."

"I sense you might be a bit envious. Perhaps you care for him more than you first thought?"

The prosecutor objected, although with little conviction. It was overruled.

The court held its breath for Faith's response.

"Perhaps," she said.

Wells took a moment then asked, "You were dancing with Mr. Colter just before his altercation with Mr. Cabot, who was dancing with Miss Faye, correct?"

"Yes."

"Do you have any idea what may have incited Mr. Colter to confront Mr. Cabot the way he did?"

"I do, but I'd rather not say."

"You're under oath, Mrs. Cassidy. If you refuse to answer, you may be charged with contempt."

"But it would cast dispersions upon my friend Mr. Cabot." Faith turned to the judge who showed her no sympathy.

"We're all adults here, Mrs. Cassidy," Wells said with an assuring look.

Faith gave a fidget, a sigh, then said, "I mentioned to Billy that Jonathon was...homosexual. That's when Billy hurried across the dance floor, they argued, and Billy hit him."

"That's it?" Wells asked, as surprised as anybody. "He knocked Mr. Cabot down simply because he was a homosexual?"

"Yes."

I gestured for Wells to argue her statement because it was not true. He ignored me with a befuddled frown and told the judge he had no more questions, then sat back down beside me.

For his final witness, Kopecky called Annie Mendoza to the stand.

I was confused and unsettled. *What connection did Annie have to this mess?* I thought. *What were the lawyers going to do to her?*

She approached the stand with confidence and grace, things she had learned running a motion picture studio. As she sat, her eyes met mine and she gave me the hint of a smile in hopes of instilling me with equal confidence. It worked for only a brief moment, before the prosecutor spoke.

He began with questions to clarify who she was and what her role was with Sheldon Pictures. Once that was done, he got to the task at hand. "Were you at Mr. Sheldon's party on the night in question?"

"Yes, I was," Annie said.

"And could you tell the court what you saw and heard."

"I saw a lot of people from the movie business. And a lot of food, enough to feed all of Los Angeles. And I heard a lovely orchestra."

Kopecky gave a look indicating he did not find her amusing. "In regards to Mr. Colter and Miss Faye," he said.

"They danced, and mingled, and appeared to have a splendid time," Annie answered.

"Miss Mendoza, were you or were you not in close proximity to the couple during their heated argument later that evening?"

"I was."

"And would you please share with us what you observed."

"Well," Annie began and paused in a teasing way. "They weren't arguing. It was more like a lover's spat. Quite innocuous, really."

An awkward hush went through the courtroom. Kopecky gave a resigned sigh and asked, "Innocuous?"

"You know, meaningless." Then with emphasis, she added, "*Innocent.*"

"What were they saying?" the prosecutor asked, maintaining his patience. "What was the argument about?"

"Honestly? I have no idea. They were whispering and

they were drunk. I couldn't understand a single slurry word. But we had just been playing charades. They had lost because of Billy's poor clues. Perhaps that is what their spat was about."

"Your Honor," Kopecky said as he stepped to the bench, "I'd like to charge Miss Mendoza with contempt for withholding evidence by refusing to testify the facts."

"Your Honor," Annie interjected, "during my interview for Mr. Kopecky's investigation I only told him that I was close enough to *hear* Billy and Rebecca. I said nothing about what it was I heard. He was merely making an assumption. And a bad one at that."

Giving a stern look to the prosecutor, the judge said, "Mr. Kopecky, do you have any evidence to the contrary?"

The whole court could see Kopecky chewing and swallowing his ego before answering the judge. "No, your Honor. No more questions."

Annie gave me a wink. The kind she had always given to let me know things would work out fine. Like when I fell off the back of a train during a stunt. As Annie might say, it was an *innocuous* gesture, but anyone observing the two of us in a moment like that could infer any number of things, which is exactly what my lawyer, Harvey Wells, did.

He rose quickly and said, "Miss Mendoza, you've known Billy for quite some time, haven't you?"

"Yes. Yes, I have. Most of my life. I was but a child when we met."

"So you've grown up knowing him, through your formative, impressionable years."

"I suppose you could say that." Annie became wary of where Wells might be going with his questions.

"He's spoken quite fondly of you on numerous occasions," Wells continued. "He considers you a good friend."

I could see she was touched to hear that as she looked at me. "And I him," she said.

"But is it really possible for an impressionable young girl to be merely friends with such a handsome, personable man as Billy Colter?" Wells asked.

I hoped at that moment Kopecky would object to the things my lawyer was asking, but he was as interested in what Wells had to say as much as the rest of the court. My unsettled feelings began to boil.

"I don't see why not," replied Annie.

"Was there anyone else close enough to have heard the spat between Billy and Rebecca? Or was it just you?"

"Just me."

"And why was that? How was it you just happened to be so close?" Wells asked, but before Annie could reply he went on. "Could it be because you were concerned, worried about Billy's well-being?"

"Of course. He's my friend. Friends worry about each other."

"*Jealousy* works the same way, Miss Mendoza."

Simultaneously, Kopecky made an objection and I leapt from my seat shouting, "No!" It didn't come out that way, however. With my damaged, unused voice it sounded like an impassioned ogre's groan.

The court went silent, all its eyes on me. Wells quietly said he had no more questions and returned to our table. I remained standing. Annie averted her eyes from me as she was lead from the stand. The judge called for a recess.

While the rest of the court cleared the room, I confronted Harvey.

"WHY?" I firmly wrote, pieces of my chalk falling to the floor.

"I need to show that any number of people could have shot Rebecca besides you," Wells stated, "for any number of reasons."

"NOT ANNIE!"

"Billy, I'm not trying to point the finger at anybody here. I'm just trying to point it away from you. You, my friend, are the only one on trial. You are the only one who could hang for Rebecca's death."

I showed him the last thing I wrote again, this time

with less conviction. I was surprised myself by the level of ire I felt in defense of Annie.

"Your outburst, by the way? Kopecky will use it to show how passionate you can be regarding another woman."

I sunk into my chair, embarrassed and foolish.

Wells was right. In his closing remarks, Kopecky would remind the jury of my conduct in the courtroom, as well the "impassioned, violent behavior" I exhibited during Mr. Sheldon's party.

After the recess, Wells moved that the court rest for the afternoon and resume the next day due to the strain upon my emotional state. "Being on trial for the murder of his beloved, a murder he didn't commit, is proving too much to bear," Wells pleaded. What he truly meant was that he wanted the jury a chance to forget about my outburst before presenting his side of the case. Fortunately, the judge approved and the court was adjourned. I was glad to be back in the confines of my jail cell that night, but my emotions wrestled my exhaustion and made for a fitful sleep.

ಎ   ಎ   ಎ

The next morning, one of the officers presented me with a letter, explaining it had arrived the day before. It was from Maggie.

The writing was mostly unreadable—smeared ink, crooked penmanship scrawled across a single crumpled page. Only one sentence was vaguely legible. *"How could this have happened?"* it read. And then her tear-stained name at the bottom. I read the letter repeatedly in hopes of deciphering more than those few words, but my hopes blurred through my own tears and my own broken heart. How much pain could one person endure, I wondered. I knew I was ill from sorrow, but what of a mother losing her only daughter?

Wells saw my distress. I told him, or rather, wrote him about the letter.

"It may be little consolation," Wells said, "but I intend to prove you innocent today. Perhaps that will give Mrs. Faye a bit of comfort."

It was but little consolation, yet I needed all I could get.

Wells began the presentation of his case by calling Jonathon Cabot back to the stand.

Cabot was even more agitated than the day before, and he appeared to be wearing the same suit. Or maybe all his suits were the same dull brown. He looked just as he had that night the police took him away from the front of the restaurant as Rebecca and her mother and I dined.

Wells didn't waste time with pleasantries. He held up several newspapers, each with a headline and a photograph about the restaurant incident. "**MAN ACCOSTS COLTER AND FAYE!**" announced one. "**CRAZED FAN!**" read another.

"Is this you, Mr. Cabot?" Wells asked. "In these photographs, and the subject of these headlines?"

Cabot nodded.

"Could you please answer aloud?"

"Yes," he replied, with as much dignity as he could muster.

Kopecky objected. "I don't see the relevancy. Mr. Cabot is not on trial."

"Your Honor, I think I will show it relevant," Wells explained, "if the court would be patient."

"Overruled," the judge stated.

"Mr. Cabot," Wells continued, "we all know headlines can exaggerate. In your own defense, could you tell us what happened?"

Cabot took a breath, relishing the chance to redeem himself. "I'm a fan. I just wanted an autograph. I tend to get over-excited though."

"It would be exciting for anyone, I think, to meet the caliber of stars like Billy Colter and Rebecca Faye."

"Yes, yes. It is!" Cabot replied with an awkward laugh. "But, I shouldn't act the way I do. I'm sorry, I truly am."

Wells removed a file from the stack on our table. "According to the police report, you were carrying a revolver when you were arrested. Is that correct? A Remington?"

"Y-yes. I'm...I don't feel safe sometimes."

"This city can be a daunting place, can't it?"

"Yes, it can."

"So, you're familiar with shooting a firearm."

"On occasion, I've fired at tin cans in the desert."

Wells replaced the file to his stack and approached the stand. "What is your relationship with Mrs. Cassidy?" he asked.

"Oh, we're friends."

"For how long?"

Cabot squirmed. "Not long, really."

"Years? Months?"

"Four or five...months."

"Five months!" Wells returned to our table as he spoke. "That would be shortly before Mr. Sheldon's party, and the death of Miss Faye. How did you and Faith Cassidy meet, exactly?"

"We just got to talking in a store as she was shopping one day. We got on so well. A couple of weeks later she asked me to escort her to a party. Her husband was under-the-weather and, of course, she couldn't go alone."

"Of course." Wells thumbed through a page of notes, pretending to read. "Her husband being Arthur Cassidy, an executive with...Paramount, I believe."

"Well, no. He's with Warner Brothers."

"Oh, yes. I stand corrected." Wells then slowly, casually made his way back to the stand. "Being a fan of motion pictures, I imagine you know a lot about the industry."

"Yes, I suppose I do."

"So, you're aware Mrs. Cassidy had acted in several movies herself?"

"Of course, but she was Faith Monroe then."

"You are knowledgeable, Mr. Cabot," Wells said with a smile. "Isn't it true that, in her earlier pictures, Billy Colter starred with, the then, Miss Monroe?"

Cabot laughed. "Oh, he wasn't a star then. He was only an extra, doing stunts."

"You've seen all those pictures, haven't you?"

"Oh, yes!"

"But not because of Faith Monroe. But because of Billy Colter. You've seen all of his movies, haven't you?"

Cabot turned as sickly green as the Martian in *A Man of Mars*.

"Isn't it true you had sought out Mrs. Cassidy that day she was shopping, following her, because you knew if you could meet her, you then might be able to meet *the* Billy Colter?"

Kopecky rose. "Your Honor! This is absurd!"

"You're more than merely a fan of Billy Colter, aren't you, Mr. Cabot?" Wells continued. "You're in love with him, aren't you? Enough to stalk an innocent woman."

"Objection!"

"Overruled," stated the judge.

"And how fortuitous it was that she would be attending a party along with Billy."

Cabot became hysterical. "No, no, I didn't know that!"

"But you knew a lot, Mr. Cabot, didn't you? You knew where Billy lived. You've even been in his house when he wasn't around, haven't you? You knew he had a gun and where he kept it, didn't you?"

"Objection!" shouted the prosecution.

"No, no, no," cried Cabot.

Wells had no further questions.

❧   ❧   ❧

Anthony Sheldon was Wells's next witness. It had been a few months since I last saw him. He looked tired and frail, no longer the stocky bulldog. His eyes were dull, his voice flat.

"I discovered Rebecca at Brown's Opera House in San Francisco," he said in response to Wells's first question. "She was in the audience. I never noticed what was happening on the stage because I couldn't take my eyes off her. She was mesmerizing. I spoke to her after the show, and when I learned she had done a little acting in some local plays, I knew I had to put her in a movie. My instincts served me well that time."

"You made her a star," commented Wells.

"I gave her a chance. She made herself a star."

"You took a chance on Billy Colter, as well."

"He'd had a fair amount of experience in front of the camera. It wasn't much of a risk to give him more roles and fewer stunts."

"And it was you who put them together in…how many films was it?"

"A few dozen. I haven't kept count."

"Forty-three."

Nodding in agreement, Mr. Sheldon said, "They've done quite well for the studio."

"So well that you were a little nervous about them getting married, weren't you?"

Mr. Sheldon's mouth tightened. "A little."

"Why?"

"I was worried that marriage would be the death of…the end of their careers. I feared audiences would lose interest in them. There's no spark in being married. No mystery. No romance."

"It hasn't hurt Douglas Fairbanks and Mary Pickford."

"They've only done one movie together."

Wells took a moment to contemplate his next question. "Didn't you state something to the effect that it would take a tragic event to save their careers, if they did get married?"

"I was drunk," said Mr. Sheldon without a flinch.

"You're known for carrying a sidearm, aren't you, Mr. Sheldon?"

"I did not kill Rebecca. She was very dear to me. As is Billy. I loved them as if they were my own. As for my sidearm, I used to carry one, but no more. The idea of carrying something like that now sickens me."

Wells ended his questioning of Mr. Sheldon there, feeling he had succeeded in drawing enough finger-pointing away from me. The next witness he called was Detective Collier.

The typically slovenly officer had cleaned himself up for his court appearance, and he proved to be a fine-looking middle-aged gentleman. The scraggly wisps of gray were combed back into distinguished lines of silver, and his shaven face revealed a Romanesque profile. His suit, normally off-the-rack, appeared now to have been tailor-made. I'm sure I heard the swooning of a few ladies as he walked to the stand.

Wells began by asking the detective to describe the murder scene as he had found it that night. Collier's narrative was almost verbatim what he had explained to me in my jail cell. Then Wells asked him, "In your opinion, as an experienced police officer, and by what you saw at the crime scene, could Billy Colter have shot Rebecca Faye?"

"Of course," the detective answered, and my stomach turned. "He would have had to have been standing further into the house, away from the chair we found him in. But he could have then walked to the chair and fallen into it."

"And, in your experienced opinion, could Billy Colter have shot himself after shooting Miss Faye and then walked to the chair?"

"No."

"No?"

"Not in the least."

There was some mumbling about the courtroom, and I felt my guts ease a bit.

"Would you please explain to the court, how it is that Billy Colter *could not possibly* have shot himself?" asked Wells.

"He's right-handed," Detective Collier stated. "Mr. Colter's wound indicates he was shot from a particular distance at a particular angle, neither of which he could have achieved being right-handed." As he spoke, Collier put his own right hand out to demonstrate the awkwardness and impossibility of someone shooting themselves in the manner I had been. "Nor left-handed, for that matter."

"How, then, does the wound indicate Billy was shot?"

"Mr. Colter was shot from a distance of greater than a few feet, at an angle equal to something like…" Again, he demonstrated, this time putting his left arm out at an angle beyond what his right arm could manage.

"Also," the detective continued, "evidence shows he instinctively reacted to the gunshot by putting his left hand to his throat, hence the blood on his hand, as can be seen in the photographs."

"Is it possible Billy shot Rebecca and then, with the same gun, someone else shot Billy?"

"That's a pretty far-fetched hypothesis. I wouldn't bet a wooden nickel on that."

"So, no."

"Not in the least."

"Then I will pose the question to you again," Wells said with Kopecky-esque grandeur. "In your opinion, Detective Collier, could Billy Colter have shot Rebecca Faye?"

"Not in the least. The more likely scenario is that someone else was there, hiding within the house, who shot the two of them with Billy's own gun as they returned home from Mr. Sheldon's party, killing Rebecca and wounding Billy. This person then left the gun on the floor beside Billy to give the appearance of him having dropped it after shooting himself."

A wave of reactions—shock, elation, confusion—swept through the courtroom.

"Thank you, Detective. No more questions, Your Honor."

∾ ∾ ∾

Finally, Wells presented an affidavit of his own. Because I couldn't speak, he had had me write out a sworn testimony about what happened, in my own words. But he didn't leave it at that. He then called me to the stand. The jury got a good look at how disheartened and pitiful I was as I made my way across the courtroom with my chalkboard clutched tightly to my chest. Wells also used the opportunity to summarize the facts of the case, comparing Kopecky's grandstanding to his own, more grounded arguments.

As he touched upon key elements of the trial, he would ask me a question, like: "Why did you confront Mr. Cabot on the dance floor?"

"I RECOGNIZED HIM FROM THE RESTAURANT," I wrote. I made sure my penmanship was clear and straight, and I held my board up for the jury and the judge to see. The jurors would lean forward, some with a squint, to read what I wrote. Wells also had the court reporter repeat my answers aloud. It was a slow process. "I WAS CONCERNED WHAT HE MIGHT DO."

"You were concerned for Rebecca's safety, based upon your previous experience with Mr. Cabot?"

"YES."

"Is that why you hit him?"

"HE GRABBED MY ARM. I OVERREACTED."

"It had nothing to do with him being homosexual."

"I COULDN'T CARE LESS ABOUT THAT."

Then Wells asked me, "Were you once in love with Faith Cassidy?"

"YES. ONCE. NOT ANY MORE."

And later he questioned, "Have you ever had romantic feelings toward Miss Mendoza?"

"NO. WE'VE ALWAYS BEEN GOOD FRIENDS," I wrote, hoping the jurors would not notice how I paused to answer.

As he summarized, Wells brought up the argument Rebecca and I had. "Would you mind sharing with the court what was it about, exactly?"

"I'M TERRIBLE AT CHARADES," I wrote with a sheepish grin, and the mood of the room lightened.

Wells concluded by reading directly from my sworn

testimony.

"*Only a fool would think I murdered Rebecca, a fool who never knew us and saw the love we shared for one another, a fool who only believes what the papers print or the movies portray. A hole has been left in my heart much greater than the one in my neck. If I had done this horrible thing so many people think I am guilty of, I can assure you I would not have been so careless with the bullet meant for myself. I would have made a clean shot to my head, because, frankly, I do not know how I will go on without her. A part of me hopes the jury finds me guilty and puts an end to my misery. I do not know how I will go on without her.*"

I thought I couldn't cry anymore, but there on the stand I found I couldn't stop.

Twenty

In this, a man's word is gold,

Heavy as stone,

Not to be bartered or sold.

T
he trial was like something, well, like something out of a movie, a bit staged and melodramatic, fodder for those with nothing else in their empty lives. Wells never thought any of the witnesses were guilty of Rebecca's murder. He felt his case was as thin as Kopecky's. But he presented his arguments with sincere conviction, and anyone reading this with half an I.Q.-point can guess that I was acquitted of all charges. Otherwise, I wouldn't be alive to write my story today.

Kopecky didn't believe in his own case, either. When the verdict was handed down and the court adjourned, he stopped a moment to give me a knowing, even apologetic, nod before leaving the courthouse. Wells was right. I was nothing but a tool in Kopecky's political agenda. I don't know if the prosecutor ever fulfilled his plans. I left Los Angeles as soon as I could once that fiasco of a trial had settled. I only had a couple of things I needed to take care of.

First, I wanted to see Thomas.

Elizabeth met me at the front door and gave me a long embrace. "I'm so glad this is finally over," she said, leading me inside where I was embraced again by the warmth of her and Thomas's home. "The rest will take time, Billy. It may not seem like it now, but give it time."

Thomas sat at their kitchen table, looking as relaxed and alert as I'd seen him in a while. A cup of coffee steamed on the table in front of him, and a newspaper rested in his lap. I sat with him and Elizabeth brought me a cup of my own.

Thomas smiled and said, "I was just reading that Wyatt Earp lives here in California. Been here for some years."

"Yes," I replied with my gnarled voice. My throat may not have been fully healed, but I'd had enough of the chalkboard. "I believe he's been active in advising William S. Hart on his movies. Hart's a stickler for details, I hear."

"It would be nice to meet him. Earp, that is. We've nearly crossed paths enough times."

Thomas took a big sip of coffee and went quiet.

"I'm leaving Los Angeles," I told him. "I'd like to buy some land somewhere. And some horses. I'm going to visit Mr. McElroy first."

"Mac? I've wondered about him of late. There's something I've been meaning to send him."

"Why don't you come with me? You could deliver whatever it is personally. After that, we could go anywhere you like. We've done enough here, Thomas. California isn't for us anymore." What I meant was, it wasn't for me. I felt it never had been.

"That does sound nice, Billy," Thomas mulled. "I've got some work to finish up. Maybe I could meet up with you."

"Maybe," I said, knowing he wouldn't.

Feeling there was nothing left to say, I stood to leave.

Thomas stopped me, asking, "How's Rebecca, by the way?"

I sighed and feigned a smile. "She's well, Thomas. She sends her love."

      ॐ   ॐ   ॐ

The work Thomas had to finish up was his last film, *Code of the West*.

While moments of his life had cropped up here and there within all the films he'd made, *Code of the West* was as much his autobiography as anything. A young man, Tom Benedict, seeing his father gunned-down, leaves the life he knows for the ranches of Texas, the cities along the Mississippi, the cattle trails further west, and of course, Denver.

By Hollywood's standards, it was not a story driven by plot, but a tale made up of a chain of tales, all exemplified by the unwritten code of which men and women lived by in their attempt to tame the land west of St. Louis. A code defined by things like a man's love for his cherished horse and his humble possessions. A kind of wary hospitality to strangers. The trusting bond of a handshake. The love and comfort of a good companion, a family, or a friend. And work, hard but satisfying work.

Thomas changed the names of everyone, except the du Bois family. He depicted them just as I had pictured. The mother and father, firm but loving characters, and their three beautiful, tempting daughters. The scenes of Tom and the girls were the most light-hearted of the movie. What he did change was that the family did not die of cholera. Perhaps he thought it was too heart-breaking so early in the film, or it was too hard for him to relive.

He also changed the nature of his relationship with Ellen Marie. In the movie, Tom meets the delicate Mary while working a wagon train, and he does not take her to Colorado to end up a whore. Rather, they invest in a saloon together there, and Tom leaves her to run it so he can

ANSWER THE CALL OF WANDERLUST, as the title card put it.

I don't think audiences would have cared if Mary had been depicted as a soiled dove. I think Thomas was trying to honor Ellen Marie by putting the memory of her in a better light. It makes me wonder if he had regretted the life he had led her to in Denver. I'm sure he regretted not staying with her. In the movie, Tom does not revisit Mary again and again, but instead, returns at the end to take her away to a new life, together.

Mr. McElroy appears in the movie as Jake MacPherson, the coarse, ill-mannered son of the man who killed Tom's father. Just like Thomas and Mr. McElroy, the two do not get along at first. But Tom gains sympathy for Jake when he sees how poorly he and his siblings are treated by their beast of a father. When Tom kills the father, forever after becoming a wanted man, I was the only person in the audience, hell, in the world, who knew the truth. Thomas would keep their secret to his death. Eagle Heart is there, as well, only as Edward Hart. And his beloved horse, Bell Ringer, that perishes in the flash flood from which young Tom is rescued by the Osage. I can only guess that the film's depiction of life on a reservation was not only the first for Hollywood, but also the most accurate ever. It was my favorite part of the movie as it showed a world I knew nothing about.

And then there's me, in the form of a full-o'-beans cowpoke by the name of Johnny Weston. At first, the cocky Johnny follows Tom around like a wide-eyed puppy, and I wondered, *is that how Thomas saw me?* But then I was touched by title cards like THERE IS SOMETHING IN THE YOUNG MAN, QUALITIES TOM LOOKS FOR IN A FRIEND. Or, JOHNNY'S COMPANY IS LIKE A WELL-FIT SWEATER and TOM THINKS: WHEN THE TRAILS DONE, WILL I FIND HIM LESS A FRIEND AND MORE A SON?

I could only imagine it was cathartic for Thomas to make *Code of the West*. It certainly proved to be for me as I watched our life together unfold on the screen. It was all there in melodramatic reverence. Except for our time in Hollywood.

I don't know if that was intentional, or if he was never fully aware of that period of his life, but the movie ends, not with Tom as a famous movie director in a bungalow in Pasadena, but with him sitting upon a horse, looking out over his ranch in Texas and back across the span of his life and all that had brought him to that single moment of peace and clarity.

        ⎮   ⎮   ⎮

The last thing I needed to do before leaving California was to lay Rebecca to rest.

Her service and burial was at Forest Lawn Memorial Park in Glendale. I know nothing about the preservation of the dead, but Rebecca appeared just as I remembered her. She was sealed in her casket, under glass, like sleeping beauty in need of nothing more than a kiss to bring her back to me and the rest of the world.

I was touched by the number of people who came to see her. Those who knew her, of course, but hundreds who had never met her. Fans who only knew her from her movies came to pay their respects. It is one of the few positive memories left upon me by my Hollywood experience, the powerful impression a single person could make upon others, upon strangers.

Maggie did not come to her daughter's funeral, which saddened, and worried, me. I had made attempts to contact her, short of travelling to San Francisco personally, but she would not respond. I imagined her alone in a dark place. Knowing how I found comfort in being surrounded by so many people who loved Rebecca, I wanted the same for her mother.

The service was short and people could view Rebecca before the private burial. As the crowd thinned and only those closest to her remained, I noticed a man lingering just inside the entrance. He was small in stature but held himself with solemn dignity, humble yet confident. His complexion had a rich, olive hue that belied his age. His suit was of a European cut. In one hand, he held his fedora, and under that arm an envelope. He looked at me as though he had something he wanted to say, yet waited with respectful courtesy. As I approached him, I saw Rebecca's eyes.

"Mr. Colter," he said as he took my hand, "I am Jack Faye, Rebecca's father."

I was dumbfounded and speechless as we shook.

"It's an honor to meet you," he continued, "though I would have rather have done so under different circumstances."

"The honor is mine, sir," I finally said. "Rebecca told me so much about you."

He paused sympathetically at the harshness of my voice, then said, "She couldn't stop talking about you, as well. Or *write*, I should say. She wrote many letters about her life here. The nature of my work takes me many places, far from home. But her letters always found me. I regret, now, not having responded in kind."

"Well, I'm sure she would be happy to know you are here, now. She loved you, and her mother, very much."

"Thank you. It comforts me to hear that." His smile did little to hide his broken heart. It faded as he became uncomfortable and looked around the room. "About her mother…could we go outside a moment?"

It was warm in the morning sun as we stepped out, a breeze rustled the branches above. (It's funny the things you remember, and the things you don't.)

"As you may know," he said, "Maggie, Rebecca's mother, had some…nervous tendencies…um…emotional struggles."

"Yes," I said.

"Self-destructive delusions, the doctors called it."

"Yes. But I thought she had gotten better. She seemed fine when she was here."

"That's the difficulty of her condition. She *seems* fine…until…"

His hesitation made my bones go cold. I put a hand on his shoulder. "What happened?"

Mr. Faye swallowed hard. "She took her own life."

My heart sank, even further. While there had been times I'd wished I were dead to end the ache of my loss, in my grief I never considered killing myself. The sorrow Maggie must have suffered!

Then, as though reading my thoughts, Mr. Faye said, "But not just."

"What?"

This time, his hesitation was more than I could bear.

"What?" I snapped.

"Not before shooting the two of you."

The world froze. My breathing stopped. My head was in a vise.

"She'd created an illusion," he said, "one where it was you and her that were in love, and about to be married. She shot you…and her own daughter…in a jealous rage."

I walked, no stumbled, away from him. I stopped at a tree and leaned forward, feeling about to retch. My breathing became short and sporadic. My head burned. Because I remembered.

The argument Rebecca and I had at the party had been nothing but a drunken, playful spat about my poor abilities in playing charades. I don't blame anyone for misunderstanding our emotional tone. But there was no ire between us. We left Mr. Sheldon's house as much in love as ever. Perhaps more.

As we returned home, I told her about the wedding plans her mother was making for us. *A honeymoon in Paris would be lovely, wouldn't it? That's where artists go,* Maggie had said to me. The idea of going to Europe excited Rebecca. We were laughing as we entered my home.

Before we even removed our coats, I heard Rebecca say, "Mother!" and I turned to see Maggie, my gun in her gloved hands, aiming at me. It's no surprise I blacked-out the crazed look in her eyes. I can hardly bear to remember it now as I write this. Without a word, she pulled the trigger.

● ● ●

The bullet tore through my neck, and I spun around with my left hand at my burning throat as I collapsed into the chair. I heard four more shots, and then nothing else.

Mr. Faye came up beside me and stood as I tried to catch my breath. When I'd calmed, he said, "I'm sorry, Mr. Colter." He showed me the envelope he had with him. "It's all in here. Her signed confession, of sorts. It's difficult to read, as her penmanship was always a mess. But having been married to her for so long, I became adept at deciphering it. I wanted you to know, before I took it to the authorities."

I stopped him as he began to leave. To this day, I can't explain the wash of benevolence that came over me, like the warm breeze from overhead. "I'll take it," I said.

His confusion gave him pause. "But the police will need me to make sense of these," he said.

"We don't need to tell the police." I gently took the envelope from him. "It doesn't matter. There's no point in convicting her now. I think Rebecca will rest in peace just the same."

Mr. Faye resigned and gave the saddest of smiles. I couldn't help but feel a little like Thomas and Mr. McElroy, with their secret between them.

"I'm sorry I didn't find this out sooner, Mr. Colter. I'm sorry, too, that I didn't have a chance to meet you earlier on. I've missed out on many things in my life. Especially on seeing my little girl grow up."

"Please call me Billy."

"You wouldn't mind if I paid my respects to her before I go, would you?"

"What? Of course, of course. Take all the time you want."

I watched Rebecca's estranged yet loving father go inside and stand over his daughter's casket, his back to me. I could see his chest heave as he cried. It made me clutch the envelope with my fingers. Crumpling the paper tightly within my fist, the corners cutting into my palm, gave me comfort, and the peace I'd needed for so long.

And then Rebecca's father began to sing:

Ma n'atu sole

cchiù bello, oje ne'.

O sole mio

sta 'nfronte a te!

O sole

O sole mio

sta 'nfronte a te!

sta 'nfronte a te!

I later had someone translate it for me.

But another sun,

that's brighter still
It's my own sun
that's in your face!
The sun, my own sun
It's in your face!
It's in your face!

At one time, Rebecca had fabricated details about her life. But she told the truth about one thing. Her father did have a beautiful, haunting singing voice.

Twenty-one

The roar of the sea subdues the clamor of the drive
Cries of the cattle, hollers of the drover
may push and stand to stay alive
But the quieting West lies down

Settling into dusty memories,
cloudy pictures, ill-remembered tales
Re-told in dark places...

Wyatt Earp died January 13th, 1929 in Los Angeles. Among his pallbearers were William S. Hart and Tom Mix. Some historians consider his death the official mark of the end of the Wild West. I personally think it ended a few days later, when Thomas Andrew Benton died on the 17th. He was ninety-six. Hearing of his death, I realized when I last saw him, I hadn't told him goodbye.

Elizabeth had Thomas cremated, and she went on a sojourn across the country to leave handfuls of his ashes in places Thomas had once set foot in his life. His favorite places, like Missouri, Colorado and Texas. To my knowledge, she never stopped in Prescott, Arizona, though.

It's probably no surprise that after leaving California I bought Mr. McElroy's Willow Ranch outside of Prescott. I knew the first moment I saw it that it was a place where I could stay forever. There wasn't any place I ever wanted to return to more than that dry, dusty forest. I even tried to raise cattle on it for some years, against my better judgment.

As I approached the ranch on a horse I'd purchased in town (I could have driven up, but arriving on horseback seemed much more fitting), Mr. McElroy came down from his porch to meet me halfway, just as he had done when Thomas and I arrived all those years ago. He was surprised to see me, but not surprised that I was alone. He somehow knew he would never see his old friend again. His face twisted into a grimace, trying to wrangle his grief. I offered my hand, but instead he wrapped me in a bear hug. The two of us stood together like that for a time. Then we sat on the porch, and with my gnarled voice, I told him about all that had happened to Thomas and me. The only parts of Mr. McElroy that showed any of the nearly twenty years since I'd last seen him were his tired eyes. The spark they once had returned slightly as I told him my stories.

"I seen all your movies that came to town. There weren't many, but I seen 'em all," he said with enthusiasm.

Out on the secluded Willows Ranch, he had gotten

very little news about our exploits in Hollywood, and he was very patient waiting for the part where I told him about the injury to my throat. That grimace returned to his craggy face as my voice broke worse than ever recalling the saddest part of my life. I had to change the subject or I couldn't have continued.

"Mr. McElroy," I said, "I came here to see if you might be interested in selling the Willows, because I'm interested in buying it."

"Hell, yes, I'm interested in selling," was his very quick response. Then, he mused, "But what use would you have for this land, Billy. It's not good ranch land. Just pretty to look at, is all."

"That's exactly what I want. A quiet place that is pretty to look at, where I can spend the last of my days." (Little did I know I would have a lifetime of *last* days.)

We talked for so long that before we knew it the sun was setting on us, and we were both famished. Mr. McElroy fried up a couple of steaks and roasted some potatoes. As he cooked, I noticed, upon the top of a small bookshelf by the front door, Thomas's leather notebook. Inside was his poetry, and thoughts about, well, everything.
One passage in particular struck me.

"I can't decide whether fences are meant to keep us safe from dangers outside," he wrote, *"or to keep those of us on the inside from*

wandering. They seem to have become an unfortunate necessity. Building and maintaining them gives me work to do. Yet, there's a paradox in how the need for them goes against my very nature."

Mr. McElroy spied me standing there, frozen, clutching the volume of Thomas's life. "He sent me that a little while back," he admitted. "He sent nothing else. No note. Nothing."

I have to admit, I was a little hurt that Thomas didn't give the notebook to me.

While we supped we worked out an amicable deal for my purchase of the Willows. Since Mr. McElroy had nowhere to go from there, part of the deal was that he stay with me for as long as he like. Because of that, he sold me the ranch for next to nothing, as though he planned not to stay for very long.

His stay turned out to be less than a year.

Mr. McElroy, Thomas Andrew Benton's best and oldest friend, died in his sleep one cool morning, just after a heavy rain had softened the dirt and settled the dust. It was almost as though he had been waiting for someone like me to come along so that he wouldn't have to die alone, and that it would rain when he died to make it easier to bury him. Since he had no next of kin or friends that I knew of, I put Mr. McElroy into the wet ground near where Thomas and I had first seen Whites-as-Indians running around in view of

Toby Greene's camera. I also buried their secret, how Thomas had taken the blame for the murder of Mr. McElroy's father. Until now, that is, as you've read this.

The house, the corral, barn, and outbuilding all needed work done to them, so I had set in at once to restoring the Willows to its better days. I had been nearly finished when Mr. McElroy passed. I grieved by sawing and hammering the last of the planks, and putting final touches of paint upon walls and fences. I like to think old McElroy would've wanted to be mourned that way. I know Thomas would have.

With the barn once again hospitable, I then spent many a long afternoon riding my new horse over the rocky landscape, where one memory after another lurked behind a tree, along a hillside, or around a boulder. On one hillside, I could see myself falling from that horse over and over while Alan Grady yelled, over and over, for me to do it again. There were more than a few spots, deeper in the woods, where I could recall either Faith or Anna Beth and I sharing intimate time together. Of course, after every ride I took, I'd return to the barn and its corral and be reminded of our re-enactment of the O.K. Corral gunfight. Of all the movies I've done, it remains the one for which I'm most proud. And I don't think but a handful of people ever saw it.

For a while, I regularly got letters from Toby. He'd

update me on the current happenings of an industry I no longer had an interest in. I didn't care what was being produced, or who was doing the producing, or who were the latest stars being talked about. That world so quickly became a dreamy fog of memories to me once I arrived back here to The Willows because living in it had been akin to being in a fog, a kind of fantastical hallucination. Hollywood is a promising garden to those on the outside, and a sickening opiate to those within. As soon as my boots touched the dirt of the Arizona forest, I felt all my disillusions fade. And I felt sorry for those I left there, all of them as lost from the world as Thomas had been in his final years. I much preferred having my feet upon hard ground, and here I've stayed.

Don't get me wrong. I did enjoy hearing from Toby, because he was one of my few remaining friends, and because sometimes he'd share news I was actually interested in hearing. I was happy to learn that Elizabeth Jerome had taken the money Thomas left her and bought a spread up in Montana. She took the last of Thomas's remains with her, too. I hope she spread them under a tree, not too close to any fences. I meant to contact her on several occasions over the years, but never got around to it.

Toby was also the one who told me about the fire that burned down the Sheldon Pictures Studio. It was in 1933, a couple of years before the final demise of silent movies. Arson was suspected, but no one knows for sure how it started. The result was every inch of film footage produced by Sheldon Pictures being lost forever in a billow of dense, black smoke. As far as I know, the only memory of Anthony Sheldon and his legacy is what I've scrawled onto these pages here.

Shortly after the fire, Mr. Sheldon retired to a place near the California-Mexico border. While having dinner out one evening, he was attacked and stabbed to death by a Mexican as old as himself. Witnesses say the two yelled at each other from across the dining room just before the Mexican rushed Mr. Sheldon's table and started going at him with a steak knife. One witness in particular noticed the strange manner in which Mr. Sheldon, while being stabbed, kept clutching for something at his hip that wasn't there. A holstered gun, perhaps?

As for Toby himself, he had a long career filming motion pictures. "Shooting films became so much easier once they got rid of having to crank the camera," he wrote in one of his letters. "The advancements in motion picture technology have made it easy for an old man like me to keep working, and at the same time be so much more creative. It's amazing the things we can do now, Billy."

From out here, I don't know that I could agree. The

last time I went to the movies was about twenty years ago. The theater's lobby was bland and unclean, the employees obviously hated their jobs, the auditorium was tiny, and the screen wasn't much bigger than some televisions I've seen. I don't remember what the film was, some trite thing with gratuitous sexual-language and violence, nothing memorable. It somehow made me think of that actress—oh, I forget her name—that jumped to her death from the Hollywood sign because of her failing career. I'm glad I got out of there, Hollywood, I mean, before I did something just as drastic. No, I don't much miss the Hollywood life. But I do miss making those movies here in Arizona. Everything we did *was* new and amazing, without the eyes of business and profit margins looming over us. And although I would've outlived Thomas anyway by now, I do miss him, too.

I should confess at this point that I never entirely shed Hollywood from my life, or that the movies never quite left the Willows. They returned one particularly hot afternoon in 1934 when Annie Mendoza appeared on my front porch. I was returning from a ride when I saw her there, at a distance a stranger, but then my heart raced when she smiled and I recognized those big eyes, still bright with the energy and bullishness of the day I first met her. We laughed and hugged, giddy as children as all the memories of our time together rushed back. It hadn't been but a few years since I'd last seen her, but it felt as though forever. And, yet, at the same time, it seemed only a day.

Billy, you might be asking yourself, *how could you have forgotten Annie?* Well, I thought that myself for just a brief moment, and then I answered, *hadn't that always been the nature of our friendship?* We'd been a part of each other's work, and always on each other's mind. We had been there for each other, just not always *there*.

In fact, it was work that had brought us together again that hot afternoon. "I have a proposition for you, Billy," Annie explained as we sat together in the cool of my kitchen. She was working for MGM at that time, scouting locations for where to shoot films. "Toby told me about your place here, and its history. How would you like movie-making to return to the Willows Ranch?"

My first feeling was one of disappointment. Not because of my dislike of the industry, but because seeing Annie in my home, the glow of the Arizona sun washing upon her, made me realize how much I had missed her, and why I had missed her. She was no longer that tomboy of a girl, but a beautiful, mature woman. The years had been good to her, and I didn't want her to ever leave. I was disappointed, I realized, because I had hoped she was there to see me, not for business. As for her offer, I replied,

"That's a fine idea, Annie," because it was the surest way to guarantee I might see her again.

We spent the rest of the afternoon touring the property. Afterwards, I drove her into town, showed her the quaint allure of Prescott then took her to the infamous Palace Saloon for dinner and drinks. Lots of drinks. Yes, you could say I was trying to seduce her, because I was. But not into bedding-down with me, but to fall in love with Northern Arizona and the life I had made there. After dinner, instead of going back to her hotel room, she went home with me and slept on the couch.

The following day we took a drive to visit places beyond Prescott. Like Jerome, an old mining town stuck to the side of a mountain, Clarkdale, the nearby smelter, and the Verde Valley. I really didn't need to convince Annie of how great the area would be to make movies anymore at that point. I was just making excuses to spend more time with her. The best part was she didn't seem to mind. In fact, years later, Annie would confess that she used the whole location-scouting activity merely as a ruse to reunite with me.

As though she needed one.

It turned out our feelings for each other were mutual. And why not? Annie and I *had* been through a lot together. From my first miss-cued splash onto the movie-making industry to the hours and days she spent by my bedside as I recovered from a bullet to the throat, a broken spirit, and a devastated heart. We had a lifetime of bonding that I hadn't had with Rebecca or any other woman, ever. She was my Ellen Marie.

The night after our tour, before she went back to Hollywood, Annie stayed again at the house with me. This time, she didn't sleep on the couch.

ॐ   ॐ   ॐ

Several notable, and not so notable films, were shot around this part of Arizona over the years since. *Junior Bonner* (one of my favorites), *How the West Was Won* (what would've been a favorite of Thomas's, I think), *The Getaway*, *Bless the Beasts and Children*, and *Billy Jack*, to name a handful.

After her initial visit, Annie promptly quit her job with MGM, moved to the Willows, and we married at the Prescott Courthouse not but a week later. We had our first son the following year, 1935, and another son and a daughter in the years to follow. Not bad for a man near fifty-something of age. We had a life here in Arizona that, in itself, would not have made a good story. It was too idyllic, no conflict to speak of, no drama. We loved our home, our children, and each other. Yet as the end to a long, event-filled tale, it was perfect.

If keeping the memory of others is a responsibility that comes with living a long life, then its *curse* is that you see so many of those you love leave this world before you. But I still have grandchildren and great-grandchildren. They visit and keep in touch. My last wish is only that I go before I lose anyone else.

Though she had left Hollywood in body, the business remained on Annie's mind and in her blood. She served as an agent to studios interested in producing films, like the ones I mentioned, in the area. She brought a respectable flow of income into Prescott and our home. A number of times I was asked to make an appearance in a movie. Whether it was out of respect, or courtesy, or curiosity, I can't rightly say. I was just surprised anyone knew who I was. Most of them couldn't have *remembered* me. They were too young, a new generation of movie-makers.

Whatever was written about Sheldon Pictures and the movies made there must have survived all these years. From newspapers and journals, I guess. Gossip columns, most likely. The fire in 1933 hadn't destroyed everything after all. How else would the new and next generations know of me and my work? How else could the documentarians who appeared on my doorstep one day have any interest in the work and life of Thomas Andrew Benton, which spurred me to write these words here?

As for appearing in any of those films, I always declined their offers. I was truthful to Thomas the last time I saw him and told him I was done with the movie business. I wanted to get back to being what I'd been before straying into that foggy-world, what I'd always been, and what I am now—a cowboy.

Epilogue

It's no secret that my great-grandfather remembered nothing about his parents. So, I took it upon myself, with welcomed assistance from the Kansas Historical Society, to do a little genealogical research about his childhood before the age of ten.

Wichita birth records show a William John Colter born on August 13th, 1889. He was the only child of Jonathon Francis and Martha Ann Colter (my great-great-grandparents!), and commerce records note they were merchants, owners of Colter's Merchantile, a well-run business by the looks of the store's bookkeeping ledgers. It appears they lived comfortably, and Billy wanted of nothing. If they had lived past Billy's fourth birthday, one can assume their store would have been quite successful. A nearby Methodist church has record of infant William being baptized on October 20th, 1889.

On July 17th, 1893, the *Wichita Eagle* reported a fire that brought down the Colter home. The story reports an account of Billy's father getting his son to safety, then going back into the burning house to save his wife where he became trapped along with her. Both of Billy's parents perished. The cause of the fire was never determined. Court documents state that the orphaned Billy went to live with his uncle, Jedediah Colter, a farmer in Liberal, Kansas. Apparently, Jedediah wanted nothing to do with being a store owner–documents show that he sold his brother's business for a song.

"He wasn't much for farming, either," Billy recollected to me once in his gnarled voice. "Every season, whether it was a drought, locust, or his own agricultural inadequacies, the odds were against us to make a profit. As years passed he sold off parcels of his land to make ends meet."

Billy also recalled, "My uncle was not abusive, just neglectful, and he became a bit of a drunk. I got my schooling when and where I could, when I wasn't busy on the farm. I worked hard from a very young age."

As the farm struggled more and more–and Jed drank more and more–Billy realized he had to leave, to set out on his own.

"Hell, I'd been taking care of myself for years, anyway," Billy said. "I lied about my age to work a nearby ranch. I also lied about being able to ride a horse, but it turned out I was such a natural in the saddle that I even fooled myself."

Jedediah continued to toil with his farm for decades until catastrophe struck in the form of the great Dust Bowl of the 1930's. Billy's uncle died in poverty alone, having never married.

"Who'd a thought he would've lived that long," Billy said to me after reading what I had found. "I wonder if he ever saw any of my movies?"

It was at his 100th birthday that I surprised Billy with the documents of his family history. A few weeks later I received a letter from him:

Dear William,

I can't tell you how much I appreciate your gift. It was very thoughtful, and I'm sure, not an easy task. Imagine my life if my parents hadn't died when they did. I might have grown up a businessman instead of a cowboy. I probably never would have ridden a horse. And I certainly would have never been in the movies.

I've always known where I was, and I've got a good idea where I'm going. But I never had any idea where I'd begun. Until now. My story's complete. A pretty good one it's been, too, I think. And we both know how much I like a good story.

Billy

About the Author

Gordon Gravley has been making up stories all his life. Born in Phoenix, Arizona, he moved around a lot before eventually settling in the Northwest. He doesn't expect to be moving elsewhere anytime soon, but will continue to make up stories for as long as he can.

Subscribe to the author's newsletter *from...Another Writer* via his website www.gordongravley.com

CPSIA information can be obtained
at www.ICGtesting.com
Printed in the USA
LVOW03*0204020418
571912LV00001BA/5/P